DRAGON DAWNING

DEMONALITY BOOK TWO

by

Nadine Thirkell

Grosvenor House
Publishing Limited

All rights reserved
Copyright © Nadine Thirkell, 2021

The right of Nadine Thirkell to be identified as the author of this
work has been asserted in accordance with Section 78
of the Copyright, Designs and Patents Act 1988

The book cover is copyright to Nadine Thirkell

This book is published by
Grosvenor House Publishing Ltd
Link House
140 The Broadway, Tolworth, Surrey, KT6 7HT.
www.grosvenorhousepublishing.co.uk

This book is sold subject to the conditions that it shall not, by way of
trade or otherwise, be lent, resold, hired out or otherwise circulated
without the author's or publisher's prior consent in any form of binding or
cover other than that in which it is published and
without a similar condition including this condition being imposed
on the subsequent purchaser.

This book is a work of fiction. Any resemblance to
people or events, past or present, is purely coincidental.

A CIP record for this book
is available from the British Library

ISBN 978-1-83975-581-1

For the little girls who wanted to be dragons instead of unicorns.

I write these stories for you.

Table of Contents

So Much Blood ix
Chapter 1 - Lake Acantha 1
Chapter 2 - Visiting Earthside 8
Chapter 3 - Evan's New Office 11
Chapter 4 - Boys Will Be Boys 18
Chapter 5 - A Little Refresher 23
Chapter 6 - Family Time 30
Chapter 7 - New Ink 37
Chapter 8 - Recon Mission... 40
Chapter 9 - Bye Bye Baby 46
Chapter 10 - The Plan 51
Chapter 11 - Sneaking Around in the Dark 55

"Toto, I don't think we're in Kansas anymore
Chapter 12 - Astranya 62
Chapter 13 - Waiting is the Hardest Part 66
Chapter 14 - The Originals.. 70
Chapter 15 - Goodbye Brother 76
Chapter 16 - Curing Curses 81
Chapter 17 - The Ritual 85
Chapter 18 - Back To Life 91

Chapter 19 - Back To Us	97
Chapter 20 - Daughters	102
Chapter 21 - The Library	107
Chapter 22 - The First Time	110
Chapter 23 - Time to Go	114
Chapter 24 - Illthana	118
Chapter 25 - I Am A Dragon	124
Chapter 26 - Minor Healing	130
Chapter 27 - Nice Day For a Wedding	136
Chapter 28 - What Was In That?	141
Chapter 29 - Limbo	147
Chapter 30 - The Silvaer of Greenhamspire	152
Chapter 31 - Tree Hospitality	158
Chapter 32 - Artiscaena	164
Chapter 33 - The Big City	169
Chapter 34 - We Got to Get Out of This Place	174
Chapter 35 - The Blacksmith Family	180
Chapter 36 - The Secret is…	186
Chapter 37 - The Circle of the Silver Blood	190
Chapter 38 - Safe Magic Dispersal	195
Chapter 39 - Sleeping Rough	199
Chapter 40 - Acallaris War Zone (or Murphy's Law)	205
Chapter 41 - Meeting the Agros	211
Chapter 42 - I Am Not a Spy	216
Chapter 43 - A Sacrifice	223
Chapter 44 - Seeing Red	229

Chapter 45 - Musical Contemplations......................235
Chapter 46 - Negotiations...240
Chapter 47 - Armistice 247
Chapter 48 - Three Long Years................................249
Chapter 49 - The Ethereal Sanctum.........................254
Chapter 50 - A Gown For a Princess 261
Chapter 51 - Here We Go Again..............................266
Chapter 52 - Solys and Luna 270
Chapter 53 - The Honey Heist 275
Chapter 54 - When Is the Right Time? 280
Chapter 55 - Family Travels 282
Chapter 56 - Remembering 287

… Meanwhile at home

Chapter 57 - Raising Darcuna 294
Chapter 58 - Understanding Dragon Dreams 298
Before You Go...303

So Much Blood

The massacre that met Thea as she entered the building was beyond anything she'd ever seen. There was blood everywhere; the floors were slippery with it. It was even splashed on the walls. The air, so heavy with the scent of copper, filled her mouth with a harsh metallic taste. Bodies were strewn all over. Wherever she glanced, there was carnage and her heart broke seeing the faces of so many she knew, dead. A baby's cry rang out and Thea's head whipped around at the sound, listening, trying to identify what direction it came from before she ran.

"Darcuna, Little one, I am coming."

She called out to Jon, her voice rising in panic.

"Jon, where are you?"

Thea swallowed down the bile that rose in her throat when she turned a corner and saw Aliyah's throat savagely torn and oozing. Ash was laid across his mate as if he'd run to her, only to be taken by surprise from behind. The blade still protruding from his back. Their faces twisted with their final agony.

Thea backed away, and as she turned, her eyes met Gaia's sightless gaze. She lay on the floor in a pool of her own blood, only a few feet away from her parents. The poor girl must have been running towards them when she was slain. Her chest wound was so large she was almost severed in half.

Tears streamed down her face when she saw her grandfather. His mighty frame had been slashed so viciously that she almost did not recognize it as a body. His head was placed atop the bloody mass in a grotesque show of conquest. She had yet to find Gath's body but feared it was the horrific unidentifiable mound of flesh close by. The loss of her beloved guardian and closest childhood friend caused her to stumble before the thought of Darcuna and Jon forced her back up onto her feet.

She staggered as she walked over more bodies, trying not to lose hope for her child. Thea finally managed to reach the cradle, but it was empty. Darcuna's wails continued to echo around her. She again called out to Jon. Her own screams mingling with Darcuna's.

"Jon, where are you? Please! "

A hand reached out from below her. Thea looked down to see her mate leaning against a wall; Jon was bleeding profusely from a large tear in his side. Kneeling to reach him, Thea carefully tried to use her Hellfire to cauterize the wound, but the blood dribbling from his lips and his grey complexion told her she was too late and the wound was fatal.

"...came through a portal... tried to stop him... He took her..."

She held him as her daughter's screams grew fainter... "No!"

* * *

Chapter 1 - Lake Acantha

She bolted up from her slumber screaming. Darcuna began to cry. Pulling herself free of the bedclothes, Thea rushed to her daughter.

"Hush little one, I am here. You are safe."

Thea placed a comforting kiss on Darcuna's brow. The disturbing dreams had begun towards the end of her pregnancy. All manner of abhorrent visions played out in her slumber. First it was dreams of a bloody and arduous birth. Now it was images of her family's grisly deaths. They left her emotionally shattered as well as physically exhausted when she awoke.

Thea and Jon's little home was situated a small distance from the other Dragon homes at the head of Lake Acantha. The privacy meant thankfully only those within Thea's close circle knew about the nightmares. Most of the other Dragons assumed motherhood was the cause of her fatigue. Thea had been adamant about keeping the details from the wider settlement.

"It does no good to let the rest know my brothers are still attacking me. They are only dreams. They cannot hurt me."

Thea could see Jon was biting his tongue to keep the peace, especially since she had conceded over their new sleeping arrangements. Thea was still getting used to her and Jon's bed; the blankets and soft mattress were for his sake, but she had to admit she was finding it more comfortable than the rough pallet she had grown up with. If only she could enjoy it for more than a couple of hours at a time.

Their lack of sleep made them snap at each other more than either of them was comfortable admitting out loud. When she woke up screaming everyone in the house woke up with her. Jon could usually nod off again along with Darcuna. Thea found it harder to close her eyes after what she'd seen. The visions staying with her long after sleep abandoned her.

Thankfully Darcuna did not suffer from the tension that flared up between her parents. Gerard had fashioned a cradle for Darcuna—a beautiful piece of work with her name intricately etched onto it as well as sanctuary spells embedded into the wood.

"May our little Darkling's dreams never be tainted by nightmares."

Thea shed a happy tear at his use of the endearment he'd once used for her mother. Darcuna's bright blue eyes were not the only resemblance to her grandmother. Taking her hair colour from Jon, the combination made her seem like Dark Haven reborn.

"Oh Momma, I wish you could see her. I hope she takes after you in more than looks."

Levi often fondly reminisced about Dark Haven as a child.

"If she is anything like Dark Haven, she will be stubborn and wilful to the point of exasperation. But also, kind and generous. Your mother could be as immovable as her rock aspect, but she could also be as nurturing as water."

He paused briefly to gently kiss his great-granddaughter on her brow.

"Regardless of Darcuna's future aspect, she will always be loved."

Gerard doted on his niece in his own way, by lavishing her with all the gifts a magical uncle could. As well as the beautiful cradle, Gerard also made sure Darcuna slept on the softest of bedding. This little one would never know the hardship that was once the norm of her mother's existence.

Gath was as watchful as he'd ever been with Thea, but his sternness had now mellowed with age. Every reproachful glare he gave her when she managed to get into trouble was always followed with smile and a cuddle. Thea liked to tease him that he was never so indulgent with her. Darcuna's adoring uncles lavished affection on her to the point of spoiling her.

Everything was different—from where she slept to what she ate. Thea's previous diet had been mostly charred meat with a few root vegetables. While Dragons did occasionally hunt, meat was not central to their meals. Vegetables were grown in abundance in a field by the lake and were tended by all the Dragons. Thea had no understanding of farming so Ash and Aliyah instructed her as much as they could.

Jon and Thea were also learning to care for their child. Some days Thea got extremely frustrated with her lack of Dragon memories. She didn't complain, but Jon could see that line form on her brow when the exasperation set in. She would silently fume for a few minutes before taking a deep breath and pushing through.

Between all the new responsibilities she was now facing and the nightmares, Jon was impressed at how

Thea coped. Nothing was beneath her. There was no distinction between her and the other Dragons, only little Brix insisted on calling her Reyma, the old demon word for ruler, but more as a term of endearment than veneration.

***

Her magically enhanced ring-mail top and shorts, while functional, made Jon anxious. He never said anything but Thea could tell the translucence of it bothered him. His shoulders would tense up and she could see the muscles in his jaw twitch. She did didn't understand it, but since her time Earthside, and without any other attire besides what she'd accumulated there, Thea had begun the human girlfriend custom of *borrowing* Jon's t-shirts. She was reaching for one as Jon popped in to check on them.

"Are you guys ok? Was it the dreams again?"

Thea nodded as she sat down in her rocking chair, a gift from Evan, trying to lull Darcuna back to sleep. She gazed into her daughter's eyes willing her into slumber, before answering.

"Yes, they are as awful as the ones before. I know, in my waking mind, that they are false, but in sleep, they feel so real."

Jon scowled.

"Damn it, I wish my spells lasted longer."

Thea gave him a tired smile.

"I know you do, my love, I am grateful for any respite you give me, even as short as it is."

Jon was increasingly worried that the nightmares were keeping Thea from getting the rest she so desperately needed. It was his idea to let her grab naps as and when she could. He left Thea and the baby, so he could see to his guest; he'd asked Gath around to speak privately.

The gargoyle quickly looked in on Thea as she rocked her daughter and sighed. Thea looked more like a shade than the most powerful Dragon in Hell. He noted the dark circles under her eyes and her sallow complexion. When they were again alone outside the sleeping area, he quietly commented to Jon.

"These dreams are unnatural; I cannot put my finger on it, but my wager is on Black Heart having a hand in this. It is not common, but some clairvoyants have been known to be able to invade the dreams of the living, and Black Heart is the most advanced clairvoyant I know."

So far, the best Jon could do was a few protection invocations that allowed her an hour, maybe two at most, of uninterrupted sleep before the nightmares wormed their way back in, but he knew she needed more. Gath gave Jon an encouraging nod.

"I know your protection spells give her some small reprieve, but could you speak to Gerard and Fenris? Between you three, you may be able to fashion a more long-lasting ward to stop them."

The gargoyle sighed.

"But you will need to work quickly before there is permanent damage to Thea's mind."

Jon rolled his eyes.

"You don't think that was my first thought? We've tried, Gath, between our combined magical knowledge —and Fenris and Gerard have tons— we've attempted everything we can think of. Nothing works, and it's fucking killing me."

They stopped talking as Thea appeared beside them cradling a dozing Darcuna. Thea yawned, planting a kiss on Gath's cheek and then kissing Jon.

"Jon, do not berate yourself."

She knew her sleep terrors were the subject they were trying to avoid speaking about in front of her.

"The small naps do help me greatly."

She turned to address Gath.

"Your whispers carry, Gath. I know it is Black Heart who sends these visions to me; do you not remember?"

She shivered at the memory before she continued.

"He once did the same to me when I was smaller. Mother gave me a sleeping draught to calm me, and put me into a dreamless state. And when he could no longer reach me, he eventually lost interest. It seems Black Heart is trying again to break me, but something about these dreams feels different. There is a darkness about them that makes me think a simple sleeping draught will not be enough this time. I had thought our wards sufficient. They must be using some powerful, sinister magic to get passed them."

Thea's voice was jaded with her exhaustion.

"Again, my brothers show the depth of their depravity."

She stopped to give Gath and Jon a tired smile. Then adjusting Darcuna in her arms, Thea had a thought.

"Jon, would Nash know anything of such things? His enchantments have previously shown themselves to be quite effective if the magic is Faye,"

Thea pointed at Jon's protective rune tattoos.

"Nash may know a way to block it and having the spell embedded on me would allow me to move freely without being confined to a single location. And it would not affect my ability to look after Darcuna."

Jon nodded and took the idea a step further.

"I'll bet Black Heart's reach doesn't extend to Earthside... And I know Nash likes to work out of his own space. Ash and I haven't seen much advancement with the project. It's quiet enough for the time being that we could go and be back before anyone notices us missing."

Thea thought over the idea. Leaving was not ideal, but if she stayed and continued to lose sleep, it could be equally bad.

"Ok, Jon, let us see if Nash can again help us."

***

Chapter 2 - Visiting Earthside

They stepped out of the portal directly into Nash's shop. There was no longer any point in hiding the portals; too much had happened to deny the existence of magic to the human population. Nash was working on a client when they materialised. Thea was back in her jean shorts, and a cute baby dragon t-shirt Jon had found for her.

Their appearance caused a minor disruption, but only because Nash had not seen Thea since before her pregnancy. He excused himself from his client and went to welcome them.

"Holy shit, you guys went and had a sprog."

Thea had long since stopped trying to understand Nash and his Earthside idioms. She gave him a careful hug while holding Darcuna.

He smiled at the baby before jokingly punching Jon in the arm.

"Glad to know I was right about you two; didn't take you long at all I see."

He gave Thea and Jon a wink and Thea had to laugh at his teasing.

"Nash, I know you are jesting, but if you do not mind, right now I would greatly appreciate somewhere to sit. I believe Darcuna wishes to be fed."

Darcuna had begun to paw at Thea's breast. Nash grabbed a chair for her and then went back to his client.

The man was staring at Thea and Darcuna with intense curiosity. Jon coughed at Thea to remind her to cover up. Thea's continued incomprehension of nudity around others was a tender spot between them, so she adjusted her shirt to cover her and Darcuna to pacify him. Jon glared at the man before using his glamour to divert his attention.

Nash glanced over at Thea, shook his head, and continued to work while talking. Jon went into the back to grab a beer from Nash's little fridge. Nash gestured towards Jon while turning his attention back to Thea.

"So other than pilfering my beer, what brings you two here, and with a baby no less?"

Thea sighed as Darcuna's feeding began to calm her.

"It seems my brothers are still trying to harm me," she explained.

"And since we defeated them on the battlefield, they are using less honourable means to attack us. I think Black Heart is sending me dream terrors, but so far, all our protections have proven less than adequate in stopping them. Jon's incantations have given me a small measure of protection, but we seek a more permanent solution. The prevailing opinion seems to be they are possibly using dark Faye magic. Jon and I were hoping your experience with protection enchantments might be expansive enough to offer a remedy."

Nash looked over as Darcuna began to nod off. Thea's nipple popped out her mouth. Jon clenched his hands while grinding his teeth. Nash asked the couple if they could meet up afterwards.

"Look I'm almost done here; can we talk later? Give me say, half an hour, and we can see what I can do."

Thea fixed her clothing before she got up to leave. Jon exhaled before giving Nash a smile and friendly pat on the shoulder.

"We'll pop in on Evan and let you finish up; see you in thirty."

Jon called up a portal and they walked through. The human client's eyes went wide and Nash chuckled at him.

"Don't worry, they're the good guys. I'm almost done here anyway."

***

Chapter 3 - Evan's New Office

Evan looked up from his desk and his face lit up as Jon and Thea walked through the portal.

Jon noticed a few changes since the last time he'd seen Evan's office. The expansive desk was new as were the lavish visitor's chairs and coffee table. The bastard had even managed to get his own espresso coffee machine. Evan rushed over to greet them. Jon grabbed Darcuna and thrust her at him.

"Because I know how excited you were to see the baby."

Thea laughed at Jon's attempt to distract Evan. Taking her baby back, she leaned over to give Evan a small peck on the cheek.

"Forgive Jon. He still does not trust you where I am concerned. I hope we have not come at an inconvenient time."

Evan took in her shapely figure before winking at her and giving Jon a warm if a tad teasing smile.

"Never, but I am wondering if this is a social call or something altogether more unpleasant; not that I ever need an excuse to enjoy your company."

He wiggled his eyebrows at Darcuna, and she gurgled happily at him holding out her arms. Thea handed Evan the baby. He balanced her expertly in his arms and gazed down at her before looking up to smile at Thea.

"As beautiful as her mother. Now what brings you to me?"

Evan gestured for them to take a seat. Jon filled him in.

"Thea's brother is using dark magic to send her some pretty gruesome nightmares. We came here to see if Nash might have something in his magic arsenal to banish them. Seeing you is incidental."

Thea smiled at Evan.

"Evan, I also wanted to thank you for the gift of the *rock-ing* chair. It has greatly helped with soothing Darcuna back to sleep when my night terrors wake us..."

Thea shook herself awake for the second time. Evan noted the dark circles under Thea's eyes.

"I didn't want to say anything but, Thea, how long has it been since you slept? You look dead tired."

Thea sank into the plush chair, her eyelids drooping momentarily. Jon patted her arm.

"It's ok; I really don't think Evan here will mind you taking a nap while I bring him up to speed."

Without the constant barrage of nightmare images and the softness of Evan's new chairs, Thea could feel sleep beckoning her. She blinked a few times before her head fell and her breathing became slow and even.

Both men gazed at her for a few seconds before Darcuna started to fuss. Jon took her back from Evan and gently rocked her while pulling Evan away so they could talk without disturbing Thea.

"The nightmares started a little over six months ago. At first it wasn't so bad and she could fall back to sleep, but now the poor thing never sleeps more than a few hours at a time. Some days she's a walking zombie. Whatever that bastard is using is bad, like really bad."

Jon paused before his next question.

"It occurs to me to ask if I might have a peek at some of those restricted books you *don't* have."

He gave Evan a meaningful glance. Evan's eyes went wide.

"And how would a couple of corrupt Dragons have access to *that* sort of knowledge?"

Jon reminded him of Thea's brother Rage.

"The elder Dragons seem to agree he's the source. His use of chaos magic isn't a Dragon trait. His mother could have been one of the Faye left behind."

Evan shuddered at the thought.

"It's a part of our history I greatly regret. The worst of us left behind... such corruption should have been destroyed not left to fester."

Evan paced as he thought out loud.

"Well, this is worrying. Look, I need time to get you into the vaults. Give me a few hours —a day max— I'll contact you at Nash's when I've got your clearance sorted."

He gave Darcuna a little tickle and she giggled.

"But for their sake, I hope you're wrong."

* * *

Thea and Jon took some time to grab coffee and sandwiches before returning to Nash's shop. With the nightmares Thea's appetite had all but disappeared, and Jon took every opportunity he could to try and get some food inside of her.

To avoid further distractions, Nash sent his assistant home and put up the closed sign. He spoke as soon as the door shut.

"Holy fuck! Evan called not two seconds after you guys left him. He told me I have to get ready to break out the high-level enchantments, like the tier-seven shit. Thea, what have your brothers started delving into?"

Feeling better after some food and her short nap, Thea, took a seat and tried to explain.

"For you to understand, I need to first clarify my place in the family. Spawn was the first. I don't think anyone bar my father knows – knew – actually knows how old he is and as the first son he has known nothing but privilege. His gift is with vortexes and portals. Though apparently he is not as talented as the Winter males."

She looked over at Jon and grinned before continuing.

"He is the first child my father formally recognized, and then came Black Heart. He is a brilliant clairvoyant, but his influence is in the realm of the dead so he became Spawn's second. That is why they are so close. For some time, they were the only sons of Shadow Lord and because of it, they are the most arrogant.

"Then Rage was born. His gift is chaos magic, which is incredibly rare, so even though his magic is marginal, he was still recognized. His unstable mind makes him the perfect lackey for Spawn and Black Heart. He is the alleged source of the dark Faye magic.

"Afterward came Soul Crusher with his necromancy. His magic is incredibly powerful; so much so that my father made him the new heir. Spawn was displaced but still respected. He became the second to Crusher.

"The strong have always ruled over the weak and Crusher is formidable. Black Heart and Rage do not show any animosity to Crusher, but they still display deference to Spawn as he was the first. Then because of their unique gifts and because they are twins, Devourer and Destroyer, were acknowledged. There was never any bitterness because they were never in line to inherit."

Nash smiled at Thea.

"And then you were born and threw a spanner into the works."

Thea paused a moment. Her voice was low.

"There was another. Annihilator was the only one with no magical ability. It is most likely why he was never missed by my father after I ..."

Jon knew it was a sore spot for Thea. He pursed his lips and looked over at Nash before he finally spoke.

"He died the day Thea's fire aspect presented. He was the reason she was elevated to heir."

Thea gave a teary smile and nodded.

"Not quite, but yes, I, the smallest and a female, but with the duel aspects of fire and rock, upended the status quo. My father desperately wanted a fire elemental heir. I was not only an obsidian Dragon, I was one with a primary fire aspect and a secondary rock aspect, the only known Dragon in Hell with a rock aspect.

"In Hell, fire outranked all other elements, but that did not mean I was well respected. I was still a female, and females in Hell were traditionally for only two purposes: pleasure and procreation."

She looked down at Darcuna who was blissfully sleeping, an image of perfect serenity. She looked back up to continue.

"I was reluctantly shown some respect in my father's presence, but it was not considered inappropriate to make sexual remarks regarding my appearance. Lewd words were tolerated but action would be punishable by death. Due to our Dragon blood, my father kept my mother and I under guard at all times."

Thea's expression became thoughtful as she gazed down at her daughter.

"I can only begin to imagine the fear my mother felt the day I was born and then when I was recognized into that dynasty. Thankfully Darcuna will not have that kind of childhood."

Jon gave her shoulder a squeeze, and she smiled at him. She took a breath and went on.

"Black Heart can invade dreams, but Rage would provide the needed Faye dark magic to penetrate our wards, or so Jon thinks."

Jon took over.

"Not just me, but Levi and the other elder Dragons. Chaos magic is not very Dragon-like. It could only come from a Faye that was left behind when they crossed to Earthside."

Nash whistled.

"And from what I know they were some seriously bad motherfuckers, like proper evil. My dad used to tell those stories to me when I misbehaved to scare me straight."

Nash sat back.

"So that's what we're trying to block? Holy shit and then some."

He paused to let it sink in before he spoke again.

"Ok, I'm going to need a look at Evan's special collection, if that's what we are dealing with."

Jon gave him a cocky grin.

"Already in the works. Evan will call us when he's got us clearance to the vault."

Nash pointed at Thea who was slumped in her chair sleeping cradling Darcuna.

"How about we get these girls into a proper bed? I got a cot in the back and we can cobble together something for the baby. I'll forward my number and we can hang out at the bar next door while we wait for Evan's call."

Jon scooped up Thea while Nash held Darcuna who promptly woke up and started staring at him, awake and alert, before blowing a raspberry in his face and giggling.

"Shit, your kid is cute. Never mind about the baby cot. I know the guy who owns the place. He won't mind if we bring her along. His Mrs behind the bar loves kids. Let Thea have her sleep. Gods only know she looks like she needs it."

* * *

Chapter 4 - Boys Will Be Boys

Thea awoke to darkness and bolted up. *Where was she? How long had she been asleep?* As her eyes adjusted, she noticed a small makeshift cradle in the corner of the room. Nash had taken a box from his storeroom and some old blankets to make a cot. She crept over and let out a deep sigh of relief when she saw Darcuna sleeping, her expression serene.

Jon had been right; Black Heart's reach did not extend to Earthside, and she felt more alert than she had for some time. Yawning she caught Jon's voice. He and Nash sounded *very* happy. She went to join them and see why they were in such high spirits. She walked out to find Jon and Nash surrounded by several dozen bottles of what looked to be the source of their merriment. Jon shook his head to clear it.

"Oh sorry, were we being too loud?"

Jon seemed to be fine while Nash was disgustingly drunk. He giggled at Thea while trying to stand.

"I've forgotten how hard it is to keep up with this fucker. Damn you and your Faye-Dragon blood; no fair."

Nash teetered, and Thea and Jon both reached to keep him from falling face first onto the ground. Each one hooked an arm around him to hold him up. Thea looked at Jon.

"If he is, as I think he is, he will be most useless until tomorrow."

Jon let out a little chuckle.

"And with the mother of all hangovers as well. Where's Darcuna?"

Thea indicated towards the back room.

"She is sleeping soundly, and I feel much more rested. Thank you, Jon. I did not realise how tired I was until now, but I worry about going back. Do you really think Nash and Evan will be able to block whatever my brothers are doing?"

Jon adjusted his grip on Nash.

"Let's get sleeping beauty here in bed first and then we can talk. He's getting pretty heavy."

Thea and Jon dragged Nash to his cot before they noticed Darcuna was awake again and needed attention. Thea sent Jon to get them something substantial to eat.

"I will see to the little one if you could get us some foodstuffs."

Now that she had slept her appetite had returned.

"We can eat and discuss what you learned while I was asleep."

***

Thea was sitting with a freshly changed Darcuna, when Jon returned with some burgers and milkshakes. She tucked into her burger with enthusiasm as he gave her the details of what he had found out so far.

"Levi told me a little about the Dragon memories of Faye that were left behind in Hell. They weren't immediately discovered when the Dragons made the crossing. Instead they were found much later after the portals had been sealed. He called them *troublesome*."

Thea nodded.

"Yes, Grandfather told me something similar. If they are the source, it makes sense I cannot defend against it. I have no understanding of Faye magic."

Jon continued.

"Nash and Evan both say they were more like 'the worst of the worst'. Now the Faye obviously didn't just leave them wandering around Hell. They were devious not stupid. These *problematic* Faye were magically sealed up in a cavern to keep them from following the rest Earthside. Our best guess is that as the conditions in Hell deteriorated, those caverns became unstable and then finally unsealed, and that's how they got out. One of them must have caught the eye of your father and—surprise, surprise—little Rage was born."

Thea reflected on her father's mage.

"There was one called Cendre that my father kept in his court. She alone made him uneasy but her gifts were unique enough for him to retain her. With everything we have learned, I now suspect she was also part Faye. It would account for her unusual magic... and explain why my mother avoided her..."

Thea mulled over this.

"I hope Evan's books will shed some light on our problem and present us a solution so we can return. Gath will keep quiet about our travelling between the realms as long as he can, but soon my absence will be noted. Others in our camp might become alarmed and panic. If my brothers find out, they could use it to cause trouble."

Jon reached for her.

"And what about your nightmares?"

Thea placed her hand over his.

"Your proficiency with portals allows us to move easily between realms. We shall return, but I will use your ability so that I may get the rest I require, while Evan and Nash find the enchantment I need. It is the best we can do under the circumstances."

Thea gave Jon a sad smile and sighed.

"I fear we will not be spending as much time in our little home and our new soft bed as I had hoped."

Jon leaned over and gave her a quick kiss.

"Only for a short time. Hey, as long as we are together, home is wherever we need to be."

* * *

Thea and Jon decided to wait for Nash to wake and sober up so they could tell him their idea. They used the time to get some rest, crashing on the floor of the shop.

The next morning, Nash was hunched over his coffee trying to keep his head from exploding while Jon was trying to work a crick out of his neck. Thea was the only one who looked well rested. Nash took some aspirin and massaged his temples as he spoke.

"So, you're going back, but you'll return every twenty-four hours or so to let Thea sleep—ok, I get that. I'll let Evan know, and we can start our research."

Nash added as an afterthought.

"Sorry about you having to sleep on the floor. Honestly, the cot is not much better. I think we can find you some place nicer, maybe with baby facilities, for when you come back. I'll get Evan to sort it out."

Thea started to raise her hand to object but then reconsidered as she realised Jon would appreciate a more comfortable place to sleep.

"Yes, I think somewhere other than your shop floor would be best for all of us."

Jon gave a relieved sigh while Nash cooed at Darcuna.

"She really is a cutie."

He smiled wistfully.

"I still remember when Julie was born…"

His expression changed to a knowing grin and he laughed.

"…and when she got older… I can only imagine the holy hell that will be your life once this "little darling" starts dating."

He laughed even harder when Jon's face blanched. Jon hadn't begun to think about dating. Darcuna wasn't even out of diapers yet. He gave Nash a dirty look.

"You arsehole, don't say shit like that. We'll be back soon."

* * *

Chapter 5 - A Little Refresher

Thea and Jon returned to Hell to find Gath speaking with Gerard. Gerard walked over to see his little niece.

"Hello my little Darkling, you grow more beautiful with each passing day."

She giggled loudly as he planted a loud kiss on her chubby cheek. He gave her nose a tweak and another kiss before turning his attention back to the couple. He raised an eyebrow at Thea.

"Gath has told me your nightmares persist."

Thea nodded and explained her and Jon's strategy to deal with them in the interim.

"Jon's portals will allow me a temporary sanctuary against my brothers' attacks, but running away to Earthside is not a viable long-term solution. Evan and Nash are looking into some high-level Faye protection spells and devising a permanent enchantment for me similar to those Jon wears."

Gerard gave an amused snort when Jon proceeded to lift his shirt to show off his abdominal muscles along with the protection runes Nash had tattooed on him. Thea chuckled at Jon's display while pushing his shirt down.

"Jon, stop showing off. It seems Rage is not as inconsequential as we thought. His minor skills have given Black Heart a previously unknown opening in our defences. At least we understand the source of the magic, and if it is as we suspect, Evan's archive of the darker arts should give us some badly needed information, as well as how to counteract it–"

They were interrupted as Gaia came running towards them, her wooden practice sword bouncing on her belt. Her sword lesson from Gerard was due. Wanting to emulate Thea in every way, she'd begged and pestered her parents for so long that in the end it was easier for them to say yes then be subjected to her incessant pleading. Thea was flattered.

She also loved that Gaia treated Darcuna as a little sister. She loved to hold here and sing to her as she slept. Thea usually let the girls play together, but this time Gerard reluctantly turned away from Thea and Darcuna and gave Gaia a stern glare.

"Part of our agreement was you would do as you were told and already you are late for your lesson. Come along, we have much to cover."

Thea stopped them. She passed Darcuna to Jon.

"I am out of practice; I believe I too would benefit from what Jon calls *a refresher*."

Gaia gave an excited squeal before grabbing hold of Gerard and Thea's hands to drag them to the exercise field. Gerard gave Thea a covert glance of amusement.

Jon looked down at his daughter as her face contorted. His eyes watered at the sudden stench. Darcuna giggled again.

"I swear you only do that when Mum leaves just for my *amusement*."

She blew a raspberry at him, and he shook his head and laughed.

"Ok little Miss Stinky, I need to fix this or one of us is not going to survive. Either Thea kills me for leaving you in this state or I die from the fumes."

Holding Darcuna at arm's length, he started towards Gath's hut, mumbling to himself.

"Maybe the gargoyle can help..."

***

Gerard looked to his younger student.

"Gaia, I know you want to learn to fight as Thea does with two swords, but for now I think you should practice with one. Much like the adage about learning to walk before running. I think you should learn to use one proficiently before you try and wield two. If you wish to be accomplished, you need to master the basics before moving onto the more advanced techniques. But today's lesson can be useful to the advanced swordswoman as well as the novice. Today is about observation. Careful observance of your adversary's movements is crucial. The smallest details will express their next actions, and if you can read them, you will know exactly how to counter them."

Gerard turned his attention to Thea.

"Thea if you are ready."

Gerard and Thea squared off as Gaia watched enraptured from a short distance away. Before they began, he erected a barrier between them and Gaia as a safety measure. Thea reached for her swords and they materialised in her hands. Gerard gave her one of his cocky smiles so reminiscent of their first lesson. He winked at her, and Thea felt just like she was back on that day again, by the lake as her mother watched. And like that day, Thea reacted a moment too late and found herself staring up at Gerard. She gave her head a shake and grinned at her mentor.

"Enjoy that, old man; it will not happen again."

She laughed out loud at Gerard's expression of mock offence. He wasn't so old that he couldn't laugh at himself and he smiled back.

"There are always things to learn, Thea; don't be so sure I taught you everything. Old swordsmen are old for a reason."

He advanced on Thea with his long sword, and Thea brought up one of her twin blades to deflect it away. Gerard tried to lock her weapon before Thea brought up her other blade and then used them both to scissor Gerard's steel and push him back. He was impressed at her progress.

"You have improved, but don't leave yourself so open. Let me demonstrate."

With a flick of his wrist he cast a spell and she went sprawling back. Gaia gasped and Gerard called a stop so he could explain the lesson to them. He walked over to help Thea back up onto her feet.

"Never assume anything. A foe will not hesitate to use everything at their disposal; so, it is fair to say magic will be a real threat. If you use both swords to block, an opponent can use that opening to strike with either magic or even a simple dagger. Never give your foe the chance to use your own manoeuvre against you. Now that you are aware of the fact, let's start over."

Thea nodded, and again they brought up their blades. Their steel clashed for several minutes before Thea saw Gerard ever so slightly lower his shoulder; she knew he was preparing to cast. She raised a shield in time to block his spell. Then taking advantage of his momentary confusion, she released her weapons and ran towards him, closing the gap between them to counter his sword's length. She brought up her knee and knocked the wind out of him with a kick to his abdomen. Standing over her mentor, she looked down and gave him a cocky smirk.

"You and Jon have the same reveal before you cast. I mentioned it to him but it is interesting to know you share that trait."

After catching his breath, Gerard laid his head back and roared with laughter at her observation.

"I see you really have been practicing. Was this all a ruse to humiliate me in front of Gaia?"

Thea gave him a playful grin while she helped Gerard up. He nodded to her.

"So now that we are *both* warmed up, let's try again."

They stood face to face with their swords up. This time Thea made the first strike and Gerard parried. Their blades collided; each other waiting for the other to use magic first. Usually the problem was, to cast one had to lower their sword and if the cast failed and the opponent blocked the spell, it would leave the caster vulnerable. Thea took a slightly more uncommon approach. Her Dragon magic allowed her to shield without releasing her swords, so when Gerard raised his sword to strike, she raised an earth shield and his blade bounced off it. Dropping her swords, they disappeared back into her tattoos and she launched herself at Gerard. Then as she sat atop him, she conjured a ball of Hellfire in her hand.

"Do you yield?"

Gerard portalled out from under her, and then Thea felt his blade under her chin.

"Never forget your opponent's advantages as well as their weaknesses. You got overconfident and it cost you."

Thea pushed the blade away.

"You tricked me; no other has your skill. It would be impossible to fight someone who has that ability."

Gerard offered Thea his hand to help her up again.

"That is not true, even I can be beaten."

He raised his shirt to show Thea a thin scar between his ribs. It was white and almost invisible with age.

"My teacher saw how I used my talents with portals to jump around and avoid his blows until he took a moment to observe me and recognised a pattern to my movements. He could see where I would emerge, and when next I appeared, his sword slipped between my ribs. Then using his remarkable skill to heal, he mended my wound, but left the scar as a reminder. I had thought I was too smart, too strong, to be bested and I almost paid the ultimate price for that arrogance. I share that important lesson with you now so you won't pay a price for your pride. Watch, learn, act."

Thea nodded then caught Gaia as she ran to her. Thea held onto her and looked down to give her an encouraging smile.

"It seems even I still have lessons to learn but thankfully you are discovering them with me. We should both be grateful to have such a wise and patient teacher."

Gerard leaned over and gave Thea a kiss on her head and then a gentle squeeze to Gaia's shoulder.

"It's good to know you understand and are absorbing your training."

As Thea stepped aside, he gave his attention over to Gaia.

"Now, Gaia are you ready?"

* * *

Chapter 6 - Family Time

After her lesson, Thea ran home. She could not wait to relax and cradle her baby. Darcuna was due her feeding. The dark patches on her shirt revealed her body was ready to nourish her child. Jon would often stay while she fed Darcuna. Thea smiled. There were times she thought her heart would burst thinking of their little family. She picked up her pace wanting to see them even more than before.

***

Jon stood in the doorway as Thea gently rocked back and forth in her chair. Her whole manner relaxed when she settled in to this task. It was one of the few times he could see the gears in her head stop their endless turning. It was a duty she genuinely looked forward to even with all her other responsibilities. If you'd asked him when they first met if he'd ever look forward to something so mundane, he'd have laughed his arse off, but standing there, off to the side, watching her, he swallowed the lump that formed in his throat.

Now that she was getting enough rest, Thea was far more relaxed. Sure, the trips were a nuisance but seeing Thea awake and immersed again with small everyday jobs made him happy. On their last trip Earthside, Evan and Nash were reasonably sure they'd found a text with the final piece of the puzzle they needed to craft an enchantment to block out not just the nightmares, but would keep her brothers out of her head permanently. They'd even hinted it could be ready for their next trip. Evan, as usual, wanted time to test it and perfect it before committing to anything.

"We know better than most, that these sorts of tattoos can't be removed as easily as the rest—well, not without consequences. I just want to make sure we're not trading one set of problems for another."

Although initially impatient, Thea was glad they were being careful; her mother's curse had shown her all too clearly that magic could have unforeseen aftereffects. Nash had been over it at least a dozen times and was happy to move forward. She looked down just as Darcuna, full and content, lolled back in slumber. Thea could feel Jon's eyes on her and a little spark of desire flared up inside her. She loved how he could do that to her, even from across the room. Raising herself up carefully to not wake up their sleeping daughter, she placed Darcuna in her cradle. She felt Jon slide up behind her and he looked down at their daughter over Thea's shoulder before placing a kiss on her neck.

He pulled Thea out of the room before turning her in his arms to face him. Thea's fire aspect meant her passion was never far from the surface, and the incubus in Jon kept his flames constantly stoked. Jon lifted Thea as she wrapped her legs around him. A quick scan around the room and Jon smiled against Thea's mouth as he moved them towards the table. Their kisses had always been heated but with everything that had happened, there was now a depth to them as well. Right now, though, neither he nor Thea was thinking about anything other than catching a rare intimate moment before...

"Ah, looking to give Darcuna a little brother or sister so soon?"

Jon groaned and gently put Thea down as his brother arrived.

"I thought we had more time."

Thea giggled breathlessly. She gave Jon a small kiss, before turning his head so her lips tickled his ear.

"Obviously not, but we may still have opportunities when we travel Earthside."

Thea gave Gerard a mocking swat on his arm for the interruption before Jon clapped him on the back a little harder than necessary.

"I'll forgive your timing for now because you're doing us a favour, bro. Even though I know you and Gath have been fighting for time with her.

Because Nash and Evan will be focused on Thea and her new tattoo, I think it would be easier for us this time if we just go, and get it done without having to worry about Darcuna."

Thea had made sure another nursing mother Dragon was available before agreeing to travel.

"While I am happy to have time alone with Jon, I am nervous about leaving Darcuna. I know we have previously left her with Aliyah or Gath but I was always close by. This will be the first time I will leave her to travel to another realm, even if it is only Earthside."

Jon gave Thea a squeeze.

"Honey, you know everyone here will look out for her."

Thea looked back towards the bedroom while blinking back tears.

"I know. I just want to give her one more kiss before we leave."

Gerard gave her a warm and sympathetic smile.

"Of course, I understand. But Jon is right you need to get this sorted, so go and return quickly."

The brothers watched Thea disappear before Jon sighed,

"Damn it, I'm going to miss Little Miss Poopy Pants, hold on."

He went to follow Thea.

Thea and Jon stood over Darcuna's crib. Jon brushed a tear off of Thea's cheek and she pretended to not see his. She leaned over and gave Darcuna a small kiss and Jon put his hand over his daughter's chest to feel her softly breathing. Pulling Thea away so they could talk without disturbing Darcuna, Jon led her out of the bedroom.

Jon kept his voice low while he gave Gerard a last-minute reminder.

"If for any reason you need us, get in touch with Evan's office, he'll know how to reach us."

They took one final glance towards their child before Jon called up the portal and he and Thea walked through to Earthside.

***

Evan had arranged a room for them at one of the nicer hotels by his office. The council kept several rooms dotted around the city ready for visitors. High up on the topmost floors with breath-taking views and the most exclusive restaurant around, they were romantic as well as luxurious.

Thea and Jon did not waste any time undressing and making their lip locked way into the walk-in shower to finish what they had started at home.

Thea had a particular fondness for the man-made water jets having never experienced anything like it in Hell. So, after the first time when she had pulled Jon in with her, it quickly became their go to spot.

Thea and Jon both reached for the temperature knob. Jon swatted Thea's hand away.

"Sorry darling, not this time. Last time I swear you gave me third degree burns and don't pout at me I'll set it hot, just not emergency room burn unit hot."

Once Jon had the temperature set, he was treated to the vision of Thea, the water cascading down her body, and the steam rising around them. It was enough to make him almost faint from the rapid blood loss away from his brain.

Years of dragging a sword around made lifting Thea up and onto him easy work. Thea let her head roll back and a deep moan escaped her lips as Jon found his footing and began to move inside her. It wasn't long before Thea could feel the first stirrings of her release.

Jon was waiting until he felt Thea's body tightening around him so he could finally let go. With a few hard and quick thrusts, he pushed Thea over the edge and followed her.

Jon was breathless as they slid down the tiles.

"I'm sorry baby but my legs feel like jelly. I just need a second."

They lay on the tiles as the water continued to flow over them until they were sufficiently able to crawl back to the bed.

After their release, they lay snuggling on the bed awaiting the call from Evan. This time Nash would close up his shop so he could work on Thea privately.

Thea was contentedly dozing sprawled across Jon, having fallen asleep listening to the sound of his heart, while he tried to keep his eyes open when they were both startled by a loud knock on the door.

They could hear Evan on the other side of the door laughing.

"Can you open up? I arrived about twenty minutes ago... but I didn't want to interrupt you two."

Jon kissed Thea on the head.

"Bloody hell, our own friendly neighbourhood pervert is outside waiting. We need to get dressed."

Thea giggled.

"Jon after all this time how can you still think Evan is anything other than just a friend?"

Jon grabbed his jeans and threw them on. As soon as Thea was dressed, Jon opened the door.

Evan breezed in with what could only be described as a rather obvious expression of his arousal. Jon rolled his eyes and gestured at it.

"Because of that my dear."

Pulling on his shirt, Jon had a sudden thought. He raised his head and looked around.

"I wonder if there are hidden cameras... Next time I think I might book the room myself."

Evan roared with laughter.

"Don't worry. We only use them when there's a security threat or when I bring certain lady friends here. I always ask before recording. I am gentleman if nothing else."

This time Jon burst out laughing.

"Your definition and mine must be different. Anyhow, we're ready to go."

Evan held the door for Thea as Jon grabbed his jacket.

"Nash is waiting at his end. Let's see about getting you inked my dear. I think it's time you stopped having nightmares."

Thea gave him a bright smile.

"Yes, I agree."

***

Chapter 7 - New Ink

The reason for using the shop was down to the books Nash would need to refer to during the process – old tomes from the time of the first Faye. They held both powerful and, if not handled carefully, potentially harmful magical knowledge.

Evan had expressly forbidden Nash from taking the valuable books to a location as unsecure as his cabin. They even came with their own security team. Nash was sure he knew what he was doing, but still felt better having the books there to refer to, just in case.

A privacy screen was set up to avoid watchers from outside as well as nosey guards. The guards were provided to keep the books safe but none of them knew the actual contents. Thea lay back on a tattooing chair, with her arm extended towards Nash. There had been some discussion over where her wards should go and while she could have had them on her midriff similar to Jon, Nash had suggested her wrists.

"These don't have to be monstrously big to be effective and considering the content it might be better to have them small and discreet."

Thea liked the idea. Her tattoo wings often made people nervous and she didn't want to appear intimidating, so something small made sense to her.

Jon sat on the other side holding her hand and absently rubbing her other wrist while Evan sat on one of the couches at the front of the shop thumbing through a magazine. Every so often he glanced towards the security detail.

The tattoo process would be relatively quick, but the enchanting would take a little more time as Nash layered on each level of protection on top of the next, creating a web of magical shielding. This shield would not just cover Thea but anyone close to her, allowing her to protect Darcuna if the need arose.

Nash was careful with each character making sure that each one was drawn exactly as in the books. The magic these symbols embodied was the highest level of magic in the Faye arsenal. Most Faye —bar a few top-level magical scholars— would not even understand them.

When the inking was done, he carefully placed each level of the enchantment, making sure again his spells were precise.

Once the last enchantment was in place, Nash leaned back and gave a long sigh.

"That's it, we're done. I just need a few minutes."

Thea looked at Nash's worn appearance and gestured to Jon. Jon nodded and taking Nash's hand he syphoned some energy from Thea to Nash. He immediately perked up and gave Thea and Jon an appreciative nod.

"Thanks, I didn't think I would feel so rough after that, but then again I don't think I've ever concentrated quite so hard for that long. Nothing is getting passed those wards."

Thea smiled.

"We shall give these a test and report back to you on their success once we are able. Thank you both for your help. I am truly grateful to have such good friends."

Nash wrapped up her wrist and Thea stood on her toes to give him a hug.

"I hope you do not take offense but I miss my child so much I would rather leave sooner than later if it is fine with you."

Evan walked over and gave Thea a quick kiss on the cheek.

"Sweet dreams, Thea."

* * *

Chapter 8 - Recon Mission

It had been three whole days with no nightmares. Each morning when Thea awoke in Jon's arms after a peaceful night, her world felt right again. Jon slipped over just long enough to report of their success and to thank Nash and Evan. He and Thea took a few days to enjoy their little home again before jumping back into work. After everything, Thea could not fault Jon's request; and if she was honest with herself, she enjoyed the time as well. Even little Darcuna seemed happier to have both her parents with her, well rested and relaxed.

***

Thea allowed herself time to enjoy being back in her space but she could not hide away forever. Jon and Ash's previous reports about Black Heart's Morsa Ersa camp made her think it was time she properly re-engaged her brothers.

"This time Jon, I would ask you to take me instead of Ash. I want to observe this thing my brother is building out in the wastes of the dead grounds. Perhaps I might be able to identify what it is."

***

Thea sat next to Jon looking through the lenses at the machine her brother's minions were building. It was like nothing she could fathom. It was a circular object that stood larger than the arch over the entrance to Incendya Domus at the bottom of the mountain, before Thea and Jon had destroyed the compound.

It stood some distance away from the main part of the camp but was still within the perimeter. Guards were placed around it, so it had to be something worth protecting. Jon had his binoculars down, waiting to see if Thea had a clue what they were looking at.

After a few moments, Thea finally lowered hers and turned to Jon.

"It reminds me of the entrance to my old home."

She tapped the lenses thoughtfully while she mumbled to herself.

"An entrance that goes nowhere..."

Thea blinked and looked again at the machine through the lenses. Then lowering them, she looked at the lenses themselves. She continued to think out loud. She remembered something Jon had said.

"Humans have their own kind of magic. They can't fly or move as fast as other creatures, so they build these incredible machines..."

Jon didn't like where her thoughts were going. If what she was thinking was what he thought she was thinking, things had just gone from bad to holy shit worse.

"Thea, you don't think he's actually building a portal? Because that would just be... beyond nuts."

Thea raised the binoculars and looked again. Her expression became grim.

"If humans could master this magical art, then it stands to reason my brothers could as well. We assumed there was nothing in these desolate wastes, but portals do not need life to occur. If they travelled Earthside, not to attack but to observe, it is possible they discovered a way to *build* a portal."

Thea continued to reason out loud.

"But how would such a thing be able to channel magic?"

Jon noticed something about how the storm Dragons acted around it. He'd seen the same behaviour during his earlier surveillances. He shared that observation.

"Looks like some of the storms aren't too keen on it. See how they're walking around it like it was going to bite them. If I had to hazard a guess, and if he's taking a page out of the human playbook, I think Black Heart has started experimenting with it already, and he's using the storms not wholly with the program as guinea pigs."

Thea didn't understand so he had to explain what humans sometimes did with small rodents and other animals in laboratories. She looked horrified.

"This must be something they learned; my father was brutal, but this... this is something even he would have balked at. Death for experimental purposes was something he never dreamed of."

It was on the tip of Jon's tongue to remind Thea what her father had been before the change, but he let it go. Whatever he and the other Dragons did while under the curse was something probably best left in the past. The fact that these Dragons, even remembering what they were, allowed Spawn and Black Heart to experiment on their own meant that they could only be hard-core disciples.

They were so thoroughly twisted with hate and malevolence that nothing, bar death, would stop them in their quest to break Thea and anyone she loved or stood with. The ones who didn't toe the line or were wavering in their support were most likely making up the group of tests subjects. Even now it seemed class lines were being redrawn. Orwell's ominous words about some being more equal than others reverberated in his mind.

Jon wasn't one to shy from combat, but this was a level of crazy that went beyond what even he was comfortable with. If followers no longer valued their own lives or the lives of their own kind in support of a cause, it meant they were well beyond help or redemption.

Black Heart was not just creating a weapon, he was developing a cult; and that made Jon extremely nervous.

Thea stood up; she'd seen as much as she could.

"I think the time for observation has passed. We must start planning to act."

Jon got up and let out a long breath.

"Guess it's time we restart the war council."

***

Gath and Crusher both sat with their mouths agape. What Thea and Jon described was unthinkable. Because of his time spent with Jon observing the camp and its mysterious machine, Ash now also sat with the war council. He kept quiet but his grim expression indicated his worry. Gath voiced the thought they were all having.

"I know some of the devices humans have created are incredible, but what you describe is unheard of. A mechanical portal? Where would such an idea come from?"

Thea sat and looking at her hands.

"Since I took his sword arm, Spawn has only his magic to create portals left to him. Maybe the machine is a way to amplify his gift. Spawn's portals were precarious at best; the mechanics could be their way to stabilize them. Worse yet, what if they use it to assault us? They could appear here in the middle of our settlement, and we would have no way of defending against them."

She took a long drawn out breath before speaking again.

"We have no choice; our hand is forced. The period we needed to rest and regroup is over. Now is the time to act. We need to start formulating a plan and attack that machine before they can use it."

Gath questioned Thea.

"You have only just recently found restful sleep, are you sure you are up to the task?"

Thea took a deep breath and smiled at him.

"True it is only recently, but the wards Nash has given me are strong and may give me additional protections. We also have some advantages. We have most, if not all, the fire Dragons with us, we have the benefit of the rock Dragons – minus my grandfather. He is old and has earned himself a reprieve. I cannot afford to lose him in battle. In fact, I think it best if all the elders are excluded. They can protect the camp. Do any of you disagree?"

Ash and Gath agreed, but Jon and Crusher were not so easily swayed. Crusher spoke up.

"Fire, while I understand you wanting to keep the elders from harm, surely their knowledge would make them an asset in battle?"

Jon agreed with Crusher.

"We are still outnumbered. I don't think we can afford to not use the elders, especially as the young Dragons will probably still be exempted from the fighting."

Thea's expression told that her alternative was a difficult one for her.

"In exchange for keeping the children and the elders from participating in the battle, I will ask parents to fight. They are younger and more resilient."

Jon knew exactly how much it was hurting Thea to say that. As new parents themselves, it was agonizing to think they might not get to see their little Darcuna grow up. Dragons were strong and Thea was the strongest of them, but even she could be killed. Laying his hands on the table he closed his eyes. Thea was not asking anyone to do more or less what she herself was expected. Opening his eyes, he looked over at her and when their eyes met, he gave her a nod, letting her know he would support her.

***

Chapter 9 - Bye Bye Baby

Thea was walking particularly fast as they made their way back to their home. Jon grabbed Thea's hand.

"Hey slow down."

Thea turned and Jon could see she was trying not to cry. He brushed his thumb over her cheek and pulled her closer.

"We always knew there would be a chance that one or both of us could be hurt or…"

He stopped short of actually saying it, but they both knew what he meant.

"I know you say you aren't in charge, but damn if you don't take on all the responsibilities as if you were."

Thea's voice was muffled as she huddled into Jon's chest.

"I have always believed that being as powerful as I am, I must look out for those who are weaker than me, but I must confess it takes a toll. So many lives depending on decisions I make."

Jon tightened his hold.

"It's ok to doubt yourself, but if you do, just say something. I know Gath and Ash, hell even Crusher would jump at the chance to take some of the load off of you."

Thea raised her head to look at Jon.

"But not you?"

Jon gave her one of his patented lopsided smiles.

"Oh, hell no. After watching you, I'd be a first-class idiot to want to step into that shit-storm. No, thank you. I'll leave that bit of unpleasantness to those better suited, or in the very least, more eager."

Thea burst out laughing then stood up on her toes to kiss Jon.

"I will try and delegate more. And Jon, thank you for reminding me that I am not alone and that I have others who will shoulder some of my burdens...but not you."

Jon kissed the tip of Thea's nose.

"Nope, I have enough responsibility keeping you sane and happy. Now let's go see little Miss Stinky and give her tons of kisses and cuddles; that always puts a smile on your face."

Thea instantly lit up before she cocked her head quizzically.

"Why do you refer to Darcuna as *Miss Stinky*? I do not find her odour particularly unpleasant."

Jon threw his head back and laughed. He proceeded to describe their daughter's nasty habit of filling her diaper whenever she was alone with him. Thea's eyes twinkled with laughter.

"Ah I see, perhaps we should have a word with Fenris about a possible solution. I am sure he will have something that could reduce the offending aroma."

Jon smacked his forehead.

"Of course, with all those damn books of his, I didn't even think to ask him. He must have something useful in them about babies and diapers."

He pulled Thea towards Fenris' dwelling.

"It'll just take a second. We can drop in on him and see if he has any ideas."

Thea laughed at Jon as he pulled her along.

"Must we see to this now?"

Jon smiled at her over his shoulder.

"You haven't experienced the pleasure of our daughter's stink bomb yet so until you do, take my word for it; it is foul and needs to be dealt with ASAP."

* * *

Thea, Jon and Darcuna were nestled together on the bed. Fenris had found them an enchantment to apply to the diapers and now the room smelled softly of lavender. Thea and Jon were spending some quality time with Darcuna before announcing the decision of the war council.

As stubborn as each other, it'd taken some convincing, but Jon had to admit at this stage Thea's brothers had not left them with many choices. If they left the portal standing it would only be a matter of time before they were hit; it had to be destroyed or at the very least, incapacitated. Black Heart's bloody wards were the issue. They were the unknown danger that kept Thea from agreeing to a full-on assault. She was unwilling to sacrifice anymore lives to her brother's bloody campaign. Her voice was sad but determined.

"We have lost too many by underestimating his will to win at all costs. I will not put more lives in danger. The portal must be disabled, even if it is only temporary. I suggest a small team portal in to give us some badly needed time and knowledge of Spawn and Black Heart's camp, their followers, and the machine."

Thea looked into the eyes of her daughter and her heart ached. Her next words to Jon nearly choked her.

"But it must be us and us alone. If Black Heart is dabbling in dark Faye magic, my new protections mean I could keep us safe, but only us. I will not put more lives than needed at risk."

She shifted her eyes back to Jon.

"What I suggest is an inconspicuous mission similar to your previous operations to watch my father. If we go at a time of night when most in the camp are asleep, we might be able to slip in and out without raising an alarm."

Thea's eyes went back to Darcuna.

"If we can hinder their progress, I am sure we can find a way to get passed the wards. And then when we can immobilize the wards, there will be a better chance that no child will have to grow up without their parents."

Jon took Darcuna away from Thea but only to give his daughter a kiss on her cheek and a cuddle.

"Are you sure this is safe? Or are you trading our daughter's parents to save the rest?"

Thea blew out a determined sigh.

"My plan is sound, but all the same Crusher is an experienced and respected tactician and much more powerful than Spawn.

"Were we not to return, Levi is of her blood so he can teach Darcuna of her heritage. Gath all but raised me, and Gerard loves our daughter as much as we do. I believe that of all the children under our protection, Darcuna has the largest number of adults already seeing to her welfare…"

She stopped to give Jon as confident a smile as she could muster.

"But we *will* see our little one after all this is done."

She raised her wrist to look at her protection tattoo.

"I trust Nash, and Evan, and you. This will work… because it has to."

Jon stood up holding Darcuna as he went to the dresser in their room.

"I wanted to surprise you with this later, but I figure with this plan it might be nice to have a talisman, you know, for luck."

He pulled out a small simple box.

"Ok honey, give mommy her present—No, sweetie, don't eat the present."

Eventually he pried the box out of Darcuna's sloppy grasp and presented it to Thea. She pulled out a simple gold pendant with a miniature portrait of Darcuna under glass. On the back were three gemstones representing each of them. Jon explained it to Thea.

"I remember Gerard telling me about the miniature my mum had made of me and him, and I thought you might feel better having her with us."

Thea startled poor Darcuna when she jumped up to kiss Jon. As both of them worked to quiet the baby down, Thea mouthed *I love you* to Jon.

***

Chapter 10 - The Plan

After hours of deliberation they had a plan. Not everyone was happy with it, but it was grudgingly, agreed to. Crusher was the leading opponent.

"It is tantamount to a suicide mission."

He was not far off, but all signs were that the portal was finished and it would only be a matter of time before their little settlement was targeted. Their respite was gone and the portal had to be stopped, else they would have to retreat back into the tunnels and cede the progress they'd made in healing the land around Lake Acantha.

"Our hand is now forced. Going in as a group will set off Black Heart's wards and will kill most of us before we can get close enough to destroy it. It must be a small but precise attack. Jon's portal is ideal, but we cannot shift a large number of Dragons through it. This is not like the taking of Incendya Domus. This is only meant to buy us more time and right now it is our only option."

Thea touched the protection ward on her wrist without thinking.

"I have defences against Faye magic, but not for a sizable group."

Jon saw her rubbing her wrist.

"Thea, we don't know what that protection will withstand. Are you absolutely sure you want to chance it?"

Thea sighed before raising her eyes.

"I trust Nash and Evan. If they say these are powerful wards then I believe them. I can feel how strong they are. I can't describe it but I feel shielded by them. Your skills with portals will place me as close to the machine as possible. I will then use my Hellfire to disable it and, if the celestials allow, you will transport us away before they have a chance to retaliate."

Gerard stepped in.

"Why not have both, me and Jon, open a portal big enough to allow a larger force through? Why just you two?"

Thea looked to Jon and he nodded.

"No, we must have contingencies in place for a worst-case scenario. As confident as I am, to not have them is foolhardy. Crusher and you will be our guarantee that if things should not go according to plan, there will still be some form of leadership in place. Gerard, your skills with portals are just as important if not more because of your ties to the Faye council. Crusher is the only other Dragon besides me who can lead the others in battle."

Thea paused to allow herself a moment to contain her emotions. She looked towards Gerard.

"*If* anything should happen to us…it falls to you and Gath to raise Darcuna. I do not have Dragon memories but Darcuna can learn, as I did from my grandfather."

It had to be said. Dragons were not immortal. Thea would not put herself above the rest, and with her immense power she felt it was her responsibility to take on the hardest missions.

"I have sent countless to their graves to see this threat defeated…"

Gath grabbed her arm.

"You have done no such thing; we march for our own sakes."

Thea wrenched her arm free.

"No, you all placed me as leader, and it was I who bore every single death. Now I say it is time I made a sacrifice."

Crusher stood over Thea, using his size to try and intimidate her.

"No sister, you forget your daring mission to destroy Mount Pyrosis."

Thea stood her ground, staring up at her brother.

"I was never in danger; fire cannot kill an obsidian Dragon with a fire aspect."

She stepped back to try and diffuse the growing tension.

"Black Heart is not a fool. He will have wards all around his camp to protect him and his machine, and yet I know he cannot penetrate my rock magic. He has no understanding of it. Also, Jon and I are linked and that will give us an advantage; a small one, but an advantage nonetheless. My new protection wards are strong, but I can only shield one other."

Thea walked over to the table where the drawings of the camp and the machine were laid. So far, they could only guess where Black Heart's wards would be, but Thea and Jon were sure there would be none directly inside the camp. Their plan hinged on that fact.

"The machine is here, inside the compound. Never having been privy to father and Crusher's private conversations, they do not know how extensive Jon's knowledge of portals is. They do not know he can move passed certain wards. We will use that information to get inside the camp and temporarily disable the machine.

Once it is rendered inoperative, with no chance for them to escape, we can then think about a full-scale offensive to capture my brothers and end this once and for all."

Crusher spat on the floor.

"Capture? Why should they be taken alive? All of them have shown themselves to be traitors. I say burn the entire camp to the ground and be done with it."

Jon shot Thea a look and she nodded. He shared his observations.

"The last time we inspected the camp, some of the storms looked less than comfortable with the machine; Ash will back me up. I think building the machine wasn't the only concept they took from humanity."

He explained his speculation about the use of live test subjects and his deduction that Black Heart was developing a cult of sorts.

"There are always survivors. Kill Black Heart in battle and you make him a martyr. We need to capture him and the others to send a message to any followers. He isn't a god or even a ruler. He's nothing."

Thea cleared her throat and all the males looked towards her. She addressed Crusher but her words were for all of them.

"Make no mistake, brother, once they are brought to heel, I will make sure they are punished. I am also a daughter of Shadow Lord and he taught me well."

***

Chapter 11 - Sneaking Around in the Dark

They sat on the cliff edge they'd used on previous missions to observe the camp. It was still light, but Jon knew he and Thea needed to study the guard movements to plan their route to the machine. They both had their binoculars up to their eyes. Jon spoke first.

"I'll plant us there, over by that guard post to the east. I would put us closer, but they have torches, there, there, and there, and I'd rather come in somewhere that will be in darkness and then move towards it. That way we can alter our steps if we need to and keep to the shadows."

Thea had a thought.

"They must change each shift at the same time. If we time our arrival just before the evening meal..."

Jon finished her thought.

"We could use that to our advantage. The shift coming off will be rushing to eat, and the shift coming on will have nice full bellies, ready for a quiet night. If they make a mistake, *that* will be when it happens."

After the ordeal of Thea's protection ward, Nash found giving Jon his sword tattoo binding more his speed. Jon had always been envious of the ease at which Thea was able to release her swords and cast; now he would be able to do the same. He was still getting used to not having the familiar weight on his back but even a small glint of steel could give them away. The new tattoo ran down his right thigh and now he would always have his sword ready if needed.

They discussed more scenarios just in case.

"Better to be prepared for anything than have to change up on the fly. I learned that after meeting you."

Thea's eyes were still on the camp, but the side of her mouth quirked up.

"How sensible. I did not think you were so organised on the day. Had I guessed, I would say you were very surprised."

Jon snorted.

"Ya well, maybe if Evan had given me *all* the mission details, I could have handled that better. I'm just saying, better to have a few plans in our pockets just in case. See those tents to the south...?"

They came up with several more strategies before Jon was satisfied they were ready. And then all they could do was wait. Jon placed his binoculars down and leaned back against a boulder.

"We can't do anything until well passed nightfall, so we might as well get some rest."

Thea lowered her lenses but was too keyed up to sleep. So much rested on undermining the mechanical portal. Every possible scenario she could think of played through her mind. What if this night the guard movements changed? What if an alarm was raised before they could disable the machine? Thea could not turn her brain off.

Where are you? What are you planning?

Even without the nightmares, her brother plagued her thoughts. So far, she had seen both Black Heart and Rage, but there was no sign of Spawn.

***

Jon cracked an eye open and saw Thea had her lenses raised again. He had to get her to shut off. He leaned over and pulled them away from her.

"Stop it. You need to rest. I know you're worried, but we've got a solid plan—several in fact. If you're not sure maybe we should abort and try again another night."

Thea shook her head and sighed.

"No, you are right. I must rest."

She took another deep breath and gave him a small smile.

"If I am too tired it may cost us."

She lay back and closed her eyes.

"Jon, are you afraid?"

Jon gave a laugh.

"I am shitting myself."

Thea bolted up.

"Are we making a mistake then?"

Jon's eyes were closed again, and his smile was calm.

"Hun, if we weren't scared, I'd have us both checked out. It's what sharpens your mind and keeps your focus. Being scared is what keeps you alive."

He pulled Thea towards him so she was leaning against him.

"We'll watch each other's back."

He kissed the top of her head.

"There's no one I'd rather be risking my life with than you."

Thea yawned, and they both finally fell asleep.

***

Because so little Hellfire existed within Morsa Ersa, it was one of the few places where there was almost complete darkness. In spite of that, Thea and Jon were in dark clothing and covered head to foot in soot. Even Thea's hair was plaited and darkened with soot. They would become walking shadows.

The portal opened, and Jon led the way so that if needed, he could push Thea back through. She readied a shield spell. They stood inside the camp. The air was still enough that every sound felt amplified. Thea had to remember to breathe. They were relieved to see very little activity at this hour. Thea dispersed her shield, and they turned towards the machine. Jon could hear the sounds of sleeping storms in their tents as well as the murmurs of guards trying to stay awake. This close to it, the machine was monstrously large. An entire army could march through it and surprise their enemy.

Thea and Jon had briefly discussed how such a device would work. They had agreed that it could only provide one-way travel as no other portal had been discovered elsewhere. It was assumed it was purely to provide a large stable portal to travel Earthside to complete their plan to annex the Faye and Human realm under their rule. They presumed that before they would go Earthside, they would use it to attack Lake Acantha to destroy the Dragons and re-enslave the lessor demons.

The plan was kept simple: to trap her brothers and their followers in this desolate waste, Thea would use her hellfire to damage vital components and deactivate the machine. Jon would note which wards were in use so that he and his brother could disarm them. The full assault would take place before they could repair the damage, when there was no chance of a mass escape. Everything hinged on Thea's ability to nullify the mechanical portal.

Thea held on to Jon's shoulder as they crept towards the mechanism. A guard appeared for his shift. Blending into the shadows, they froze to allow him to pass. Jon reached for Thea's hand and gave it a squeeze. Once again, they moved towards the device. Jon used a Faye spell to lower the light from the torches around them. Someone would notice if the torches went out but not if he simply lowered the illumination a few degrees giving him and Thea more shadows to hide in.

Thea found what she hoped was the main panel that controlled the machine and laid her hands on it as she conjured her Hellfire. The air around them crackled with dark magic. She kept her flames small enough so as to not arouse suspicion, but they had to be hot enough to not just melt the metal but fuse it so as to make repairs more difficult. Thea could feel the metal flex under her hands and took a calming breath. She needed just a few seconds longer to completely disable the panel. Once the main panel was a useless lump she moved to try and weaken the structure of the arch.

Jon became aware of a magical shift around them. He didn't like how the air tasted. He nudged Thea to hurry up. Both of them jumped when the machine sprang to life with a low hum that started creeping up in pitch.

Jon tried to tug Thea away but she held fast. They would not have another opportunity like this again.

If Black Heart knew they had tampered with his device he would definitely place an enchantment on the machine itself. The hum grew louder, and Jon whispered in Thea's ear.

"We need to move now. Something is not right here…"

The hum was no longer quiet, and Jon could make out shapes of guards moving towards them as they came to check on the machine. Thea held fast as her Hellfire continued to melt the metal structure. As the arch of the machine warped, a strange whining starting to come from the machine, and Jon choked when he realized a sizable portal was opening up under the arch. This time he tried to physically pick Thea up but she was held in place by the force of the portal. Thea's eyes were wide with fear when she realised what was happening.

Jon tried to open his own portal so they could slip away, but the whine grew in volume and he felt the machine pull him towards the portal. He dug his heels in but then the machine started to syphon off his own magic. Jon went rigid when he heard one of the guards call out.

"We have intruders. Quickly, they are attempting to sabotage the portal; fire on them!"

The machine whined and shuddered as the structure became unstable. The force of the portal forming was actually drawing the machine into itself. Metal shards flew off the device, and Jon heard one whiz passed his ear before he made a split-second decision and using all his strength, he shoved Thea through the portal.

***

"Toto, I don't think we're in Kansas anymore…"

Chapter 12 - Astranya

Thea and Jon tumbled out of the portal into a field and found themselves surrounded. Both had the same thought. *How had they known to expect them?* A quick glance around confirmed they were no longer in Black Heart's camp. It was now day, and the sun was high in the sky. The grass was soft under their hands and the sky was clear blue with only a few wisps of clouds. A cool breeze kept the air from feeling oppressively hot, exposed as they were.

The figures wore dark cloaks with intricate runic symbols woven into them. They kept their faces hidden under hoods, but their daggers were displayed; the glint of the blades left no doubt of their sharpness and the bearer's willingness to use them if Thea or Jon gave them provocation.

Thea knew they were Faye by smell but one felt familiar. Before she could dwell on it any longer, she and Jon were hauled up to their feet.

The one with the faintly recognizable scent stood apart observing. They seemed to be in charge, and from their slight form, Thea guessed it was a woman. The voice was matronly as she instructed the others.

"Keep them separated, until we have a chance to speak to them individually."

Thea could see Jon readying a spell, and she gave him an almost imperceptible shake of her head. As much as she understood his wanting to go on the defensive, it would do them no good to antagonize their captors until they knew exactly who they were dealing with.

The unknown female leader observing Thea caught the exchange and nodded.

"I agree; you are wise to practice caution…"

Thea was stunned; she thought her movement was subtle enough to be hidden. The female Faye paused as she considered her next words.

"You are not the first to appear as you have, but you are the first to show some measure of judiciousness."

Thea caught a glimpse of the leader's smile from under the hood. While not malevolent, it did not put her at ease. More importantly, the statement confirmed Thea and Jon's speculation that Black Heart had been testing his portal for some time. The female Faye continued.

"Keep your wits about you, and I see no reason for you to come to… much harm."

Her eyes narrowed when she saw the runes on Thea's wrist and her smile disappeared abruptly.

"Let us see if you survive longer than the others."

With those last words, Thea felt afraid.

***

Thea caught a quick glimpse before her eyes were covered. Jon had been tied with what looked to be simple rope; they bound her with iron shackles similar to the ones Jon had once used on her. These bore a different enchantment; so instead of feeling calm, cold fear rose up her spine. Thea watched Jon ahead of her.

The blindfold they placed on her was not so dense she couldn't see. If she concentrated, she could make out vague shapes without detail. She noted she was intentionally being held away from Jon so they could not talk.

Her thoughts went immediately to the child she'd left behind. When they'd left to destroy the mechanical gateway, she'd given Darcuna a kiss on her forehead with promises she would be back quickly. Gath had given her a sympathetic smile and a knowing nod. She knew Gath would care for and protect Darcuna, but what if she and Jon never made it back? Thea blinked back the tears that threatened to fall, but nothing could stop the ache in her chest.

She could smell the blood of previous wearers on the shackles; the scent filled her nose—dried Dragon blood. Jon would sense it as well and she could imagine his shoulders would be stiff with agitation. Thea willed her breathing to appear slow and even, so as to not show how much it was affecting her. The route their captors were taking felt well used under her feet. Thea was sure their destination would be both secure and well-guarded.

***

Jon heard Thea give a small whimper. He flinched and tried to turn to her but was forced forward again with a shove. He balled his fists to keep from casting but the urge to protect Thea was overwhelming. That little sob could only be because she was thinking of Darcuna, and he felt his own chest tighten. They needed to get back. He felt the incubus rise in him and he silently told it to bide its time. *Don't you worry, I'll feed you soon.* The guard shoved Jon to keep him moving and the incubus growled from within. *Yep, you'll be feeding soon enough.*

* * *

After a long two-hour march, Thea could see the shape of the compound. Her blindfold was removed abruptly and she blinked to refocus her eyes. When she could see again, Thea noted that the compound was a mix of wooden structures of varying sizes with elaborately carved decorations and enchantments to provide protection. In the center, there was a single large stone structure. The group separated, and Jon was taken to one of the wooden buildings while Thea was pushed towards the stone structure. The smell of blood was stronger and she cried out. She could see Jon pulling at his bonds before the female Faye leader leaned over and spoke quietly to him.

Thea was too far away to hear, but whatever she had said to him was enough to calm him. Thea blinked back her tears. *Where were they taking her? Had they enchanted Jon to make him compliant?* Thea tried to run, but a strong iron chain attached to her restraints made the attempt futile and with a sudden tug she fell backward. The female spoke in a loud clear voice.

"Until I have had a moment to speak to her, I need her alive. Is that clear, Captain?"

Thea understood; she would not be summarily executed. They would keep her alive until they were satisfied with her and Jon's statements. Alive but not unharmed.

* * *

Chapter 13 - Waiting is the Hardest Part

In the cell awaiting her interrogation, Thea's jailers secured her restraint to the wall. *How long would she be stuck in the cell?* Her shoulders ached from the unnatural position. How would Gerard and Gath explain to Darcuna where her parents were? She was so small and Thea felt her breath catch with the thought that she might never see her baby again. She squeezed her eyes shut. She took a long shaky breath to try and calm herself, but she could not stop the tears that slid down her cheeks.

The cell was large. A few torches were dotted around but not enough to dispel the darkness. They seemed, instead, to enhance the gloom of the cell. In the dim light, she could just about see that the walls were lined with rings like the one she had been secured to. There were six along each wall facing each other with enough space in between to keep each prisoner separate, twelve in all.

When she and Jon left to destroy her brothers' machine, she'd been wearing one of Jon's t-shirts and her beloved jean shorts that Jon had given her so long ago; neither gave much protection from the rough stone beneath her or the damp cold that permeated the chamber. The stone walls were thick enough to dull all sound from outside, and the cell was eerily quiet, like a tomb.

Jon had been taken to be questioned first. No doubt they had recognized one of their own and wanted to know why he was travelling with a Dragon. If the old blood Thea could smell all around her was any indication, the Dragons they had previously encountered had not fared well, and Thea shuddered. Was it their own actions that had doomed them or something not of their making?

She had to believe that Jon would find a way to explain their appearance together and convince their captors to release them.

A movement in the shadows before the sound of chains rattling, seized Thea's attention and she called out into the darkness. Her voice reverberated in the empty space.

"You there, are you friend or foe? How long have they held you?"

As the echo's died away, Thea felt an icy finger up her spine when she heard the voice of her companion.

"I am no friend to you, and yet it seems we are to be cellmates."

Thea's voice was barely a whisper.

"Spawn? But ... how?"

He shifted partially into the light, and Thea could see him now. It was clear he had been badly abused. Unable to be shackled like her, they had fashioned a crude sort of iron sling to keep his remaining arm strapped to his chest. A chain was fastened to a collar and then looped through one of the rings on the walls. *Why was he here?* Black Heart and Spawn had always been thick as thieves. He should have been able to portal away; that he was chained could only mean something was wrong with his magic.

Seeing him as he was, she could not gather the anger she'd previously held for him. He looked so pathetic. This wasn't the arrogant Spawn of her childhood; this was a broken shell. Had he been sent here to die? She was surprised to find she felt pity for him.

He coughed. His voice was rough as if he'd not used it for some time.

"How indeed. Too late I realised I was but a means to an end…"

His words tapered off as if the energy to talk was too much.

Thea called out to him.

"Spawn, how long have you been confined?"

He sounded weary.

"I do not know, nor do I care. I wish only to be done with this life."

Thea was afraid to ask about the others, whose blood she could smell all around them, but she had to know.

"Spawn, what happened to the others?"

There was another long period of silence before Spawn finally answered her.

"One by one, they came to question them. Each one was taken and brought back bloody and then taken again, never returning until I alone was left…"

He went silent and Thea could not prompt him to speak again. It was painful hearing him so beaten, even after all that had passed between them. With no allies and alone she pitied her eldest brother. Thea called out to him. Her voice felt so loud in the dead space.

"Spawn, had the fates been kinder to us, we would not have found ourselves adversaries. I…?"

Thea was interrupted when the door to the cell opened, and a Faye came to collect her for her interrogation. She turned to finish speaking to her brother.

"Spawn, please, say something."

Instead she heard laughter—bitter, defeated, sad laughter.

"Go on Fire; run along. I am done with this life. Leave me."

***

Chapter 14 - The Originals

As the Faye pulled her out of the cell, Thea could not stop the tears as the door closed on the sight of her brother waiting for death. Unnoticed by her, the jailer took note. Thea was led across the compound and into a room. She sighed in relief to see Jon was no longer bound. Her throat tightened with emotion. At least the fates had seen fit to keep him safe.

He stood to the side of the female she'd glimpsed before. She still wore her cloak but the hood was now pulled back to reveal her face. The female rose and instructed the jailer to remove Thea's shackles and nodded to Jon that he could approach Thea. Unable to contain herself, Thea rushed to Jon. She held onto him, shaking, as tears streamed down her cheeks. She kissed him over and over while mumbling.

"Thank the stars".

Jon pulled away, but only long enough to check and see for himself that Thea had not been mistreated. He looked at her face and ran a finger over the bruise on her cheek before he pulled her back to him in a crushing embrace. The jailer and the female supervisor watched patiently before the female spoke.

"You are in Astranya. You may call me Caris. Jon has explained who you are and how you came to be here in this realm, and he assures me you are not connected to those who came through before you."

Thea tried to keep her voice even.

"Where is Astranya?"

Thea was startled when Jon answered.

"Thea, this is going to sound cracked, but these beings are Faye and this realm is, pardon the expression, a hell of a lot farther away than I thought possible to travel."

Jon gestured toward Caris.

"Caris has tried to explain to me that somehow your crazy-as-shit brother built a portal that is more powerful than we first thought."

Thea's expression became panicked.

"What do you mean? We can't travel? We need to get home. What about Darcuna?"

Jon tried to give her a reassuring smile. Only his eyes belayed his sadness.

"She's safe. She has Gath and my brother and Aliyah... Hell, she has an entire Dragon village to look out for her."

Thea wasn't convinced.

"But her parents are here! Jon, I want to go home to my baby!"

Thea turned to Caris.

"Please, we will leave. Send us back to where we came from. The portal that brought us is destroyed. It is no longer available to us. We need to go back. We have a young daughter."

Caris shook her head sadly, and Jon held Thea as she cried. His heart was heavy, being away from Darcuna, but he had to stay strong for Thea's sake. So, he swallowed down his own grief so he could redirect Thea's thoughts from their daughter.

"Thea, listen to me. I've been talking to Caris... and she's sort of related to me."

Thea had known there was a connection from her scent, but still did not understand why Jon trusted her.

"Jon, I know she *seems* familiar, but do *you* trust her?

He tried to explain.

"These are the Faye that chose to stay. Me, Evan, The Olde Ones—fuck, the entire Earthside Faye population—share the same descendants as these Faye. A group left and went looking for someplace... less restrictive. From what Caris tells me, they found Hell, and when that went sideways, well you know the rest."

Thea was unconvinced and Jon saw he needed to explain further.

"I'm still getting to grips with it all myself, but it seems they know things; things about the problem Faye Evan and Nash talked about; even about me and my family and —this is important— a way to lift the curse off of you."

Thea turned and studied Caris. She could not doubt her scent and if Jon was sure, Thea would trust his judgement. But she needed to ask about Spawn.

"While I am grateful Jon is unharmed... I am... concerned over the volume of Dragon blood in the cell..."

Thea knew it was a precarious question, but she had to know if she could save her brother.

"I am safe, but there is one left. What is to happen to him? Will he be destroyed? Like the others?"

Thea swallowed before continuing.

"The one you hold is known to me..."

Thea glanced quickly at Jon.

"He is my brother..."

Jon's jaw dropped when it dawned on him who Thea must have encountered. The only one missing when they observed the camp.

Thea's voice trembled.

"I have no reason to ask for him. We have not had an easy relationship and yet it pains me to see him chained like he is."

Caris and the jailer exchanged a knowing glance.

"Jon said you were not a threat and that you had a soft heart. The one left has said nothing in his defence since his appearance. The others did not interact with him. We have not yet decided on his fate."

Thea pushed even though Jon's expression pleaded with her to leave it alone.

"He is no threat, not anymore."

Caris nodded.

"We will take your comments into consideration."

Thea felt anger rising inside her. They spoke about Spawn as if his life were of no consequence. Pulling herself away from Jon, she stood to face Caris.

"I have greater reason than you or anyone to wish to see him dead. Jon can tell you what he did to me, and if I am willing to pardon him, then *that* should be enough of a reason to offer absolution. *That* is the only consideration you should need."

Caris beckoned another forward from behind Thea and Jon. They turned to see Spawn being led into the room.

In the light, Thea could see the fullness of Spawn's injuries and her lips trembled with sadness and rage.

Spawn had never been handsome, but his wounds made his already unpleasant face grotesque. One eye was so swollen, it was fused shut, and his nose was badly broken. His face was covered in varying shades of purple bruises and he was missing an ear. She rounded on Caris.

"How could you do this? You said he gave no fight…"

Thea was interrupted by Spawn. His voice was still hoarse but firm.

"It was not these Faye that harmed me."

He took a moment to clear his throat.

"No, it was our brother, Black Heart, to whom you should aim your fury. Once he had his army and his machine was ready, he syphoned my gift before turning me over to those who once served me. A cripple, no longer able to fight, stripped of both my strength and my magic, they turned on me, battered and molested me. And then he sent me here to die."

He gave a pitiful laugh.

"How ironic that the fates saw how I treated Father and thought to visit the same insult on me."

He looked at Thea. She alone saw how empty his eyes were. The scorn that once burned bright was gone replaced with a hollow and desolate gaze. He'd died long before now. Like one of Crusher's walking corpses, he was waiting for permission to die.

"No sister, I do not wish to continue this wretched existence, but I *will not* die by some Faye executioner."

He paused and sighed. He looked at Caris, but his words were for Thea.

"I will ask for one courtesy, that I should be executed by one of my own."

Jon could see the exact moment Spawn's words hit their mark, and Thea's heart broke at the request. If she fulfilled it, it would haunt her for the rest of her life. The evil bastard wanted one final dig at Thea. Jon had heard enough.

"No."

***

Chapter 15 - Goodbye Brother

Thea tried to speak but Jon held his ground. His voice was low and menacing.

"No, take this piece of shit back to his cage and let him rot there for all I care..."

Time seemed to stop for Thea. She blinked, and in that moment, she could hear her mother's voice so clearly, she could almost believe she was standing next to her.

"It is not in our nature to be cruel. You have a soft heart and while others will criticise you and make you feel it is a hindrance it also gives you great strength. Your emotions run deep. You love as strongly as you hate. But hate destroys and if you let it, it will destroy you."

Her mother's image dissolved and then she saw her father as he lay dying, his face contorting with pain.

"You shall be my legacy."

Thea blinked again. Her parents were gone and she was back in the room with Jon and the others. The jailer was taking Spawn back to his cell. Before anyone could stop her, Thea's sword materialized in her hand. She spun Spawn to face her and she ran her brother through, her sword slipping in just under his restraint and up into his chest. Tears ran down her cheeks as she leaned into Spawn. He bent down and she was able to touch her forehead to his.

"I forgive you and may you find the peace you were denied in this life. Farewell brother."

She released her sword, and then before his body hit the ground, she called up her Hellfire and he dissolved into ash. Caris and the jailer watched in stunned silence. Jon caught Thea as she crumpled to the ground. He held her as she howled in grief.

Cradling her, Jon's expression was of stunned disbelief. "Why Thea? He didn't deserve your mercy. I don't get it."

It took a moment before she was able to speak, her tears streaming down her cheeks.

"Because we were pawns in a game not of our making. I could not deny him that one small concession."

Jon could not fathom why she thought she owed Spawn anything.

"Small concession? What the fuck, Thea? Why would you do that to yourself?"

Thea took a shaky breath.

"I cannot pretend that this will not hurt. And yet if I left him to die alone, part of me would have died with him. I have not forgotten that his past actions were cruel, but I am not like them, Jon. In that moment I heard my mother's voice and then saw my father's face as he died in my arms."

Thea stopped to wipe her eyes.

"I needed to show myself that I am my mother's daughter and that I am worthy of my father's trust. That after everything that has happened, I am still capable of mercy because if I am not, my hate would eventually overwhelm me."

Jon was speechless as he held Thea. Caris and the jailer nodded to each other. They saw what Thea was capable of—her true nature. Caris waited until Jon pulled Thea up to stand before speaking.

"Thea, Jon did not lie, you are nothing like the Dragons that came through before you. You are like the Dragons of long ago that our stories told of. I believe we can trust you. It is time you regained your full Dragon memories."

Thea held onto Jon as she turned to face Caris.

"I have no use for my past. I must look to my future and what I wish is to see my daughter again."

Caris understood, but her reply was not what Thea had hoped for.

"We do not possess the means to send you back, if we did, I would. But it is possible that your Dragon memories may provide you with a clue to how to get home to your child by yourself."

**

Alone in their room, Jon watched Thea pacing.

"And you are absolutely sure we can trust her?"

Jon nodded.

"We talked. I said the same thing as you, I told her we would be more than happy to go home and never look back, but she said it would be impossible—that there were complications."

He walked over to Thea.

"I was surprised that she knew you were a Dragon, but then they were shocked to find out I was half Dragon. So, I explained what happened, and why we were here and everything about your brothers and the war—anything to convince them to let you go. I told them we just wanted to go home."

Thea was still unsure about Caris.

"Why do you believe her? I know she has a familiar scent, but why do you trust her?"

Jon pulled Thea to sit down next to him.

"She asked me something that may not sound like much but it reminded me of a conversation I overheard between my mother and Gerard. At the time I didn't understand, I was just a kid. Mum seemed to think it was something to hide. Caris asked; *'What do you know of the Highborn?'* I never got to ask my mum what it meant, so I was curious.'"

Thea looked confused so Jon explained.

"My mother, Camille, was a type of Faye called Highborn. It meant that her magic was sort of special, intense. Sometimes those Faye were even confined for the good of the community as a whole. It was part of the reason they left. Even after arriving in Hell, the council felt that to have that much power was unnatural and tended to keep a close eye on them.

"Her magic was particularly extreme, even for most Highborn. Evan knew about my mother. When she was pregnant with me and she ran, she freaked out a lot of people. Gerard told me our family was special, but he never said why. It was like some dirty secret no one talked about. Until Caris asked me, I'd never heard that title used in my presence. That caught my attention.

"Caris said the women in her family were all Highborn, and that I was the only male Highborn she'd ever met. Something about my Dragon blood must allow me to tap into it. That and her resemblance to my mother got me thinking, so I asked her about the ones who left and sure enough she and I share an ancestor."

He smiled suddenly and gave a little chuckle.

"She was a bit surprised that I knew our family tree off the top of my head while she had to refer to a book. My mum kept a written ledger of her family's history hidden, but I was a curious little shit and I found it. I may not have Dragon memories, but I do have the ability to remember more than the average Faye. The important thing is, I'm pretty sure we can trust her."

Thea nodded and let the feel of Jon's arms around her soothe away her last doubts.

"I hope your faith is not misplaced."

***

Chapter 16 - Curing Curses

The ritual to remove the curse was a tricky one because of the protections Nash had given her. They were designed to keep others out, but to get to Thea's Dragon memories, Caris needed to get in.

Caris bent over to closely examine the runes on Thea's wrist.

"Thea, you said the one who gave you these protections was a friend. Well, your friend was remarkably skilful when he applied them. Did you see *how* he applied them? Do you understand exactly what they do?"

Thea glanced at her wrist and the tattooed symbols. They meant nothing to her other than a means to end her nightmares; she'd never given them much thought because she trusted Nash and Evan.

"Yes, well sort of, my brother is a master clairvoyant, he sent me the most awful night terrors and used my other brother's Faye chaos magic to inject some sort of intense darkness into them. Our Dragon wards could not shield them, so Evan and Nash said that this type of enchantment was needed. Are they dangerous?"

Caris sighed.

"No, they are not inherently dangerous but it does make our task difficult. We banned this sort of grey magic for a reason; it often comes with a cost and can cause all sorts of problems for the uninitiated. But there is no doubt they are strong defences to have."

Thea's eyes widened with worry.

Jon patted her hand and whispered in her ear.

"Nash and Evan would never give you something they thought might hurt you. Besides, not all alleged darkness is inherently evil. We're proof of that."

Thea nodded and Caris patted her hand reassuringly.

"You are lucky, these particular runes are fairly innocuous but do offer pronounced resistance to most dark spells. But due to their grey nature, I am not sure they can be reapplied once removed. We have some options, we can discharge them; it will be a chore, but it can be done."

Caris ran her fingers over Thea's wrist.

"I'm sorry but the tattoo will remain. We can remove the magic but not the ink. Or the more challenging option is we can try and work around them. They do, after all, provide you with powerful protection.

Caris paused before continuing.

I would be remiss if I did not mention that we cannot guarantee if the side effects of removing them would be any less harmful. The choice is yours."

She left Thea and Jon to discuss their options. Jon tried to be supportive.

"It's your decision, Thea. You know I'll back you whatever you decide."

Thea closed her eyes and sighed.

"I know, but I have no grasp of Faye magic. I cannot decide because I simply do not comprehend it. This time I really do need you to help me, Jon."

***

Jon paced the room. He'd watched Nash as he placed each layer of the enchantment and while he understood bits and pieces of the spells, they were mostly beyond him. Caris said they were safe enough and to remove them could have side effects. If getting Thea's Dragon memories was the prize then maybe going with the more difficult but possibly more rewarding choice was the way to go. Putting on his most confidant smile he turned to Thea.

"Onward and upward, I say."

Thea looked confused and he gave a little chuckle.

"We'll see if they can work around them. I think it's better if they leave them."

Thea looked comforted. Jon felt a little sick to his stomach.

* * *

As they sat over a meal, Caris tried to describe the ritual to Thea and Jon as best as she could.

"We are all in unknown territory. This is the first time we are attempting to remove a curse, not from the original source, but from one whom has been affected by it."

She squeezed Thea's shoulder and smiled at Jon.

"Jon will be our link through the wards – and with his Dragon Blood – a route to your memories."

Jon looked rather nervous about his part.

"And I only have to stand near Thea?"

Caris patted his hand.

"Yes, sort of. You are my conduit. You will also keep her in the moment, so we don't lose her when her Dragon memories come flooding back. You will act as a tether for her to us and keep her grounded. Memory is an intoxicating kind of magic. It can take us back in time, and most don't understand how powerful that can be. Get stuck in a memory and you can be trapped in the past."

Thea had always been amazed that Dragon memories were so magically potent, but it did make sense because of how absolute a Dragon memory was—every detail perfectly suspended in her blood. She grasped Jon's hand even tighter and he squeezed back in response. Nothing short of a complete separation at the wrist would break his grip. They both nodded to Caris. Jon gave Thea a wink with his usual bravado.

"Let's do this."

Thea added her own prayer.

"And may the celestials watch over us."

***

Chapter 17 - The Ritual

Thea was laid out on an old large stone altar where several weathered runes carved into the rock could still be seen. Jon stood just behind Thea's head, holding her hand over her shoulder. A ring of salt crystals surrounded her providing a purified space that Caris assured her would keep her safe but also contain the damage if things went wrong. Several hooded mages chanted quietly as they continuously circled the altar, provided a second barrier. Caris spoke her incantations over their murmurs.

Thea could not understand the Faye words, but Caris' voice and Jon's tight grip on her hand was enough to reassure her. She looked up at him and he winked back. Glancing towards her, Caris gave her a confident smile, and Thea slowed her breathing allowing a calm to settle over her. It wasn't long until Thea's eyelids drooped and she felt herself drifting off. Caris had warned her that it might happen and told Jon to keep hold of her no matter what. Thea could feel Jon's hand tighten and she sluggishly responded.

***

Thea found herself looking up at Gerard. At first, she mistook him for Jon, but no, it was Gerard. She was aware of pain throughout her body, and she inhaled quickly as she realised these was her mother's final moments. Gerard was holding her mother and crying.

"We saved her. He cannot reach her anymore."

His words meant to ease her mother's passing. She could feel her fading and her heart ached. Dark Haven would have known her father would send for her that night.

***

Thea felt her mother's fear facing Shadow Lord and his unbelievable fury. Dark Haven was on her knees and frightened as her father stood over her and roared with rage. The walls shook with his wrath. How dare she sneak behind his back? The girl was his and spiriting her away was a punishable crime. Thea trembled as her father exploded at having his prize stolen away. She could not block out the sound as her mother cried out with each blow until Dark Haven fell blissfully into oblivion.

***

Thea's body was then wracked with a familiar pain; she was remembering her own birth. To the side she could see Gath and she smiled. He looked so small and frightened, and while she already knew it ended happily, part of her wanted to comfort the old gargoyle. She watched him take a knee and pray for her mother. It occurred to Thea that Gath loved her mother and they were more than close friends. He must have been devastated to leave her, knowing what would happen. Her throat felt tight at the idea that his devotion to her mother was strong enough for him to carry out her last wish, regardless of the cost. Gath did not just lose a master, but the closest he had to family.

Thea scowled as the demon midwife berated her mother, but Dark Haven was able to see past the bravado presented, to a midwife baffled by a Dragon birth. Even as she struggled with each contraction, she had encouraging words for the demon.

***

The demon midwife's face dissolved and another face appeared over her, coalescing into her father, but his expression was strange and she realised she was experiencing her mother's memories of her own conception and she gasped. While it was heartening, seeing her mother's memories, she was unnerved by the sensations her mother experienced in those memories, as her father hovered over her.

***

Thankfully, the memory was then superseded and instead she remembered how Gerard held her mother before they crossed over and as she made her way to Incendya Domus, Dark Haven could feel Gerard watching her, and she felt safe.

***

It was dark and she felt Gerard squeeze her hand under the table. They sat as a group with Evan, planning their daring mission over a meal.

***

A young Gerard stood in front of her. She smiled. Gerard was a handsome Faye when Thea met him but in her mother's memories, he was shy and not so cocksure. Her mother felt a rush of tenderness as she caught a glimpse of Gerard watching her. Dark Haven had been so happy and so in love.

****

Another memory took over, and Thea was surprised to see her grandfather but not as she knew him. This was a younger Levi and as she relived her mother's childhood, a flood of tears began streaming down her cheeks. Her vision remained clear though, as she was seeing through her heart and not her eyes.

***

She took a shaky breath as each memory tugged at her heart. Most were happy and tender, but then she was thrown into a memory further back when she was cowering in a secret hole while humans searched her village. She could hear the cries of children separated from their parents, and her heart broke when they were quickly and ruthlessly silenced. The smell of charred Dragon flesh made her choke on remembered smoke. Thea could feel the fear of her ancestor and the sad relief when the humans and Faye finally left.

***

Jon watched Thea's body twitch and her face change. It was strange to see her react to each new flashback. He had no idea how far back Thea's memories would go, but a small bead of sweat was forming on Caris' brow at the concentration needed to carefully hold back all the layers of protection while maintaining their integrity to release the recollections. Thea's body started to violently spasm and her mouth opened in a silent scream. Was she reliving the time during the Dragon Purge? Or even the Earthside wars?

Her ancestors survived, but they must have seen others–friends and neighbours–taken and murdered for their precious blood. Children and adults alike destroyed, their bodies burned not with Dragon fire as was custom but human fire; their Dragon souls trapped and unable to find peace. Jon used his free hand to brush the tears from Thea's cheeks, and he became aware he was crying himself. He would never have Dragon memories like Thea but he could feel the emotions without context. She was so sad, and he felt his own heart break with hers.

Thea's next memory caused her to jerk violently with such force Jon almost lost his grip. Her body bowed almost completely in half. She was convulsing so hard he was afraid he would lose her. To keep his hold, he was forced to climb up onto Thea and straddle her. Using his own weight to keep her steady, he was now in the center of the spell.

Jon was very nearly overwhelmed with the sheer mass of magic swirling around him. Thea's runes were glowing and he remembered Nash's comments that they would protect anyone close to her. She was protecting him even as she was going through hell herself.

Caris noticed the glow of the runes as she made a final push to release the last of Thea's memories. The air crackled with energy and then it went quiet. The chanting stopped; everything was silent. The only sound he heard was Caris' breathing and his heart hammering away in his head.

Until Thea awoke, there was no way to verify if the curse was lifted permanently or if Caris' ceremony had simply allowed her a temporary glimpse. Jon could not explain how he knew, but something had changed for both of them. He leaned over and placed his forehead against Thea's and whispered to her.

"Come back to me."

※ ※ ※

Chapter 18 - Back To Life

After three days and three nights, Thea was still unconscious. Jon kept up his vigil while Thea continued to convulse and tremble, though nothing as intense as during the ritual. Caris came often to check on them.

"Has she woken yet?"

Jon was exhausted and yawned. He'd not moved since Thea was transferred into this room. His back and neck ached, but he refused to leave her. He was the reason Thea had gone through with this ritual, and he'd be damned if he'd let her suffer alone.

"No nothing yet, but I can see she's still dreaming. Is this normal?"

Caris gave a noncommittal shrug.

"Who can say? This is an unusual situation. Our records only say that the one having the curse removed will need time to recover but not how long that should take. And if her memories stretch further back then we first thought, it's possible she may never wake. She may travel back further and further as she recovers those lost memories. This curse was not designed to be used on Dragons, and as such we are observing and documenting along with you."

Jon choked with those words. Did he just doom Thea to spend the rest of her life going back to relive a possibly brutal past? Would he be forced to watch her wither and die? He looked down at her and felt like he couldn't breathe. Caris saw the colour leave Jon's face and laid her hand on his shoulder before using her glamour to rein in his panic attack.

"She means a great deal to you."

Jon just nodded; he couldn't talk.

Caris raised his chin forcing him to look at her.

"The fates don't often make their wills known to us, but what little I saw during the ceremony makes me believe she will come back to us. Her family has been through much, and the celestials never burden us with more than they know we can manage. She is stronger than you or she understands. True, her magic is great, but it is her heart that is her greatest source of strength."

Jon gave a jaded laugh.

"She said her mother told her the same. But if she never wakes up…"

He could not bring himself to finish the thought. Caris patted his shoulder.

"She will come back, give her time, Jon. Do not fear, we will continue to give her small amounts of water and nourishment while she recovers her memories."

Caris affectionately brushed Thea's hair aside.

"The curse placed on her was strong; someone did not want her mother to ever be able to access those abilities that can only come from a Dragon in their true form. This realm may be far, but even we know of the Dragons and their unique gifts."

Jon had no idea that Dragons were so well thought of. Caris gave him a knowing smile.

"The celestials gave each race a realm, but we were scholars, so we made it our business to learn about the others. Each realm was given the tools to maintain their home and thrive. Some did, like the Dragons, and others..."

Caris' eyes lowered in shame.

"... tried to take short cuts. Many sought out the Dragons for council, but their home had always been Earth realm or Earthside as you know it, and they were afraid of what would happen to the balance of their home if they ever left. The Faye who departed were given the choice to stay and try and rebuild this realm— and we have with hard work and sacrifice— but they chose an alternative route.

Caris moved away and leaned against the wall.

"First they stole Hell from the demons and then they stole Earth realm. We argued amongst ourselves if we should have warned the other realms, but ultimately, we made the decision to allow things to play out. We never imagined they would slaughter the Dragons.

"Dragons had the most difficult realm because they shared it with humanity, a stubborn and troublesome lot. Humanity were constantly pushing back against the boundaries the celestials placed on them. Dragons were meant to enforce that will. The deserters, as we called them, used humanity to their own end. They understood human nature and used it to undermine the Dragons.

"I am glad to know the deserters have finally settled. In the end they made a home for themselves and are thriving. I am very happy to hear they are also making amends for those transgressions long ago, as evidenced by your friends."

Jon attempted to smile, but he was too tired to try and be pleasant, and the thought that Thea might never wake up was too much for him to pretend to be civil. Caris pushed herself away from the wall.

"Do not give up so easily, Jon. Hope is the one gift the celestials gave to all of us to see us through the dark times, if we give up hope, then we are truly lost."

Jon nodded and waited for Caris to leave before he crawled into bed with Thea. It was the only way he could relax because he could feel her breathing and her heartbeat against his chest telling him she was still alive. He was so tired, but every time he closed his eyes the thought that Thea might not wake up jolted him awake. Eventually he did what he'd been doing for the last few nights, and settled in for another night of dozing interspersed with moments of jarring wakefulness.

He was just about to drop off when he felt Thea move against him; nothing obvious, almost as if she was changing positions in her sleep. He held his breath and she moved again settling herself against him.

"Thea? Are you here?"

There was no answer, but her breathing was different; it felt relaxed, serene. Maybe she was finally coming out of her magic-induced coma but when he shook her, she remained comatose. He had to rein himself in.

"Take it easy, Winter; keep your cool."

Then a sound, a quiet sigh; and a small smile. No, she wasn't going to wake up at this moment, but for the first time Jon felt like she could wake up soon. He placed a kiss on the side of her head and slept like the dead.

***

Thea didn't wake for another two days, but Jon knew she was coming back into herself. When he lay next to her, she gravitated toward him. He knew Thea was coming back, so, he waited patiently, and he waited, and waited. The moment Thea's eyes finally opened, Jon had to sit on his hands while Caris checked her over to make sure there were no residual symptoms from the ritual.

He apologized for putting her through everything with that first gentle kiss.

"I promise I will never take you for granted ever again."

***

As Thea emerged from her room, she found the light from the sun almost too bright after so long away in darkness.

Jon, happy to watch her eat, was ecstatic to have her back, awake, and next to him.

But then Jon's inner incubus awoke. Since the ritual, Thea appeared fragile. Jon willed the incubus into submission. He was worried about jeopardizing Thea's recovery, so he denied his own desires to allow Thea time to heal. To play it safe he began to keep a little distance. Thea was sort of hurt but he told her to take time to mend.

"We got time, holy shit, that's one thing we have loads of. Don't think I don't want to take you seven ways from Sunday, but fuck, I will not risk a set back because I was feeling horny. I can wait. It's ok."

Once Thea understood his reasons it became easier to allow Jon his space. She felt vulnerable and knew she needed the time, but it didn't help the ache she felt when he was away from her. She laughed to herself that she'd become so needy. Maybe they could both do with a little time away from each other. At night when they went to sleep Thea could feel Jon's arousal. She would move closer to him only to feel him pull away.

Most mornings she woke to find the space next to her empty and while she accepted that Jon was trying not to hurt her, part of her was sad.

***

Chapter 19 - Back To Us

Caris now trusted Thea and Jon enough to allow them to explore their temporary home. Jon had never been one for hiking, but without any other mode of transport, it was either that or sit around the compound thinking about all the firsts he would miss with Darcuna: her first proper steps, the first time she said "Daddy", the first time she went potty. At this moment he would give anything just to lay his hand on her back to feel her breathing as she slept.

***

In the month or so they'd been stuck there, Thea had managed to find a surprising amount for them to see. Jon knew it was her way to avoid thinking about Darcuna. Thea's body was still adjusting to the lack of feeding. She tried to act like she was fine, but at times her sadness radiated off her in waves. Add to that, her sallow complexion; some days she looked like a ghost flitting about.

***

Thea loved the wooded areas and how the sunlight would filter through the trees. She told herself that one day she would be able to tell Darcuna all about them. One day she would hold her baby, and smell her skin again. If she closed her eyes, she could remember that smell so clearly that her chest would constrict and she would gasp for breath.

***

Jon was more interested in watching Thea than the trees, but he smiled at her as she marvelled at the timber giants. For the moment she was relatively happy. She still looked like a stiff breeze could knock her over but if she was walking, he knew she was mending.

"Jon, I don't think we've been this way before. Where do you think that path leads?"

He blinked at Thea. He'd not had a decent night's sleep in weeks. They would start the night with a gap between them. But when she fell asleep, she would shift. The feel of her body pushed against him was making resting difficult. He was worried the incubus would pull too much energy when Thea was still mending. Now he was spending most of the night awake trying to keep it under control.

The monster rebelled at the forced celibacy the only way it could and tortured him with memories of all the times he and Thea had been intimate. To keep himself from losing his mind he'd been sneaking off at night to relieve the tension which then became two or four times a night. It was juvenile and a little depraved but it was either that or jump Thea in her sleep, which he was not comfortable doing.

Jon was so lost in his thoughts when he stopped and looked around, he realised he'd lost track of Thea

"Thea, where are you?"

He heard a splash and ran up the path she had previously pointed out and found her splashing about in a large pond.

"Look Jon, a swimming hole."

Her clothes were carelessly tossed on the side and she was stark naked in the water. Jon blinked for a few seconds, thinking he was having a stroke from his blood suddenly moving south from his brain. Thea saw the colour leave his face and rushed out of the water to make sure he was ok.

"Jon, oh my stars. Jon, are you ok?"

Thea was standing next to him bare as the day she was born, and he couldn't breathe for keeping the incubus under control. He was almost white and gasping for air.

"Jon, you're scaring me. Please, do I need to run and get Caris?"

His eyes were closed and he finally got his breathing under control. He opened one to carefully look at Thea. His voice was low and measured.

"Thea, for the love of all that is holy, please step back before I jackhammer you into the fucking ground!"

Thea's expression was puzzled until she felt Jon's obvious arousal pushing against her and a startled, "Oh," escaped her lips before she finally clued into the feral look in Jon's eyes. It had been so long since they had lain together, and Thea felt that familiar warmth start to curl its way from her belly outwards. There was a split second where they stood still, neither one willing to make the first move before they came together at the same time in a crushing kiss.

For a change Thea knocked Jon over and grabbed hold of the front of his trousers. There was a moment of fumbling before Thea was able to pull him free. Jon let out an animalistic groan as he felt her slide down onto him. It was like that first time in the forest next to Nash's cabin; neither of them thinking, only acting on instinct. Thea rode him until Jon couldn't take anymore and flipped them over so he could take control and thrust into her.

Giving his inner incubus full vent, he felt Thea move under him and her nails raking over his back so hard he briefly wondered if she would tear his wing tattoos off. The thought gave him an idea and he felt his wings materialize and he used them for additional leverage.

Thea's screams went up an octave and then he felt his whole body go ridged before a release so intense rocked him and made him think he was actually having a heart attack. Thea followed him a few moments later. Jon rolled off her and they lay next to each other panting. Jon's wings held Thea to him. She turned her face and breathlessly whispered into his ear.

"I missed this between us."

Jon pulled her even closer and gave her a silly delirious smile.

"Oh my god, I missed you. I love you, but oh my god, I needed this."

Thea laughed at his ramblings even while a tear ran down her cheek. This caught Jon's attention and he immediately sobered up.

"Did I hurt you? Are you ok?"

Thea nodded and wiped the tear away.

"I did not think it would ever be this way with us again. Between possibly never seeing Darcuna and the ritual, and then afterward. I was afraid we would never be intimate like we were."

Jon brushed his finger on her cheek and caught a second tear. His throat tight with emotion.

"I literally almost died thinking I'd lost you. And then you woke up and you seemed so frail. Like if

I touched you like this, you would shatter into a million pieces. So, I kept my distance, but it kept building inside and the more it built up the more afraid I got of hurting you."

He stopped to kiss her gently. Thea deepened the kiss, and they stayed locked until the need to breathe was overwhelming. When they broke apart, Thea nestled into the crook of his arm, her hand splayed over his chest feeling his heartbeat.

"We have been through so much that I feel like you have always been part of my life, that we were somehow matched at birth. Those fairy tales Fenris told me of, with heroes who save their lady loves and then they live happily ever after. I laughed at the stories and yet …"

She reached for Jon and they shared another long drawn out kiss. When they broke apart again, she ran her finger along his jaw.

"I can no longer imagine a life without you. That should make me vulnerable, but instead it makes me feel invincible, like no matter what I face, if you will be with me, and together we will prevail."

Jon sighed.

"I said it before and I'll repeat it for good measure. Home is anywhere, as long as we are together. We'll find a way back to Darcuna, I promise. But for the time being I am just grateful I still have you."

Chapter 20 - Daughters

The pain that Thea felt every time she thought of her daughter was constant; but instead of a sharp stab that would take her breath away, it became a dull ache that never left her. When Jon spoke of Darcuna his voice would catch and Thea would see his eyes shimmer even as he smiled. Their little girl may not be so little if they ever saw her again. Caris was genuinely sad for them. Her own daughter had been taken two summers past in an unfortunate hunting accident.

Caris could see her daughter in her mind's eye.

"My Eloise was so full of life. Her laugh could crack even the most sullen person. One day she was there and then, she wasn't. I did not think I would ever smile again and yet, when I think of her now, I can."

Caris stopped to look at Thea.

"She would have liked you, she always fancied herself more a warrior than a mage. I wish I could send you back to your little girl, but the reach of our magic was intentionally restricted so we would never be tempted again. We keep our magic use to a minimum while continuing to study it so we never forget who and what we are. It is a fine line we walk and yet it has served us well for as long as I can remember. Speaking of memories, have yours provided any insight?"

Thea shook her head sadly.

"No not really, but it does give me comfort to finally have that link with my mother. When she died, I felt like she was ripped from me and having her memories makes me feel like she is still with me. I am also learning about my father in a way I never thought possible. He was far more complex than I was aware of. It makes me think I may have judged him too harshly. I only wish I had the chance to tell him as much."

They sat for some time in silence each one thinking of their families. Thea was curious about something Caris said.

"If your magic does not reach as far as Earthside, how did you know of Dragons?"

Caris gave a thoughtful sigh.

"Once we knew how to reach any place within the known cosmos in the blink of an eye. As scholars it was a useful way to study and learn of other realms. But then other races began to tempt us with all number of riches to acquire this power. Some even stole it by force. Warlike races developed and we saw our gifts used to plunder or maim so we took back our gift. It was a long arduous process. Many sacrificed their own lives.

"We destroyed all trace of it and burned the pages where it was written and any who knew it were silenced. Some even willingly had their own tongues removed so they could never be forced to speak the spells, others were not so eager to give up that power. While we value knowledge, we also understand its responsibility. The Dragons taught us that."

Thea turned and saw Jon coming towards them. Caris gave her hand an affectionate squeeze.

"Go and be with Jon; he makes you smile and it's harder to be sad when you are smiling."

Caris' eyes shone with unshed tears as she smiled. Instead Jon was looking for her.

"Actually, I need to speak to you. I've been sort of negotiating with the elders about looking at some of your older texts. I know you don't like to practice, but they could hold the key to getting us back to our realm. I'm not looking to use your magic per say, but if we are ever going to get back, we need to know where we are in relation to Hell.

"You told me you were academics and maybe one of those texts has a map we can use. I can't do the jump in one hit but I could leap frog our way back. My ability to portal is finite and having a map, so I know where I am going, would be a huge help."

Caris nodded.

"While your theory has merit, why seek me out?"

Jon shrugged.

"The short answer is they don't trust me and my ability to portal makes them nervous. I kind of hoped you might put in a good word for me and explain what exactly I'm looking for. And then maybe help me find it."

Caris laughed.

"I think I can assist you, but I cannot guarantee the answer. And I would think, once I make your case, they will still need time to discuss it."

She touched Thea's cheek.

"But I will ask for expediency for the sake of your young child."

Thea wrapped her arms around Caris, and Jon laughingly joined in. Once she was able to untangle them from her, she grinned.

"I will do what I can."

※ ※ ※

Jon stood before the elders as Caris spoke on his behalf.

"I understand Jon wishes to have access to the Library. He does not wish to access spells or magic but hopes to find maps in our volumes of the locations we visited and studied."

One of the elders spoke.

"This deserter's wishes are suspect. He is after all one of them. What if he takes knowledge back to the others?"

Caris addressed the speaker.

"He is not a deserter; he is descended from them. We cannot hold him in judgement for things done long before he was born. And as a precaution, I will oversee him, as will the Librarian. That should assure you. Besides, we all know the truly dangerous magic has long since been removed."

Jon tried to speak in his own defence.

"Look, I understand why you are nervous, but really my only intention is to find maps. I can portal but only short distances—across two maybe three realms at most. We just want to go home."

Caris spoke for Thea in her absence.

"They have a young child—left behind—that they wish to go back to. I believe them to be trustworthy. Moradon will corroborate my observations. Thea has shown a similar nature to the Dragons of old. We trusted her enough to allow me permission to carry out the Ouvon."

Another elder spoke this time.

"You removed a curse placed on her by another deserter. She was never given access to any sensitive information not already known to her through her blood. This one asks to be allowed inside the Library."

Jon was getting a headache dealing with these bureaucrats. He was close to losing his temper. He rubbed his temples in frustration.

"My daughter, my *less* than a year-old daughter is waiting for her parents to come home. I just want to get home to her before she is old enough to have her own babies. Surely that much we can all agree on?"

Several elders nodded before one spoke.

"Of course, we understand your frustration, but we must be careful. The information housed in the Library is vast and many would pay dearly to know what we have kept locked away. Caris will have told you of our history and the cost we paid for allowing our knowledge to be taken. We must discuss this further. We will give you our decision soon."

Jon and Caris left them to deliberate.

※ ※ ※

Chapter 21 - The Library

It had taken several days for the elders to make their decision. Once they had been given access, Jon and Caris were led to a table in the Library where they would have texts brought to them. Even though she was unable to read the language, they were still wary of her Dragon memory, so Thea was left to amuse herself while Jon and Caris poured over the old Faye manuscripts. Neither he nor Caris mentioned to the elders Jon's Dragon ability to remember. He was forced to take notes to cover up.

Jon was stunned at how much information there was. The Library was an underground repository of all the Faye's knowledge. It was seven levels in total. The oldest and most powerful spells were kept in the lowest and most secure section. He would only be allowed access to the first level.

Standing on the stairs looking down, Jon stifled a laugh.

"I know a guy back home who would literally sell his body to get a peek at this. But I just need maps of the realms so I can safely portal. I'd hate to wind up inside a mountain or worse."

Caris nodded and led him to the reading table.

"The oldest information is on the lowest level. Before we start, I should warn you that you may find gaps in some of the information. We have tried to preserve as much as we can, but as I said we removed and destroyed the tomes we deemed most dangerous and powerful."

Jon found himself looking at several stacks of books, scrolls, and loose paper before he dove in and grabbed a random book. He flipped through, but the pages he needed were missing so he picked up another book and again pages were gone. Jon grabbed a scroll and scanned it before tossing it aside with the books.

After several hours, Jon felt like he was going cross-eyed after squinting at the pages.

"I need a break and so far, I haven't seen anything that even resembles a map. Parts of the books are gone and these loose pages are a nightmare to try and follow."

Caris gave a dejected sigh.

"I was afraid of this. Several years back we had a particularly harsh winter which led to an infestation. Rodents destroyed whole swaths of our remaining records. And by the time we were able to get them under control, we had lost a good portion of our remaining archives. At the time we did not regret the loss. We took it as a sign from the celestials of a further purge of still dangerous information.

"I had hoped some of the information you required had escaped, but it seems it did not. I am sorry, Jon. We have provided all we can. Now it is up to you and Thea. She has had some time with her Dragon memories. Maybe what you seek is there only waiting to be discovered."

***

Jon sat with Thea as Caris told her about the maps.

"I am afraid we cannot provide you with any more information... I'm sorry, Thea."

Thea swallowed the lump in her throat. When would she see Darcuna again? Jon laid his hand on her shoulder.

"Has anything popped up that might be useful?"

Thea tried to describe what her new Dragon memories felt like.

"The most recent ones are the easiest to understand; the ones from my own lifetime because I shared them. I now also have Spawn's memories and his final thoughts were of thanks. I did not feel any malice at the end, only peace. For that I am grateful. But older memories are harder to decipher. Even though Dragon memories are absolute, it is like wandering in a vast archive.

"Imagine a space as large as a mountain filled with books. First, you must find the volume you require. Then, once you know where the volume is kept, you must still climb to reach it. And then once you have the volume in hand, you have to seek the exact pages. I have the memories, but they are substantial and having received them all at once, I am having trouble sorting through them. I am sure with some time, I will begin to make sense of them, but right now they are a jumble of faces, feelings, and impressions without context."

Jon squeezed Thea's shoulder.

"This is just a setback, I can still technically portal but our landings might not always be as soft as I'd hoped, and I won't have a clue what will meet us on the other side. We *will* get home, somehow. I'm just not sure how long it will take or what exactly we'll find along the way."

Caris tapped her finger thoughtfully.

"I have an idea, but let me confirm if it is possible before I raise your hopes."

***

Chapter 22 - The First Time

They had yet to test if Thea could take her true form. She knew how to from her restored Dragon memories; this was part of every Dragon's core memories. But knowing how to, and actually doing it were very different things.

Having never experienced her true form, Thea was frightened. What would Jon think when he saw her? Her wings were black but would her scales be the same flat black? Would she be grotesque? Would he fear her? So many questions, but as usual Jon spurred her on.

"I won't push you if you really don't want to, but if it was me, I would definitely give it a try."

He gave her such a confident smile, she decided to go for it. She closed her eyes and concentrated. Jon stood back as the air around her began to shimmer. A large form started to take shape. Jon could make out wings, then a tail, and finally a head. Thea's human form faded as the large shimmering cloud solidified into Thea, in her Dragon form.

She was not as big as Ash; she was hardly taller than a large horse at nine feet tall. But compared to her usual diminutive stature and with her wingspan she appeared bigger and the combination of her deep black scales and fire Dragon aspect had the most unimaginable effect. Between each scale was a glow from the fire within her.

"Holy mother fucking shit!"

Thea flinched unable to tell if Jon was impressed or afraid. She began to back away from him and he reached out to her.

"Hey, Thea, it's ok. Please really, it's just like nothing I've ever seen and the effect is... incredible. You're as beautiful as ever, I promise."

He could see in her eyes how nervous she was, and he smiled and moved closer to her. Placing one hand on her head, he ran the other over her scales marvelling at how the glow intensified and he laughed as she purred.

"You like that, huh? Come on, let's really run you through your paces."

And with that he unbound his own wings and gave Thea a wink.

"Are you ready?"

Thea gave him a snort and began to beat her wings. Airborne, Thea felt like a key had slid into place. Jon tried to keep up with her, but in her true form Thea moved through the air effortlessly. Her tail gave her a stability she'd previously lacked, her scales streamlining her to the point where everything was a blur as she raced through the sky. Instinct allowed her to navigate faster than she thought possible. She turned and tumbled in the air before spiralling high into the clouds only to dive back down.

She raced passed the compound and several children squealed as she flew past them. Even Caris could not contain the bubble of laughter as she saw Thea enjoying her first flight as a Dragon.

Thea looked over to find a flock of geese racing along with her, using her slipstream to pull them along in the higher winds. She snorted as they honked at her.

She broke off from them and climbed higher again until she was even looking down on the clouds. She sailed through the air enjoying the feel of it as it rushed past her. Thea then plunged down and dove into a crystal-clear lake before she broke the surface startling the animals drinking at the shore. They bleated and whinnied their disapproval, but Thea just snorted back at them.

She looked down to see a pack of wolves running and remembered the alpha she-wolf by Nash's cabin. Thea raced passed them and gave a roar and the wolves howled back at her. Finally, she delved into a wooded area and found she could weave and dodge around the trees with ease. The animals, startled by her appearance, ran and Thea chased them before she turned back towards the compound.

When Thea landed, Jon ran over to her. She transformed into her human form and exactly like Ash had cautioned, her clothes were gone, destroyed when she took her Dragon form. Before anyone could see her, Jon pulled his shirt off and quickly threw it over Thea as she excitedly tried to explain what she felt.

"Jon, I wish I could describe it to you, it was incredible."

Jon laughed at her enthusiasm but had to point out she had essentially ruined the only clothing she had.

"Thea, while I am genuinely ecstatic for you, we are going to have to have some rules regarding your future clothing needs. Either we ask Caris to enchant any new clothing or you are going to have to remember to remove your clothes before you take your Dragon form."

Thea threw her arms around Jon's neck.

"I am sorry, Jon; I shall be more mindful next time, but this is so exciting."

He laughed at her animated squeal as she danced around in his shirt describing her experience for him. He loved that she was smiling and that she finally had something to feel happy about. He would just have to make sure he could keep her clothed until they got home.

* * *

Chapter 23 - Time to Go

The going had been slow but eventually Jon had found enough information in the archives that they could begin planning their departure. But as much as he wanted to go home, part of him knew leaving Caris would be hard. Jon had spent so little time with his mother and being with Caris felt like he was getting a second chance, but Darcuna was waiting for them as well as Gerard.

And there was still a war going on, and they had no way of knowing how their disappearance had affected that. Were Black Heart and Rage laying waste to Hell and everyone they knew? Would there be anything left? He gave his head a shake to dispel his negative thoughts. No matter what, Gerard, Gath, Levi, Ash, Aliyah and even Brix and Gaia would make sure Darcuna was safe. Yes, he would miss Caris greatly, and he was genuinely glad he'd had the chance to meet her, but it was time to go home.

***

Thea's new clothing was a gift from Caris. Her daughter, had been of a similar build to Thea. Eloise had often made her own clothes from the hides of the animals she caught. Caris' daughter had been a skilled hunter and leatherworker and her garments were often praised for their beauty as well as their attention to detail.

Because Thea had been so used to her old jean shorts and t-shirt, Caris thought it best to stick to something similar, so she gave Thea a pair of shorts and a hunter's shirt with laces up the front. It only required a few minor alterations and was woven with Faye runes and enchanted. It would disappear when she took her true form and reappear when she took her human form. It was as attractive as it was practical.

Jon looked at the runes and chuckled.

"Good to know they are enchanted like my clothes. No more unintentional nudity."

Thea ran her hand over the soft leather.

"Thank you, Caris, this is lovely; I will treasure it always."

Caris beamed at Thea.

"I am glad to know that some part of Eloise will continue to travel the realms like we once did — all be it in a more benign fashion."

Caris had one more gift for them—an enchantment that she hoped would help lead them home.

"The first day when you fell through, we found something which I believe belongs to you, Thea. It was damaged, but we have been able to repair it, and it may hold a key to helping you get back home to your daughter. Much like your clothing, I've made sure an enchantment allows it to be kept safe when you take your Dragon form."

Thea cried out when Caris pulled out the keepsake pendant that Jon had given her before they left. In the confusion of finding themselves thrown through the portal and then being marched off, Thea had assumed it was lost forever and seeing it now she could not stop the tears in her eyes. She reached for it and held it gently. She could see where Caris had replaced the glass over Darcuna's image and turned it to see that while the stones were gone, there were more Faye runes etched into it.

"I could not bear to destroy the image of your little girl, but your gemstones did offer something. They provided me with an idea. Each realm is unique. I used the stones to craft an enchantment that will act as a compass to lead you home."

She gestured to Thea to hold it up.

"When held up like so, it will turn until it locks onto your realm. Your daughter's face should face towards you. Hold it still and it will begin to sway of its own accord. It may start slowly but as you move closer to your own realm it will sway faster—pointing your way home.

Jon smiled.

"The stones are from Earthside. I thought it would be a nice reminder where the Dragons originally came from, but Hell isn't that far from Earthside…"

Thea excitedly finished his thought.

"If we can get to Earthside, we can get home."

***

Everyone in the compound gathered to see them off. Caris wrapped her arms around Thea and Jon.

"I am so happy I got to know both of you. It's good to know that the deserters have found a new home, and past mistakes are being made right. I will never forget either of you. I will add your names and what you told me about the Earthside Faye to our texts, so your stories will never be forgotten. Who knows, maybe one day we might attempt to travel and we will meet again…"

Caris paused as tears threatened to overcome her.

"Your daughter and your families are waiting for you. If the celestials will it, may our paths cross again."

Jon opened a portal, and with tears in their eyes, they waved at the group and walked through.

***

Chapter 24 - Illthana

Thea stepped through into a blizzard. She had never seen anything like it. Snowflakes landed on her eye lashes, almost blinding her. The wind whipped her hair across her face and was bitterly cold. The ground was covered in white powder that crunched under her feet. She shielded her eyes from the wind as Jon stepped through after her.

"Motherfucker, it's cold. The books said this realm was *cooler* than most, but this is unreal."

Wrapping his arms around himself, he looked over at Thea. Her teeth were chattering.

"I have never felt cold like this. I must do something before we both freeze."

Balling up her fists Thea called up her Hellfire and her skin took on that red glow that Jon remembered from their very first meeting. The temperature of the air a few feet around them went up almost ten degrees, and the snow melted at their feet.

"Ah that is a little better, but I do not know how long I can maintain this. Do you know of any settlements or places we can shelter?"

Jon looked around and blinked as his eyes were watering.

"I could have sworn there was a village or something in the area, but I can't see it with this bloody wind in my eyes. Hold on I think I see something over there."

He pulled Thea along towards what looked like a little hut.

"It's not a village, but it *is* shelter."

The wind pushed the door open just as Jon reached for the handle. Thea bumped into him when he stopped abruptly in the doorway. Jon was looking down the bolt of a crossbow while the other cabin inhabitants held an axe and a shotgun respectively. The owner of the shotgun put his weapon down and ordered his colleagues to do the same.

"Lads, it's not the magbear. Put your weapons down, and bolt the door this time. These guys look half frozen."

Jon exhaled when the crossbow was no longer pointed at his head but pushed it further aside so it was not aimed at his crotch either. The men all rushed to help Thea in before closing and securing the door.

"What in all that is holy are you two doing out dressed like that? Where are your furs, your boots? She barely has leggings."

Jon tried to think of a response before Thea spoke, using one of Jon's favourite expressions.

"I believe the term is *it's complicated*. I am not sure how to explain our attire without further confusion, but I hope it is enough to say, we did not expect such a harsh environment when we set out."

The man with the shotgun laughed and shook his head in disbelief.

"Ok I'll accept that — for now. You two look like you got chased out before you could dress. You aren't wanted by the law, are you?"

Jon grinned.

"No, I've been accused of bending the rules and even pushing a few boundaries, but we are not running from the law. Like she said, it's kind of complicated. I'm Jon and this is Thea."

The owner of the shotgun gave a casual salute.

"I'll give you the benefit of the doubt for now. I'm Gunther and these are my mates, Worth and Laithem. This was supposed to be our men only hunting weekend, but I'd feel like a right beast for sending your girl back out into that, especially if that magbear is still wandering about. Are you one of those travellers?"

Jon nodded.

"Yeah, sure, let's call us travellers. We're trying to make our way home, but we are sort of flying blind. Where are we?"

Worth laughed.

"You're kidding right? This is Illthana. Where do you think you are?"

Jon pursed his lips.

He wasn't keen on sharing too much but he also knew he and Thea would not survive long out in the cold. Living on his own as a mercenary for the Olde Ones had sharpened his ability to read people. There was nothing to indicate anyone in the cabin was a magic user, but that didn't mean magic was unknown in this realm. He weighted their options before coming to the conclusion that if things went pear shaped, as difficult as she would find it, he and Thea could easily overpower the three men and dispatch them before anyone knew.

He bit his lip before exhaling.

"Ok, I'll try and explain, but it's a long story."

Gunther pointed at the door.

"That storm will be awhile. Have a seat. Laithem just put some food on, and I'm sure we can stretch it to feed two more. Nothing like a good story by the fire, hey lads?"

***

"...and so now you see why we are dressed like this."

The men in the cabin tried to take in what Jon had just told them. Gunther scratched his head.

"So, you are from Hell, but you were sent to Astranya and now you are here? That's crazy. You aren't deranged, are you?"

Gunther lifted his shotgun back up slowly and Jon raised his hands.

"Woah! Mate, put the gun down. We are not crazy."

Jon turned to see Thea making her way towards the door.

"Wait, Thea! Where are you going?"

Thea unbolted the door.

"We cannot expect them to believe us without proof."

Jon carefully pushed Gunther's gun away and went after Thea.

"What kind of proof? Thea? Thea, where are you going?"

Thea opened the door and stepped out. The wind seemed to have died down, but snow continued to fall. The men followed her outside before Gunther shouted out.

"What in all that is holy is she doing? You both really are crazy. That magbear is out here..."

There was a roar as the beast reared up from behind Thea. Standing, it was eight feet tall with coarse black fur. It had viciously long claws and razor-sharp teeth. Thea turned and the animal roared again.

Jon readied a spell but already he could see Thea changing and taking her Dragon form. Once transformed, she roared back at the magbear and butted it with her head, pushing it back and away from the cabin. Before surrendering, the beast took a swipe at Thea. Its claws skittered uselessly over her scales, and Thea gave another warning growl.

Gunther had his gun up and Worth and Laithem also pulled their weapons out. Jon stood in front of them with his arms out to block them.

"Hold on. Thea is trying to help. I don't want one of you numpties to shoot her by accident."

Gunther turned his gun on Jon even though his hands were shaking.

"What are you two?"

Jon saw Gunther's finger on the trigger and portalled away, appearing behind him. His sword materialized in his hand and he raised the blade under Gunther's chin.

"Look, I don't want to hurt you. You seem like a nice enough guy, but I will not let you or your mates kill Thea, especially as she is trying to save our arses. So now tell the other guys to put down their weapons and let Thea deal with that thing and then we will get the hell out of your realm."

Gunther nodded at Worth and Laithem.

"Ok, ok, I get it. Lads, do as he says."

Jon took Gunther's gun away and lowered his sword. Thea was using her wing claws to corral the animal away from Jon and the other men, snapping at the magbear every so often to keep it moving. Once the creature was gone, Thea returned to her human form and joined them.

"I am sorry if I frightened you. I could not take my true form in the cabin for fear of destroying the only shelter we had. That I was able to chase off your predator was timely. Do you still wish us to leave?"

Gunther was shaken at what he had just seen.

"What are you?"

✷ ✷ ✷

Chapter 25 - I Am A Dragon

Thea glanced towards Jon and he shrugged.

"Go on, tell them. That train left the station the minute you transformed."

Thea gave a hesitant smile.

"I am a Dragon. Have you heard of my kind?"

Worth's mouth hung open until he was finally able to speak.

"By all that is holy. A Dragon, here, in this realm?"

Laithem crossed his arms.

"Are you drunk? Dragons are myths."

Gunther was staring and pointing at Thea.

"I know what I saw, lads, and that girlie turned into a Dragon right here in front of us. I haven't had a drop to drink yet, so I *know* I'm not drunk."

Jon held his sword out to block Gunther when he tried to approach Thea.

"I'll respectfully ask you to keep your distance."

Thea pushed Jon's blade aside.

"I do not believe he means to hurt me, Jon. And besides even if he did, I am not without defences."

She conjured a ball of Hellfire and then closed her hand to extinguish it as a demonstration.

"We only wish to rest and then we will move on. We will leave immediately if that is your desire, but truly we mean you no harm."

Thea had the idea to make them more sympathetic. She pulled out her pendant from inside her shirt.

"We only wish to go home to our daughter."

Gunther gently took the jewellery and looked at the picture.

"She's cute. Ok, let's say we believe you. Why don't you just," he waved his hands about, "and go home?"

Jon groaned.

"I can't, my magic can only take us so far in one hit. We are going as far as we can each time we jump. I need a break to recharge each time. Look, help us, don't help us, but we are not here to cause shit. We are just trying to get home."

Gunther passed the pendant back to Thea.

"Fine, I get it. Ok, since Thea took care of that magbear, we can go back inside and figure out what comes next."

Thea smiled gratefully.

"Thank you."

***

"Is it always so cold in this realm?"

Worth shook his head.

"Only up here in the mountains. Down in the valley where we live it isn't quite so harsh, but this is the only place to hunt dadyr. Gunther was going to present it to..."

Gunther elbowed his friend.

"We were tracking a dadyr until that magbear showed up."

Thea was enjoying her stew and spoke between mouthfuls.

"I am glad we could help. Maybe you can resume your hunt if the animal has not run too far. I am sure your family will appreciate the meat. Do you have any children?"

He smiled and shook his head.

"No, not yet."

Worth laughed.

"Not for lack of trying though. How long have you been mooning over Lina?"

Gunther swatted his friend.

"She'll come around."

This caused Worth and Laithem to double over hooting with laughter. Laithem was laughing so hard, he was crying.

"She has to date said five words to you, and of those five, three of them are not fit for polite company."

Thea tried to be supportive.

"I am sure there are others who see your gifts."

Even as his friends continued to snicker, Gunther wore a dreamy, starry-eyed smile.

"Lina is unique. Beautiful like a goddess, with a quick mind..."

"And a sharp tongue. She has snubbed you so many times, we're starting to think you enjoy it."

Laithem and Worth started guffawing again. Jon took a different approach.

"You need a hook, my friend. Something she won't be able to overlook. Something she can't resist."

Gunther's shoulders dropped.

"I've tried everything to catch her eye. The meat was for her and her family. It's that damned blight. It's hard enough for her family to run their farm but it's damn near impossible with the blight. As long as her family's farm remains afflicted, she won't even take the time to look at me."

He paused and shook his head.

"That farm is all her family has, and it's part of the reason I love her. Family means everything to her. She would be such a devoted mother and wife but only if she could stop worrying about her parents and the farm."

Thea pulled Jon closer and spoke to him quietly.

"We could help him win this Lina. Grandfather said your Faye water magic and your Dragon storm magic makes you similar to an obsidian. We have all the elements between us. We could never heal a large area but maybe we might be able to help this farm."

Thea smiled confidently at Gunther.

"I think Jon and I could help you win Lina. We Dragons have the ability to heal the land. It would usually need many of us, but for a small farm we may be able to with just us two. And if she no longer had to worry about her family, she may be more open to your entreaties."

Jon laid his hand on Gunther's shoulder.

"And it wouldn't hurt your cause if you were the one to introduce us."

Gunther's eyes were wide.

"And you would do this for me? A stranger?"

Thea and Jon beamed at him. Jon made one request.

"In exchange, maybe you could allow us a place to rest before we portal again?"

Gunther jumped up and hugged both of them.

"If you can help me win Lina, I'll carry you both home if I have to."

***

Thea and Jon clarified to Gunther and his friends that they might not be able to completely remove the blight from the land but they should be able to slow the progress. Either way they would put Gunther in good stead with Lina, and for that he was more than happy to offer them a small room in his home to sleep in until Jon was able to portal them to the next realm.

They found the object of Gunther's affection marching across to the barn with a covered basket on her arm. Lina was indeed a beautiful girl. Her golden hair was tied up at the moment, but when left loose it would be long enough to fall down the length of her back. She had soft cornflower blue eyes, and she would have had a pleasing face except for the frown she wore as she caught sight of Gunther. She gave an exasperated groan.

"I don't have time to listen to all the reasons why we should be matched. We lost another poulchen. The poor little thing died after it got into the tainted grain before we could burn it. Now I need to burn the body and make sure nothing else gets into the grain…"

"Lina, these people are here to help."

Gunther pointed at Thea and Jon.

"They have gifts that could help repair your land."

Jon held his hand out to Lina.

"We can't guarantee anything, but we'd like to try."

Lina pushed past them.

"I'm sorry Gunther has put you strangers up to this. He can be trying. I suppose he means well, but I don't have time for games."

Thea grabbed Lina's arm.

"Truly, we carry the ability to heal the land. We are not sure if just the two of us can, but we would like to try. Gunther has told us how important this farm is to you. He only wishes to ease your burden. Will you let us try?"

Lina stopped and turned to face them.

"How could you heal our soil? It is dying. I wish you could, it kills me to watch my father toil only for more crops to dye or become polluted like the grain that killed poor Glissy..."

She wiped her eyes.

"I need to get back to work. I don't know how long we have."

Thea conjured her Hellfire.

"We are Dragons; it is what the celestials made us to do. In our realm my kind are known as the ones who purge decay and disease. I can try and remove the sickness that plagues your farm, and then Jon and I can attempt to restore it to some measure of health."

Lina dropped her basket.

"By all that is holy!"

Thea knelt down to give a demonstration.

"I'm sorry but the basket has most likely become contaminated."

Using her Hellfire, she burned the little animal and the basket leaving nothing but ash.

She looked up at Lina.

"I can take the sickness away, but the fields must be empty. Can the animals be locked away for their safety?"

Lina nodded mutely. Thea continued.

"I will attempt this but I have never done it before."

Lina's voice was barely above a whisper.

"Dragons here, by all that is holy."

***

Chapter 26 - Minor Healing

It had taken some persuading, but eventually Gunther had explained who Thea and Jon were to Lina's parents and what they would try to do.

After the animals had been cleared off the land, Thea walked to the center of the field. It had taken her a few minutes to find the memory of how fire Dragons removed sickness. It was not altogether difficult, but having never done it before Thea was nervous. Everyone was far enough away to be safe, but they were all watching her.

She knelt down and placed her hand on the soil and closed her eyes. The ground was cold under her and she called up her flame to warm her. A familiar feeling rose inside her as her Dragon memories took hold. When she'd healed the land around Lake Acantha she was following instructions. This time memory and instinct drove her.

Reaching out with her Dragon senses, she tried to find the cause of the sickness. In her mind she could see the infection like a root growing under the surface of the soil. The cold of the season seemed to have slowed the spread, but once the weather turned warm the disease would extend out until the land would support nothing. Thea felt the fire in her veins flare up, and then it moved out to seek the infection.

Jon watched Thea with the others. After his lessons with Thorikill, Jon was now able to subtly syphon energy off from multiple sources and direct it. At the moment, he was focusing it toward Thea. He knew it was technically wrong, but he also knew Thea would be drawing from her own reserves of energy to help these people. He reasoned he was letting them help themselves.

Lina and her parents were awed at the sight. Thea's veins seemed to glow and the fire in her burned into the ground resembling tiny snakes of flame. They could see them moving in the dirt, killing off disease where they found it.

Jon noticed a grey-black tinge creep up Thea's skin. She then took on that familiar red glow, and Jon understood she was drawing the worst of the disease into her and burning it from within. The fire snakes moved in and out of the soil. At the moment every trace was eliminated from the field, Thea collapsed, no longer having the strength to hold herself upright. Jon ran to her and pulled her into his arms.

"Hey, don't you dare die on me. Thea, are you ok?"

Thea was deathly pale, and her eyes were closed. She was breathing like she had run a marathon but smiling.

"It is ok, Jon; I am just exhausted. The memory of how to cleanse the land came to me, and then it was like I had done it a thousand times before. I could not leave any sickness. I could sense it would spread to neighbouring farms if not completely eradicated. But right now, I would greatly appreciate some assistance standing."

Jon helped Thea up, but he could feel she was relying on him to keep her vertical. She really was wiped, so he lifted her up into his arms. Thea laid her head against his shoulder and promptly fell asleep. The sounds of her soft snoring assured him she was shattered but would heal. Gunther and the others rushed to see if she was ok. Jon gave them an encouraging smile.

"She tends to push herself pretty hard trying to help others, but I try and keep her from doing serious harm to herself. She said she removed all the blight from the field and when she's rested, we'll try and restore some of the balance. She just needs a nap right now."

Jon kissed the top of her head.

"You did good, baby. Go on, get your rest."

***

Thea woke after a few hours feeling more like herself. When she appeared, everyone asked after her.

"Truly, I am fine now. I feel ready to attempt to restore balance to the field."

Jon whispered in her ear.

"Are you sure? You didn't sleep that long. We can leave it a day…"

Thea cut him off with a kiss.

"I know how you worry, and I assure you I am ready."

She gave him a wink, and he chuckled.

"You know you're really are starting to get rather cocky."

Thea beamed at him.

"I learned from the best."

Jon couldn't help the roar of laughter.

"Fine, if you're sure, then by all means let's get this done."

Once everyone was assured that Thea was recovered from her previous cleansing of the land, she and Jon walked out together to the center of the field. The others watched from the edge. Standing facing each other, they called out the words of the healing in unison.

"We are the blood that flows. We are the breath that moves. We are heart that burns. We are the bone that supports. We are the spirit that binds."

They knelt together and placed their hands on the soil. The air around them was instantly charged with magic. The crops that still stood withered and died but only to nourish the new life that would soon be planted. The ground shifted as if a million small creatures were burrowing out, and slowly small blades of grass began to sprout from the earth until the field resembled the meadow it had been before being tilled. They collapsed from the exertion, laughing.

"We did it! We actually did it!"

Staring up at the sky, both of them enjoyed the high of from carrying out a healing together. The feeling of being connected, heightened because of Thea and Jon's relationship. Thea rolled over and kissed Jon.

"Yes, we did. In truth I was unsure we would be able to without the others. But we have done it and now I would like nothing more than to celebrate with you."

As tempting as it was, Jon turned Thea's head and pulled her close to whisper in her ear.

"Later on, I'll make sure you're calling out to the celestials, but right now I can see Gunther and Lina walking towards us. We'll baptize the field when we don't have so many people around."

Thea's grin was all the confirmation Jon needed that she was in agreement. Thea rolled off of Jon and allowed Lina to pull her up as Gunther gave Jon a hand up.

Lina's parents stood, eyes wide, staring at their new field.

"By all that is holy, you really are Dragons. We had heard the stories, but this... this is beyond anything we could have imagined. Dragons here, just when we thought we had lost everything. How can we ever thank you for what you've given us?"

Jon smiled at Gunther.

"Your daughter has caught the eye of our friend here..."

Thea cut him off again with a tug on his arm, and he gave her a glare.

"You know your habit of interrupting me is getting really annoying."

Thea shrugged.

"It is only that to put Lina in such a position is wrong."

She looked at Lina.

"I know Gunther's love for you is true, but I do not think it right to make you do anything against your will. Lina, do you have any affection for Gunther?"

This took Lina aback. She never expected to be asked her feelings. She knew that Gunther had chased her since they were children. But since the blight on the farm had begun, she had never given a thought to if she had any fondness for him. Gunther read her hesitancy and acted. Dropping to his knees, he pled his case.

"Lina, I have loved you for as long as I can remember, and I will do everything in my power to make sure you feel like the princess I think you are."

Lina looked at her parents. Her mother and father's marriage had been arranged, and they eventually grew to love each other. Because of the farm she'd never been forced to marry as they had nothing to offer as dowry. Now she would have her pick of suiters, but Gunther had always been there, worshipping and worrying for her when she had nothing.

Other suitors might find her beautiful, but her heart told her Gunther's love was pure. Then she looked at Thea and Jon. He had his arm protectively around her. Thea was almost incandescent every time she looked at him. Lina made up her mind. She wanted a relationship like that. She looked down at Gunther and smiled.

"Yes, I will join myself to you, Gunther, but I shall hold you to your word."

Seized by the moment, Gunther hoisted Lina up and whooped.

"I promise every day to remind you of how much I love you."

Lina giggled but struggled with Gunther.

"Gunther, put me down. Please, people are starting to gather."

He was so happy he started to twirl her around in the air.

"Let them look. I am going to marry the most beautiful girl in the world."

He then let her down but only so he could kiss her. It wasn't long before she was kissing him back. Jon leaned over to whisper to Thea.

"It feels nice helping them out. And I think they'll be a wedding sooner rather than later if that kiss is any indication."

***

Chapter 27 - Nice Day For a Wedding

The entire village turned out to watch the joining of Gunther and Lina. Laithem and Worth stood beaming next to their friend. There were very little decorations and the ceremony itself would have been a sombre event, if not for the giggles from the intended couple.

Lina and Gunther were dressed very simply in white. Lina's hair was unadorned but it had been brushed until it shone like spun gold down her back. Gunther's breath caught the moment he'd turned and seen her, and since then the smile never left his face.

Standing in the back with Thea, Jon studied her. Because they had no other clothing, he was wearing borrowed clothes from Worth, and Lina had loaned Thea a simple dress. She was so beautiful, and she was enthralled by the ceremony. Dragons did not have weddings; they simply chose their mates without any fanfare. Thea had never seen a wedding before and her eyes shone with tears of happiness watching Gunther and Lina pledge to each other in front of their friends and families. Jon had an idea. He took Thea's hand and started to whisper the words of the vows, personalizing them for her.

"Today, surrounded by new friends, I choose you, Aurrynthea Shadow's Fire, to be my partner. I am proud to join my life with yours. I vow to be your kin and your partner in life as we move forward. I give you my hand trusting that even though we started as strangers, in time we came to know each other completely. I give you myself for better or worse, in sickness and health, for richer or poorer, as long as we both shall live."

Thea smiled up at Jon as she whispered back to him.

"Today, surrounded by new friends, I choose you, Jon Winter, to be my partner. I am proud to join my life with yours. I vow to be your kin and your partner in life as we move forward. I give you my hand trusting that even though we started as strangers, in time we came to know each other completely. I give you myself for better or worse, in sickness and health, for richer or poorer, as long as we both shall live."

As Gunther and Lina kissed to seal their vows, Jon leaned down to kiss Thea. Maybe it was the wedding or maybe it was the after effects of the healing they had done, but Jon felt very emotional at the moment.

"I don't have a ring to give you, but it's ok because you already have something of mine."

Thea looked confused.

"I do?"

"Yeah, my heart."

Thea melted against him and sighed.

"I did not think you were one for such poetic words."

Jon gave a shrug.

"I think I read it in a greeting card."

Thea blinked up at him.

"Jon, what is a greeting card?"

He chuckled and tightened his arms around Thea. He kissed her on the tip of her nose.

"Never mind."

***

Unlike the ceremony which had been quite plain, a huge feast was laid out to celebrate Lina and Gunther's nuptials. Jon was impressed with the last-minute preparation. The tables groaned under the weight of all the food. Fresh flowers of every colour were placed in between dishes as decoration. And pretty lanterns made of hollowed out gourds stood ready for when the sun set.

Gunther and Lina were seated on a raised dais overlooking everyone. No one missed how Gunther and Lina gazed at each other, and they often had their heads bowed together tittering at some private joke. Thea and Jon were given places of honour for their part in restoring the farm and facilitating Gunther and Lina's match.

Because they had already met, they were at a small table with the closest friends of the groom. Thea sat next to Laithem while Jon was next to Worth. There was a lot of laughing at stories of when they were younger. Most of them involved being caught in compromising positions with young girls. Jon caught Thea's eye and she felt a flush creep up her face at his silent yet blatant proposition. She lowered her head before raising her eyes in an answering gaze. Jon wasn't sure if it was a trick of the light, but for a brief second, he thought he saw her eyes flare up and understood she was also biding her time until they could be alone.

Most foods were familiar enough to Thea and Jon, but there were a few that had to be explained. Thea was eyeing up a grand looking concoction in the middle of the table. It looked to be about a foot tall with colourful icing and edible flowers dotted around it for decoration.

"What is that?"

Worth rubbed his hands together.

"You are in for a treat. That is Kriegagolly."

Thea dipped her fingers in to taste and groaned in pleasure.

"By the stars! Jon, it tastes like chocolate cake but with some spice I cannot place."

Worth nudged Jon and gave him a conspiratorial wink.

"This dish is only served at weddings. It's meant to make a woman more responsive to romantic pursuits if you get my meaning."

Thea had already eaten half a portion before Jon swiped the plate away from her.

"Ok, that's enough for you."

Thea squeaked in protest. Jon smiled at Worth.

"Her fire aspect means she does not need anything stoked. Trust me on this."

Thea shrugged.

"Was that not your intention?"

Worth and Laithem let out loud guffaws causing some of the other guests to turn and stare at them.

After eating, several guests brought out instruments and space was made for dancing. A strong drink made of fermented fruit was passed around and after a few large glasses of it, Thea was flushed and giggling. After the revelation at the table, Laithem and Worth decided it would be amusing to keep Jon and Thea from sneaking off too soon. So, once the music started Laithem pulled a startled Thea towards the other dancers while a dismayed Jon could only watch when Worth pulled him towards some other guests. Thea tried to turn back towards Jon.

"I do not know this style of dance."

Laithem laughed and gave her an affectionate grin as he held her hand.

"Don't worry. I'll show you how it's done and then later you and Jon can have your fun."

Thea sighed and allowed herself to be spun around like the other dancers. The ladies stood in a circle facing out to their dance partners. As the music played, Thea was spun around and with every turn, she found herself with a new partner. This continued and before long she was dizzy and laughing. Copying the steps of the other ladies she finally found herself again facing Laithem. The alcohol was making her unsteady on her feet and all the spinning meant she wrapped her arms around his neck to keep from tripping over her own feet.

Eventually the mix of the music and dancing and the drink magnified the effect of the cake. Her lust was becoming unbearable, and she needed to seek out Jon. She saw him over by the side speaking to Gunther and Lina. He'd been sipping the same drink and watching her over the rim of his cup. Laithem followed her gaze and recognised when the joke was over. Still, Thea did not want to be rude.

"I'm sorry, Laithem, but would you excuse me."

He laughed.

"Of course, I think we've tortured you enough. Go on, you two. I don't think anyone will miss you if you go out behind the barn."

Thea gave him a friendly kiss on the cheek.

"Thank you for the dance, but I think it is time you found another dance partner."

***

Chapter 28 - What Was In That?

Thea stumbled towards the barn. She leaned against the wall to stop her head from spinning. The wall on the opposite side would be far enough away to offer them privacy. But instead Jon pulled her towards the now dark, new field.

"I believe we still need to bless the field."

As drunk as Thea was, she was still worried about being caught.

"Will we not be seen?"

Jon was already undoing the laces on her dress and sliding his tongue along her shoulder.

"Half the group has already gone to bed and the other half is so wasted that they'll be looking to hook up anywhere. This dark field is probably the last place anyone will think to look for us."

"But Jon…"

This time is was Jon's turn to interrupt her, as his tongue slid between her lips. Thea sighed as she was finally able to quench her growing desire. They slid to the ground as they undressed and Thea gasped as Jon entered her. True to his word he had her calling out to the celestials several times, but by then she was one more voice in a chorus.

***

Thea woke to find Jon hovering over her. He was smiling with a dreamy look on his face.

"You are so beautiful when you sleep, and did you know you have the cutest little snore?"

They were still lying in the field with their clothing scattered around them. From the snores emanating around them Jon's prediction of them being left alone had not been so accurate. Only the long grass hid them from the other sleeping couples. Thea covered her mouth to stifle a giggle.

"It seems we are not alone and without our clothing. Usually you would be quite agitated but you seem very calm."

He leaned down and kissed her.

"I'm trying to not sweat the small stuff. And for the record it's weird when you are naked in front of my friends, but out here, we're one of probably thirty anonymous couples."

He leaned over again to trail a few kisses down her neck and along her shoulder.

"And right now, for whatever reason, I just cannot be arsed to care."

"Jon, are you still drunk?"

"Mmm, probably."

"It would seem the effect of whatever was in that drink was not hindered by our Dragon blood."

"Mmm, so what?"

"I think I like being drunk."

"Thea?"

"Yes, Jon?"

"Shut up."

***

Several hours later the pleasant effects of the alcohol wore off. Thea and Jon were now dressed and lying in the barn with several other guests who had overindulged in the powerful drink. Thea had never suffered a hangover and even Jon who was usually ok, even after some of his more legendary benders with Nash, was feeling rough.

"Jon?"

Jon was holding his head and shading his eyes from the light coming into the barn to keep his head from exploding.

"Yes?"

"I do not think I like being drunk anymore."

Jon laughed but immediately regretted it.

"Ugh, yeah, at the moment I'm trying to remember why I thought this was fun."

"This is not fun, Jon. I feel horrid."

"Time to pay the piper."

"What?"

"Nothing. Never mind. It does eventually pass, but in the meantime, it helps to…"

The last thing he saw was Thea bolting outside to empty her stomach. After retching for several minutes, she came back shaking and pale.

"I do not think I want to be drunk ever again if this is the result."

"After this I don't think I ever want to be *that* drunk again."

Gunther wandered in to see them.

"I take it you are now suffering the after effects of our local brew. It's a powerful concoction that we affectionately call the Tempest—it feels great for several hours, but like a violent storm it leaves devastation in its wake. You can see why we don't tend to serve it often. You two are new to it."

Gunther let his eyes travel around the barn and he raised his voice.

"But the rest of you should have known better."

Several of the other barn occupants moaned in response.

Gunther helped Jon and Thea rise and guided them towards his home. Once inside he gestured for them to sit.

"I have a special mixture guaranteed to make you feel better."

Jon was sceptical as he watched Gunther search his cupboards.

"You mean if it doesn't kill us first."

Gunther chuckled as he pulled the bottle down from a shelf.

"Ah, here it is. You don't see me holding my head or vomiting. Trust me, you've given me something I treasure dearly. I'd never harm you."

Lina breezed in and saw Thea and Jon looking worse for wear.

"I see you have overindulged in the Tempest. Gunther's remedy will make you feel much better. He was kind enough to give me some this morning, and as you can see, we both are fine."

Thea sipped at the cup Gunther gave her while Jon sniffed at his.

"What was that stuff? I don't usually get drunk like that."

Gunther smiled.

"Everyone in the village has their own recipe, but the difference is mine has been sitting and brewing for several months while most gets drunk after a few weeks."

Thea began to feel sleepy. She looked over to see Jon yawn. Gunther explained their reaction.

"You'll need an hour or so to let my remedy calm the worst effects of the Tempest, but afterward, you should feel fine."

Gunther and Lina helped Thea and Jon to a spare room to sleep and allow Gunther's tonic to calm their hangover.

***

When they woke up, Gunther and Lina had a small meal ready for them.

"Food also helps. Not too much, but some bread and cheese should restore you."

Thea was beginning to feel a little better. She tried to explain why it was worrying that they had been affected at all.

"We Dragons don't usually suffer the effects of alcohol. This makes me wonder if since leaving Hell we will encounter other foodstuffs that we may react with."

Jon's head felt much clearer.

"We'll need to be careful with what we eat and drink from now on. We can't afford to be incapacitated at the wrong time."

Thea nodded.

"Yes, the outcome may not be so forgiving next time."

Thea and Jon rose feeling considerably better than they had earlier.

***

A day and a half later, rested and fully recovered, it was time for Thea and Jon to move on. Jon and Gunther shook hands and Jon gave Lina a congratulatory kiss on her cheek.

"We've stayed as long as we can, but we need to get moving. We have a long way to go still, and no way to know how long it will take us to get home."

Thea kissed Gunther's cheek and turned to hug Lina.

"Gunther, Lina, as much as we have enjoyed taking part in your celebration, we need to get home. Our young daughter and family are still waiting for us to return. May the celestials watch over you and keep you safe."

Lina gave Thea some fruit to take with them before Jon opened the portal and Thea waved before walking through. He nodded to the startled couple before he followed her and they disappeared.

❊ ❊ ❊

Chapter 29 - Limbo

For the first few months it had been easy to stay positive, always hoping the next realm would be home. But every time they walked into another new realm, Jon's confidence was knocked down a peg. Jon could see Thea trying to stay positive for his sake, but each night when they bedded down it tore at him to feel her shaking with silent tears.

They walked through the latest portal and stood in another empty realm, the occupants long gone or perished. The ground was hard with small rocks. The only life they could see was some scrub vegetation. In the distance they could hear insects chirping. Thea gave a dejected sigh.

"Another abandoned realm. I do not even see much in the way of food. At least we ate well yesterday and it should be safe enough to rest here."

Jon knew Thea was struggling to hide how much she was suffering. Being away from Darcuna was taking its toll. Every time they came across a little girl with dark hair and blue eyes, it felt like reopening the same wound. He could see Thea falling deeper and deeper into depression, and he had no idea how to help her. So instead he pushed them, sometimes to the point of breaking, hoping if she was too tired to cry, she would also be too tired to dream. And it worked for a short time, however it also put them under tremendous strain, and they began to snap at each other.

"Why are you crying? Can't you even go one day without crying?"

"I *am* trying Jon. I do not cry to make you feel guilty, but I cannot always control it."

Jon rubbed his temple.

"I *know*, I'm *sorry*. I *know* you want to go home, and I *know* you're tired. I'm tired too. So much so that I can't see straight and even though I *know* you aren't doing it on purpose, your bouts of crying are just exaggerating my bad mood."

"If you need time to rest then…"

"No, if we stop you get weepy, I feel bad, we fight —wash, rinse, repeat—it's a vicious cycle."

Thea did not let the tears fall, but her lip was trembling.

"We cannot keep up this pace. We are both drained: emotionally, physically, mentally. We must rest, or the result will be catastrophic."

Jon yelled at no one in particular; he just needed the release.

"I know, I know, but this is so fucking frustrating. I don't know if we are moving forward, backward, or in fucking circles."

Jon kicked at the ground as Thea pulled out her pendant. The swaying had been consistent over the last several realms, so it was hard to gauge if they were making any progress. Putting it away she sat down.

Jon looked down at her sitting cross-legged in the dirt.

"What the hell are you doing?"

Thea glared up at him.

"I am trying to see if my Dragon memories can offer us a solution beyond a slow death from sleep deprivation. Each day they become more organised, but because I have been so tired, I have not had a chance to concentrate and try and see if any of them can help us. I just need a moment's rest to let my mind quiet and allow my memories to flow and then maybe the key to our problem will make itself known. So, as you have so often yelled at me in recent days: shut up, sit down, and let me think."

Jon made a face at her but otherwise did as he was told. He twiddled his thumbs for a while before speaking.

"Anything yet?"

Thea answered through gritted teeth.

"No, but it has *only* been a few minutes."

Jon held up his hands.

"Fine, fine."

***

"I have it!"

Jon woke with a start and rubbed his eyes. It was dark, the only light coming from a small amount of Hellfire that Thea had set down next to herself.

"How long was I out?"

"Several hours I think, but that is not important. We have been so blind. We have been portaling under the assumption that we move through the realms in a linear fashion like moving along a straight road, but what if we should be moving more like a river as it winds around obstacles on its way to the sea."

Jon looked confused.

"How else are we supposed to move? I don't get what you mean."

Thea lay back and again pulled out her pendant.

"We assume the only way the compass works is to hold it like we would if we were standing in Hell or Earthside. But what if we have been wrong?"

Jon's eyes went wide when the pendant swung up and remained suspended over Thea before swinging on the opposite axis. It was swinging substantially faster than it had before. Jon tilted his head and stuck his hand under it to make sure he was actually seeing what he thought he was seeing.

"Motherfucker. This changes everything."

They were making progress. Thea and Jon jumped up and he twirled her around.

"You amazing, awesome, brilliant woman. I take it back. If you need a good cry to come up with more ideas like that, I can give you a good hard spanking to get the tears flowing."

Thea's crying was now out of happiness and she laughed at his suggestion.

"Thank you Jon, but I believe I do not need any assistance at the moment."

Jon hoisted Thea up and whooped to the sky before he lowered her and kissed her. He grabbed hold of Thea's hair and deepened the kiss. Thea was confused and pulled away.

"Jon, I don't understand your change in mood."

Jon gave her a beguiling grin.

"Hon, you've never had make-up sex."

His eyes were bright as he slid his hand under her top and ran his fingers lightly over her back.

"Up until now we've mostly always agreed. This was our first big fight and after a couple has a big fight they always make up. The only thing possibly better is angry sex, but between the two of us and our magic I'm not sure that would be a good idea…"

He moved his mouth to her neck and sucked on the spot just above her shoulder, and Thea gave a groan before she continued to query him.

"I do not understand how you have gone from being so angry at me to now hungering for me."

Jon moved his mouth so he was hovering over her lips.

"You don't question it; you just do it."

Thea held Jon's face, staring into his eyes, searching for some trace of his earlier anger. All that she saw was love—and passion. In that moment she did not question why his mood had changed but understood that if they lost their faith in each other they would never get home. She turned his head so she could whisper in his ear.

"I know you will get us home. Not because you are one of the most powerful mages I have ever known. But because I love you and I trust you."

He ran a finger across her lip and she kissed it. She moved her hands down to the fastening of his trousers.

"Now, at this moment, I wish to remind you of how much I love and trust you."

Jon groaned as he felt her hand on him. He lowered her to the ground. Before he allowed himself to let go and lose himself in her body. He stopped to brush the hair from her eyes.

"Whatever I did to deserve you wasn't enough, not by a longshot."

***

Chapter 30 - The Silvaer of Greenhamspire

Thea walked out of the portal and was immediately struck by the colours. This realm was filled with lush greenery. Since their argument and the subsequent make up, they had travelled through at least a dozen more realms. The last one had been little more than a desert with individual towns built around oases. Everything had been the colour of sand and stone with a few small splashes of green and gold. The inhabitants though had been friendly enough and had offered them food and a place to rest for a few days.

They had seen every possible type of landscape: from a realm in perpetual night where individuals were born blind, to a land with very little dry earth inhabited by creatures born in swamps pools. With each new realm Jon insisted on keeping their identities a secret until he judged it safe. Thea complied but once they'd established the citizens were friendly, they found most were amazed to see Dragons so far from home and were eager to welcome them.

Thea was still sad.

"I know Darcuna will have my memories of these places, but..."

Jon put his arm around Thea.

"I know, I wish we could share it with her too. We can talk about her. I know sometimes it's hard to, but it's ok. I get it."

Thea gave a little sniff, and nodded.

"Yes, she is safe and with people who love her. I miss her."

Jon tightened his arm around Thea.

"I miss her too. I miss our bed and cuddling with her on it. Unfortunately, here's home for the next couple of days."

He stumbled and Thea grabbed him.

"You have been overexerting yourself again. How many realms did you attempt to cross this time?"

Jon allowed Thea to help him sit.

"Four, maybe five. I just wanted to see if I could."

Thea sat next to him. She leaned back against a tree and pulled his head down to her lap.

"I know you want to move quickly for my sake, but I do not want you to hurt yourself."

Thea viewed their surroundings.

"From this vantage I cannot see anything past these trees. This vegetation is so dense that a city could be just a few miles away and we would not know it…"

Thea looked down to see Jon had passed out and was snoring softly. Placing a few simple wards, she leaned over and gave him a small kiss before closing her eyes. Her wards would alert her if anything malevolent approached, and her runes would initially block any attack.

***

Thea became aware of voices around her and Jon.

"They are huge."

"Ooh, she's pretty."

"Do you think they're dead?"

"No stupid, she's breathing."

"What about that one? His clothes look funny."

"I like hers, they don't cover much… Ouch!"

"Pervert! Don't make me tell my sister what you said. You're already in enough trouble with her."

Thea couldn't keep her face straight any longer and opened her eyes. She was surprised to find that it was not a group of rowdy youths, but spritely, elderly men. They all stood no taller than a few feet with hair and beards that were long enough to cover them completely to their feet. Their faces were almost hidden under wild unkempt eyebrows and whiskers. One was staring at Thea wide-eyed like she was a siren, the entire impression would have been comical had they not all been carrying very lethal looking weapons.

Jon yawned and opened his eyes to see the group.

"Have we landed in Oz?"

He sat up and was already taller than most of them. In response they all raised their spears. Jon pushed one aside.

"Look, Lollipop Guild. No one appreciates waking up to a spear in the face."

Thea nudged Jon to correct him.

"We are travellers making our way home. We did not mean to trespass."

The apparent leader of the group gave a deep bow, which almost caused him to topple over.

"Ah this one has breeding. Not like that lout."

Thea tried to hide a smile with her hand before straightening her face.

"Forgive Jon, he is not so hospitable when he first wakes, but I assure you he is an honourable Faye."

This made them all take a step back.

"Is he dark or light?"

Jon's face screwed up.

"Why you little…"

Thea stopped him.

"I believe what he means is, do you practice the dark arts or a more noble path? Jon is my mate and I know him to be good. But not everything born of the dark is evil, as not all things of the light are virtuous."

The leader smiled at her.

"Beautiful and elegant speaking, she must be a Dragon. Though why she is in company of a Faye…"

Jon pushed himself up and then helped Thea.

"I'm half Dragon, small fry. That's why she's with me."

This caused every bushy eyebrow to shoot up. This time Thea couldn't help herself and giggled, before straightening up her face.

"I am sorry I should not laugh so. It is rude."

The leader shook his head.

"No, my lady, it's quite alright. We understand what we must look like to your kind. My name is Fernhorn. I am the chief in this province."

He took Thea's hand and the others followed leaving Jon standing there wondering if them knowing he and Thea were Dragons would be an issue.

"Ah, Chief Fernhorn, where exactly is here?"

Fernhorn waved his hand and the greenery swept aside to show them a small town.

"Why this is Greenhamspire."

The town was built into the trees. Nothing looked shaped or formed by hand. It was as if the entire town was grown into being.

"I see you are admiring our homes. They are clever, our trees. Sentient trees, we care for them and they care for us. They can even defend themselves if the need arises."

Thea pressed her hand to one and could almost feel the sap running through the tree like a heartbeat.

"Astounding!"

Thea and Jon were led through the village. Everyone stopped to look at the tall strangers in their midst. Chief Fernhorn waved them off.

"Go about your business, nothing to see here. It's very rude to stare…"

The grass beneath their feet was so soft it felt like they were walking on clouds. There were no roads or carts with wheels. Elbowing Jon, Thea pointed to a little sled-like contraptions that seemed to glide along. Each one was carried by hundreds of tiny caterpillars, moving in seamless formation. Their movements leaving no trace on the grass. Chief Fernhorn proudly explained.

"Everything we desire moved is carried by the dimmi. They can carry more than their individual weight when they move as a group, and as you can see nary a blade of grass is disturbed. We don't require much, certainly nothing bigger than the dimmi can transport. Our trees provide most of what we need."

As their hosts steered them towards the center of the village, Thea and Jon admired how each dwelling was unique. Some were bright and vibrant while some were subtle and subdued, each catering to the unique personality of the dweller. The air was perfumed with the fragrance of abundant flowers that bloomed everywhere, and Thea took deep breaths enjoying the scent.

"There is something familiar... but it can't be, not so far away from home."

Thea followed her nose and when she turned Jon could see tears in her eyes.

"Daisies! By the stars, Jon, there are daisies."

Jon carefully picked one of the little flowers and placed it behind Thea's ear.

"We are definitely moving in the right direction. This just proves it."

* * *

Chapter 31 - Tree Hospitality

"So that's it in a nutshell."

Chief Fernhorn nodded after Jon explained their situation. They were sat around a table that resembled a large mushroom; each seat a smaller version, like stools around a bar. Each stool grown to the perfect height for its seater. Jon was still trying to get comfortable on his. Fernhorn asked for drinks and food to be brought out for them.

"Ah yes, what an adventure. I am still amazed to see Dragons so far from home, but I won't lie. It's rather prestigious to have such exalted guests. Even the trees are impressed. Look at the bounty they have given us. We only eat what the trees drop for us and never take anything off the branch, but look how much they have provided."

Chief Fernhorn nodded at no one.

"Ah, of course. Yes, I agree very fortuitous."

Jon shot Thea a sideways glance. *Who is he talking to? The trees?* She shrugged before turning back to their host.

"After the ruin of some realms we've passed through, it is truly wonderful to find one so much in balance. Were you conversing with them just now?"

The old man smiled.

"Yes, they tell me they are so very excited to meet an actual Dragon."

Thea was curious.

"Tell me Chief Fernhorn, how did you learn to speak to the trees?"

Chief Fernhorn puffed up his chest with pride.

"It is the reason my family were raised to Chieftains; my ancestors were the first to learn to listen to the trees, in this province at least. Once we began to understand, we taught the others and now we live entirely in conjunction with the trees. But as a Dragon surely you must be able to understand them as well?"

Thea looked up at a large dark oak tree and concentrated but so far as she could tell it stayed silent. Chief Fernhorn followed her gaze and chuckled.

"Oh, don't mind Burnbow, he's as stubborn as they come, he barely talks to me."

He pointed towards a beautiful tree with an explosion of blooms in every imaginable colour.

"Now Cherryspine is much more social. She'll talk the leaves off most of the trees."

He gave Thea an impish wink.

"I think Burnbow is sweet on her, but he won't admit it."

Thea gave a loud snort and covered her mouth to stop herself from further laughter. Jon watched her face and his heart melted at her delight. It had been a long time since he'd heard her giggle at anything. He even felt himself smile. He stared up at the old oak and thought to himself. *Kind of reminds me of guy I know. Wonder how Nash worked up the courage to ask his ex out. He'd know what to say...*

I am not sweet on her.

Jon's head shot around.

"Who said that?"

Ahem, up here, Faye. I said I am not sweet on her. I just find her foliage nice to look at.

Jon narrowed his eyes and looked up at the tree again. He poked Thea with his elbow. He whispered to her.

"I think that tree talked to me."

Yes Faye, I talk, like you, well more intelligently and certainly more refined than you.

Jon fell over, pointing up at the old oak.

"That oak actually talked."

Perhaps I should attempt to converse with the Dragon, at least she seems polite or in the very least more intelligent.

Chief Fernhorn saw Jon's reaction and guessed what was going on.

"So, he does speak, just not to me anymore. Seems he found someone more to his liking."

Jon crossed his arms while glaring at the tree.

"More likely he found someone new to fuck with."

Jon stood and was about to yell something rude at the tree before he caught himself.

"Ok, the train to crazy town has just entered the station. I am arguing with a fucking tree. I must be way more tired than I thought."

Chief Fernhorn gave him a sympathetic smile.

"No, he can be unpleasant. I've called him out on it, probably why he refuses to answer me anymore."

He wagged his finger at the tree.

"Burnbow, you behave yourself with our guests or maybe I should ask them to teach you some manners."

Chief Fernhorn leaned over and whispered to Thea.

"Could you give a small demonstration of your Dragon fire, if you would be so kind?"

Thea opened her hand and small flame appeared. The leaves in the oak moved as if caught by a small breeze.

"That's enough. I think we got his attention. Now Burnbow, we have guests, stop acting like a child. Apologize to them."

Jon waited and heard some rustling. He called up to the oak.

"I can't hear you!"

...I am not sorry... and if you ever breathe a word of what I told you I will strangle you while you sleep.

Jon narrowed his eyes at the tree.

Mate, that is a dangerous threat to make to an incubus Faye. Don't fuck with me or I'll turn you into kindling.

Jon flicked his finger and allowed the incubus to taste the tree. He never got an answer but it felt like they had come to an understanding. Burnbow never spoke to him again.

***

Thea sat in the middle of the clearing, nodding. Jon was impressed that she seemed to be following what was going on. He'd lost track of the conversation after he'd picked up the sixth voice, but Thea was coping and, in some cases, responding out loud.

"It is difficult to describe. Before I had no memories but now, I do. No, I always had the memories but they were magically blocked. Yes, I am very happy to have them now. I am not sure. One of my ancestors must have travelled through this realm."

Thea's eyes dropped momentarily.

"After the purge, it seems many Dragons left Earthside. I have discovered my family was flung far and wide across many realms. I am hopeful that as more of my memories take shape and I am able to understand them, I might find additional family."

Even though Jon was born long after the actions, he still felt guilty over what the Faye had done to the Dragons. There was no way around it. It had been a really shitty thing to do. The only consolation was that the Faye still in Astranya must have helped smuggle Dragons out of Earthside prior to their magical clear-out. Jon swore his head would explode with all the new information. His world had expanded exponentially ever since meeting Thea. He took nothing for granted, because when he did, it had a way of coming back and biting him in the arse.

Thea looked relaxed even though her expression was sad. She smiled through her tears. Getting her memories back was proving to be more valuable than just the knowledge she was gaining. She was connected to her family now in a way that made being away from everything and everyone she knew bearable.

The possibility of not getting home kept nagging at Jon, but he refused to let it take root. No matter what, he'd keep trying. He'd promised her he would get them home, and with everything they had been through, he be damned if he would break that promise.

***

Thea took advantage of the balance between nature and the Silvaer to recharge. Jon used the time to catch up on his sleep. Feeling refreshed and recharged they felt ready to continue their trek home. Jon opened a portal and Thea walked through. But just as he was about follow, Jon got an unexpected surprise. The old tree offered him some advice.

I do not care for you, Faye, but she apparently deems you worthy. I will shed no tears at your leaving, but I will feel her departure. It is a lucky man who finds a partner who makes them better than they are; take care of that one. She is unique.

Jon looked over at the old oak and gave it a genuine smile.

"Don't I know it."

He crossed his fingers that the next realm was home.

***

Chapter 32 - Artiscaena

Thea exhaled with fatigue. This was the two hundred and seventh realm they had entered since the night Jon had pushed her through Black Heart's mechanical portal. Nothing smelled familiar to Thea and it was pitch dark so she opened her palm and a flame of Hellfire illuminated a small area around them.

The ground was covered in little more than scrub vegetation, and the air was cold and dry; the season of the year felt autumnal. Thea could just make out the lights from a settlement but was too weary to walk the distance to reach it.

In the Hellfire light, Jon could see the exhaustion on Thea's face. He'd been pushing them hard, sure that each time they jumped through, this would be the time they found Hell, but each time they walked into another new realm. The last one had been a complete disaster forcing Thea and Jon to run before they'd had any time to rest. He'd only been able to jump with Thea's help but now they were both running on fumes. Jon yawned.

"I would never have guessed there were so many realms between us and home."

Thea leaned against Jon, blinking to keep her eyes open.

"I could fall asleep right here on this spot."

A cool breeze made Jon shiver. He grabbed hold of Thea's arm to direct the light.

"Unlike you, I prefer a little shelter. Over there, I think I can see some caves."

Thea was too tired to argue. Since their near escape her heightened emotional state meant she was always on guard. Jon knew, when in a hostile or unknown realm Thea used her rock shields to keep them safe when she was awake, and the Faye runes sapped her strength when she slept.

"You look shattered."

Thea observed Jon's haggard appearance.

"I am beginning to understand the price Caris spoke of, that these protection runes extort. You also look in need of rest."

At that moment Jon's stomach gurgled and Thea gave a tired giggle.

"I think we must also find food stuffs soon before that growl becomes a full roar."

They stumbled towards the caves using Thea's Hellfire to guide them. Once inside, Thea slid down the wall. Jon sat and pulled her towards him so they could sleep using their body heat to keep them warm as neither of them had the will or the strength to build a fire. Before long both of them were breathing deeply and asleep.

* * *

Thea awoke to find Jon gone. Rubbing her eyes, she followed the sound of Jon's voice as he sang to himself. While not possessing the most pleasing singing voice, since they'd left Hell, he often sang to himself when he thought no one was listening. Thea loved when he sang to her. She gave a long stretch and smiled. If he was singing, it meant he had slept well.

While Thea was used to sleeping in the rough from her time growing up in Hell, she knew Jon missed their soft bed greatly. Thea felt like she'd not properly relaxed since their brief stint in Greenhamspire. Now her mind felt clear enough to properly decide their next move. Lifting her head, she could smell something cooking and her mouth watered. After sleep, food was always welcome. Jon turned as Thea came out of the cave.

"Just in time for breakfast. I know we've been trying to be careful since that episode in Illthana but I think these are safe, they sort of look and smell like yams. I found a patch of them growing wild. The ground is so hard I had to dig them up with my sword. Thankfully bound weapons don't dull like ordinary swords."

Thea reached into the fire and grabbed one of the root vegetables and bit into it, savouring the sweet earthy flavour.

"Who cares, they are divine."

Jon laughed at her expression of pure bliss. He conjured his sword and pulled another tuber out of the fire. Laying it down and hacking it in half to let it cool before he ate. He watched as Thea grabbed a second out of the fire.

"Hey slow down, I only grabbed a few of these and I have to wait for mine to cool down."

Thea laughed at him before reminding him he was half storm Dragon.

"Can you not bring the temperature down using your magic? While I realise, we are trying to conserve our resources, surely at the moment eating is a priority?"

Jon grabbed one of the roots he'd sliced. Blowing a cold breath, he felt it cool down in his hand. He took a tentative bite and groaned with pleasure."

"It worked. Mmm, holy crap these are good but right about now I'd kill for a nice big smear of butter. We definitely have to grab some of these before we leave. If they are anything like Earthside yams, they should travel well."

They finished eating and begun discussing what to do next. Both agreed that Jon was pushing his portaling ability to the limit and after a few close calls it was paramount that they find some place relatively safe until they could portal again. Recently Jon had had to rely on the incubus, but the monster was becoming more demanding. He could stamp it down, but he would eventually have to feed it properly, especially if he was calling on its strength.

After digging up a good supply of the yam-like tubers they fashioned a crude basket to carry their bounty along with them. Jon looked towards where Thea had seen the town the previous night. What had looked like a little town just beyond the hills, now appeared to be a sizable city much farther away. Thea blew out a sigh.

"I must have been more tired than I thought. The city did not look that great a distance last night, but I do not think it is wise to fly."

Jon agreed.

"No arguments here, at least until we know what or who we are dealing with."

Before they started walking, Jon pointed at her pendant.

"Better hide that away, no point in taking chances with something so precious. In my opinion as soon as you get progress, the criminal element follows."

Thea tucked the pendant away in her shirt. They walked with the basket between them, chatting as they made their way towards the unknown city. Thea was upbeat.

"This is the first large advanced settlement we have seen. They might have technology that could help us get home."

Jon wasn't so trusting.

"Thea, being advanced doesn't always mean willing to share. Humanity can't be the only developed species to have pulled their way forward using the bodies of their conquered foes to build themselves up. Just be careful about how much you share."

He stopped to get Thea's full attention.

"We've been lucky so far, but I don't trust our luck to last. We both need to remember we are strangers in a strange realm. We've found out Dragons are known well beyond Hell and that magic is practiced and *that* means our blood has worth. If the wrong person were to find out, it puts a target on our backs."

His look told her he was being serious. Thea bobbed her head in agreement.

"I understand what you are saying, Jon. I may be powerful, but even I can be killed."

She gave him a teasing poke in the ribs.

"And then who will keep you warm in this cold and foreign land."

Jon poked Thea back.

"Hey, I didn't hear you complaining that night in Amul. In fact, I'd go so far to say you were enjoying it."

***

Chapter 33 - The Big City

They continued to joke as they walked towards the settlement. As Jon and Thea got closer, they met up with other travelling vendors making their way to trade in the city markets. The most talkative was an older man named Tibor. From his well-made clothing and fancy cart, Jon guessed he was good at selling. He was overly proud of his home city.

"That jewel on the horizon is Artiscaena, the largest and most profitable trading city for miles. People travel from all over to buy and sell in their markets. To trade there is a badge of honour. Only the best products are allowed. I occasionally have to journey to check on my other properties, but it is always nice to return home."

Thea and Jon's clothing got them some odd looks, but most of their travel companions were polite enough to not say anything outright. The women marvelled at the runes woven into Thea's clothing. When asked what they meant Thea responded with a shrug.

"I do not understand them, but the one who wore them before me was much loved, and they were given to me with love."

The women nodded knowingly. Because Thea's clothes were charity and with their little basket, they appeared to them to be poor farmers. They had a harder time explaining exactly where they came from. Jon took to using his Faye glamour to subtly divert questions.

The group of traders suddenly stopped, and Jon and Thea saw they were being checked before entering the city. The walls surrounding the city stood roughly twenty feet high with entrances every so often to allow the flow of people in and out. Each one was manned by two guards. They arrived at the main city gates and were asked for trading papers. Tibor took pity on his two new friends and chided the guard.

"Look at the pair of them; they barely have enough to clothe themselves and it's just a basket of darra roots. The quality of their goods are sound, and I'm sure the masters will not mind a single basket for trade from such poor farmers."

Jon tried another tactic. He waved a yam under the guard's nose.

"Would a few of these buy us our trader's papers?"

The guard looked at their basket suspiciously and took two of the nicest bulbs before waving them through. Tibor gave Jon a covert wink.

"Good thinking, it was wise to remember the fourth rule."

Neither of them had a clue what the fourth rule was, but accepted that it worked in their favour. Jon tried to appear casual as he spoke to Tibor.

"Remind me again, what are the rules?"

Tibor was more than happy to tell them about Artiscaena's laws.

"My city prides itself on its order. You are already familiar with the fourth rule: Work is its own reward. Charity is for the weak and the feeble. I do not consider my bargaining with the guard charity. The largest traders – myself included – started with a single stand."

Thea wasn't sure how she felt about these rules and chewed her lip. Tibor didn't seem to notice as he continued.

"The first rule is, trust the authority of the Circle of the Silver Blood; they serve the whole. The second is magic is not for the common people; it is only for those born into the Circle of the Silver Blood. And the third is, dabbling in magic breeds discontent."

Jon looked to Thea. His back stiffened, and Thea understood they would have to watch what they said and did while inside the city walls. Their benevolent benefactor was now someone to be wary of. When they walked through the gates and got their first look at Artiscaena, both their jaws dropped in awe. Most of the city appeared to have been built from some sort of gleaming white stone. When it caught the sun, the stone shimmered like pearls.

Towering over them were the stately homes of the wealthiest merchants. They were the ones who dealt in large luxury goods such as furniture and carriages along with fine fabrics like silk with gold thread laced through it. Finely dressed ladies sat under awnings on their little balconies above all the people. They sipped drinks brought by their servants. Tibor most likely lived among them.

Farther in were smaller, less intimidating buildings nestled between the white giants. They were made from some type of white wood to mimic the grand merchant homes. These were the artisan workshops. Each workshop was fronted by the artisan's public shop.

They were filled with all sorts of wares. They sold everything from brightly woven blankets and pots and pans to pastries and cordials.

They walked through the common district to reach the Trader's Market. This housed the humblest buildings that were made of cheap slate or dark wood and were hidden away to minimize their effect on the overall landscape of the city.

Thea peeked down an alley and saw a small family working away in what appeared to be a forge. Because of the black smoke and noise, the smithy was hidden amongst the slate homes. A woman pumped a pair of bellows while her husband pounded away on an anvil. Two small children sat nearby ready to run to action if called on by their parents. The little girl was barely tall enough to reach the woman's hip. Thea instantly thought of Darcuna and bit her lip. These would be the shops and homes of the common labourers.

Trees with crimson and gold leaves were planted around the buildings adding colour to the city and the cobbled streets had the same gold and crimson colours running through them along with more simple grey slate chips. The most striking structure was the black citadel high up on a hill at the center of the city overlooking the Trader's Market.

Tibor followed their gaze and gave them a sombre nod.

"The Circle of the Silver Blood live up there, studying the old texts, trying to summon magic back into this realm. They say that once magic was common and our peoples travelled to other realms, but then an evil race of Faye stole our magic and we've been confined to this realm ever since. The Circle toil trying to get us back our magic, so that we can once again take our rightful place as the most feared traders in all the realms."

Jon could feel the hair on the back of his neck stand up. They were in one of the realms Caris had warned them about. They called themselves traders but what they really practiced was piracy. Raiders who pillaged other realms for their own gain and his eyes met with Thea's. Thankfully she'd had the same thought. Feigning a need to rest, they let the group move on. Tibor offered to stay with them, but Thea assured him she was fine.

"I am just tired; we've travelled a great distance. We shall look for you in the market."

* * *

Chapter 34 - We Got to Get Out of This Place

After they watched Tibor turn a corner, Jon pulled them further into the shadows of a quiet alley. Once they were sure they were alone, they spoke. Jon wore a grim expression.

"This complicates things. So far no one has any clue of what we are, but I don't relish spending any more time in this place. My vote is we ditch the yams, I'll use my glamour to hide us, and we get back to our cave. Then, as much as we need a rest, I think it's better if we jump sooner than later."

Thea nodded and pointed toward the other alley.

"That small family forge we passed. The children looked hungry. Perhaps instead of discarding the yams we could give them to that family? They looked like they could use the food..."

Jon shook his head and grinned at Thea.

"Yeah, yeah, I know. They may not think much of charity, but we still do."

A guard shouted down the passage to them.

"All trading is to be done in the main square! No gypsy stalls outside the market. We don't like gypsy traders in our city. Artiscaena has a reputation to uphold."

Jon pointed at the basket.

"Just making a delivery. Everything has been bought and paid for. No laws being broken here. We just got a little turned around –Hey!"

The guard cuffed him on the back of the head.

"I said move it!"

Thea saw Jon's fingers curl as if he was about to cast and she squeezed his arm.

"We mean no harm. We are simple farmers delivering food that was purchased by the family that runs the forge. We simply got lost."

The guard grabbed hold of Thea's arm and yanked her so hard she lost her hold on the basket. The yams fell onto the ground.

"*That* family bought all these?"

He brought his foot down on one of the yams. Thea's eyes flashed with anger.

"Why would you do that?"

The guard laughed at her.

"Because the Circle gives me the authority, gypsy. I ought to haul you in for disturbing my peace."

Jon could see Thea was shaking with suppressed rage. There were a lot of things that made her upset and a few that made her angry, but when she saw that sort of flagrant abuse of power it was like a red cape to a bull for Thea. He knew her history would compel her to act. He took a step back. The guard called out to him.

"Hey you, gypsy scum, where are you going?"

Jon held up his hands.

"Mate, I'm the least of your worries right now."

The guard stepped towards Jon, but Thea had already conjured her Hellfire in her free hand and thrust it into the chest of the guard.

"I do not take kindly to persons who misuse their authority."

The guard opened his mouth to shout but was dissolved into ash before he made a sound.

Jon blew out a breath.

"Well that was close…"

Two more guards appeared at the entrance to the corridor.

"You two, what are you doing?"

Jon smacked his forehead.

"Oh for fuck's sake."

The guards charged at them, and Jon grabbed Thea and pulled her through a portal. They appeared in front of the forge. He knew they didn't have much time before the guards started searching the adjacent roads looking for them, so he negotiated with the startled labourer.

"Look, in the other alley is a basket full of darra roots. If you help us hide it's all yours."

The blacksmith took a few seconds to comprehend what was happening before he gestured for them to move to the back of the shop and nodded to his daughter. The little girl ran towards the alleyway opening and shouted at the guards.

"I saw them, I saw them."

Jon readied a spell, and Thea called up her Hellfire. The woman whispered to them.

"Please don't hurt her."

The blacksmith threw a large tarp over Thea and Jon and knocked them down. Pulling them towards the back of the shop, he kicked the tarp a few times. He kept his voice low enough so only they could hear.

"Be quiet, you two."

The guards ran towards the little girl.

"What did you see?"

The little girl screamed at the guards, making as much of a fuss as she could to distract them.

"Magic users! I saw them. I saw them. They appeared out of thin air over there and then they ran towards the gates."

One of the guards threw a few copper pennies at the little girl before they ran off. While the little girl dropped to her knees and scrambled to collect the coins, the blacksmith tugged the tarp off of Thea and Jon.

"I'm sorry but we were only trying to help, and I did not want you to hurt Anke by mistake."

Thea looked over at the little girl and nodded to the man.

"I think I understand. Thank you for hiding us."

The blacksmith smiled.

"We are used to them. Visitors are not regarded well inside the city. It's better to send the guards off with false information than pretend we saw nothing."

The blacksmith's wife grabbed hold of her daughter protectively.

"Why was the city guard chasing you? Are you thieves? Did you steal your magic from the Circle?"

Thea looked at Jon before he nodded. She pulled out her pendant.

"This is our little girl. Her name is Darcuna. We are just trying to get home to her."

Jon wrapped his arm around Thea.

"We're travellers. And yes, we do wield magic but it's our own. We didn't steal it. We were born with it. We didn't know about the rules. We need to get out of the city, but I'm properly tapped out after escaping from those guards. I need to recharge my magic before I can attempt to open another portal."

The blacksmith held out his hand.

"My name is Horst. This is my wife, Lene. You already know Anke and this is our son, Niko. We are Sommner. Most are traders, we are simple labourers. That is why we live in slate not ivory. We don't have much, but we can share what we have until you are strong enough to leave. We don't follow the fourth rule as strictly as others."

Jon shook his hand.

"I wasn't lying. There is an entire basket of those darra roots in the next alley. It's all we have, but if you hide us, just for a few hours, we'll gladly give them all to you."

Horst smiled and sent the children to grab the basket.

"Niko, go with your sister and gather those roots before someone else finds them."

The little boy and girl took off to collect the yams.

"Trade has been slow, and the food is appreciated. Most in this city follow the fourth rule. Come inside and tell us how magic users such as yourselves come to be here in the Lower Schond District. We don't often have such exalted visitors. We usually see servants or occasionally artisans. You are the first magic users we've ever met."

The children returned hauling the basket between them. Anke's face was red from the exertion but beaming.

"Look Papa, there's enough darra roots to last us until Saint Warnerus's Feast."

Niko carried the basket inside while Anke gazed at Thea and Jon before pulling them down to hug them in thanks.

"No one ever comes to visit us with such gifts."

Lene pulled her daughter back and cuffed Anke to silence her.

"Be quiet, child. We don't need city guards hearing your boasting and coming to inspect."

Anke shut her mouth but gave Thea a grateful smile. Again, Thea's chest felt heavy. She blinked back tears.

"Do not be so severe with her. She is still young. I know what it is to fear for your child, but she is truly a blessing."

Lene, tried to stay firm but Thea's tears softened her.

"How old is your daughter? Is she yet old enough to talk back? Anke is a talkative child, but I do love her. She just tries my patience at times."

Lene tweaked Anke's nose. Thea watched the affectionate display and sighed.

"No, Darcuna has yet to speak. She was still in diapers when we left her... It feels like ages since I kissed her goodbye. I do not even know if she will remember me when we finally return home."

Lene patted her hand.

"Children never forget their mothers. It's both our curse and our blessing."

Thea gave a small laugh, even as the tightness in her chest remained.

"I know you are right. I simply miss her terribly."

Jon put his arm around Thea.

"Once we get out of this city and I get my strength back, we'll try again."

※ ※ ※

Chapter 35 - The Blacksmith Family

Horst had to return to his work so he and Lene resumed labour at the front of his forge. Jon and Thea hid in the shadows just inside. Horst continued to talk to Jon and Thea covertly, speaking between each strike of his hammer.

"How long have you been trying to get home?"

Jon counted on his hand.

"If your calendar is the same as ours, just over a year and a half.

Thea let out a whimper and bit her fist to try and keep her emotions in check. Jon tried to comfort her, but he felt his own chest tighten. If he stayed any longer, he'd lose it. He moved towards the door before his own feelings came out in a torrent.

"I need to get some air."

Thea tried to stop him, but he gently pulled his arm free. He tried to keep his tone light.

"I'll be careful. I just need to walk. I'll be back. You stay here and stay out of sight."

Thea nodded numbly. Once he was gone, she could not stop the sobs. Lene left her place at the bellows and went to her. She gave Thea a handkerchief. Once she was able to, Thea spoke.

"He blames himself for this, and my tears do not help. But, when I think of all the time we have been away from Darcuna, my heart breaks and I cannot help myself. I know his heart also shatters being away from her and yet he does not allow his emotions to so easily affect him."

Lene patted her hand.

"Men are not so easily given to tears, but it does not mean they hurt any less. I'm sure Jon does not fault your tears. He'll return when he's ready."

Thea wiped her face and tried to smile.

"I know. We only have each other now, and to abandon the other would surely destroy us both. We agreed it was unhealthy to bottle our feelings and usually he bears my outbursts…"

She sighed.

"I just need to find a more useful way to express my grief instead of making the man I love suffer any more than he already is."

Thea stood, sniffing and wiping her eyes.

"I will go to him and apologise."

Lene frowned.

"Didn't he ask you to stay hidden? What makes you think you know where he has gone?"

Thea straightened herself up.

"Because after all this time, we have learned to read each other's thoughts as if they were our own. We will return soon."

Thea strode purposefully out of the forge and went to look for Jon.

***

Jon looked over as Thea sat down next to him. He was sitting on a roof and using his Faye glamour to hide his form. Thea was only able to know where he was by his scent. Once she was sat next to him, he extended the spell to hide her as well.

"Damn it, Thea, I thought I told you to stay hidden. Can't you do anything I ask you?"

Unable to face Jon, Thea swallowed the tears that threatened to fall yet again. There was something she needed to say to him.

"The fault lies with me. Had I stopped when you told me that night by the portal, we would not have been discovered. We would have left the portal broken and unusable, and we could have left and attacked at a later time, but my pride and my impatience once again put us in harm's way. You only did what you had to, because I left us no choice."

Thea reached for her sword. She slid the blade across her forearm in a neat line. Once her sword had vanished, she used her Hellfire to cauterize the cut leaving a small line before she finally turned to face Jon.

"It is my fault, not yours, that we have missed so much of Darcuna's first year. And it will be my fault if everyone we loved is now dead because I refused to listen. I should bear the marks of my mistake. I am sorry, Jon."

Jon sat silent for a moment. Thea assumed he was even angrier at her than she'd previously thought. Instead he ran his finger over the raised edge of Thea's new scar and let out a long sigh.

"It's both our faults. You never listen and I never push back hard enough. We are as bad as each other. We might bring out the best of each other, but fuck, if we don't bring out the worst too. The problem is, it doesn't matter whose fault it is anymore.

We are stuck here, and we'll be stuck here until I can get us out."

Thea looked at Jon.

"Why do you not syphon what you need from me or from these people for that matter?"

The same thought had played out in his mind. He'd done it so many times before. Why was now any different? He knew why. The problem was he could usually control the incubus if he let it out every so often, but he'd recently felt a shift. He was worried that if he let it out for too long, it would start to get greedy. And worse, if he let it gorge, it would want to be let out more and more. It was powerful and the monster inside of him could so easily take over if he wasn't careful.

He could never go back to simply bottling it away like before; that would be impossible. It was a balancing act, allowing the monster out to feed just enough to fuel him when he needed a boost but not leaving it out to binge until it overwhelmed him completely. He tried to explain to Thea.

"The more I let the incubus feed, the easier it is to leave it out until it kills someone. When I'm with you it's different. You are usually strong enough to withstand it. Redirecting the flow helps but these people, he'd eat them alive. I did it once, when we helped those farmers, but it was such a small amount and I was passing it on to you. It's hard to describe, but if I keep it to myself it feeds the monster and if I feed the monster too much it expects to be fed like that all the time. It *demands* to be fed like that."

Thea placed her head on Jon's shoulder.

"Then we will wait until you are rested and ready, so we can get out of this city."

They sat watching the people below as they scurried about, unaware of the invisible strangers watching them from the roof.

***

Thea and Jon returned to the forge looking and feeling better. While Niko took her place at the bellows, Lene and Anke were preparing some of the darra roots for their evening meal. The little girl was standing on a small stool next to her mother, prattling away. Anke could have been a twin to Darcuna with her dark hair and bright blue eyes. And for a brief second Thea imagined Anke as Darcuna. That mischievous twinkle in her eye heightened the ache in her heart. Jon read her thoughts.

"Anke reminds me of her so much. Do you think she'll talk our ears off like that?"

The comment made Thea smile.

"I do not know. I was a quiet child, unless I was provoked. Were you talkative when you were young?"

"Who me? I could talk for England if they let me. Mum loved to listen to me waffle on, asking all sorts of questions. I think Gerard actually gagged me a few times to shut me up."

He stopped. An old memory made him frown.

"I stopped talking like that after my incubus manifested."

The thought of that change made him realise something and he took a long deep breath.

"When we get back, no matter what, I don't ever want her to stop rabbiting on. I don't care if she never stops... I miss her."

Thea laid her head on his shoulder.

"I know you do and you will get us home. I will try to control my outbursts better. They do nothing but lower both our spirits."

Jon gave her a kiss on the side of her head.

"Thanks, I appreciate that, even though some days I feel like joining you."

Thea gave a small chuckle.

* * *

Chapter 36 - The Secret is...

Anke turned around and squealed.

"You are back! I am learning to cook like momma. She is the best. She makes the yummiest roasted darra roots. She has a secret, but I don't think she will be mad if tell you."

Anke jumped down off her perch and ran to Thea and Jon. She pulled them down so she could speak quietly into their ears.

"She adds sweet annona. It makes it the best."

Thea could see Lene's shoulders shake with supressed laughter. Apparently, it wasn't that uncommon, but she straightened her face before turning to her.

"Anke! I have told you that is our secret."

The little girl pouted so Thea stepped in.

"Oh, we would never reveal it, no matter what."

Anke turned and gave her mother a triumphant grin. Lene waved her spoon at Anke.

"They better not, then everyone will buy sweet annona and the traders will have to raise the price. And then you will be sorry. Now go play with your doll until it is time to eat."

This seemed to have the desired effect, and Anke slapped her hand on her mouth and ran to her little bedroll to play.

Lene spoke quiet enough so Anke would not hear her.

"I do not do this to be mean, but she is so trusting and many will take advantage of that. She is a good girl, if not always so wise. I am trying to teach her that her actions have consequences in the gentlest way I can."

Jon winked at her.

"A good tactic, we'll have to remember that for our Darcuna."

There was a commotion at the front of the forge, and Lene placed her finger to her lips. She pushed Anke toward Thea and Jon. Moving to assist her husband, she pulled the curtain closed behind her and left them. They listened as she and Horst were questioned by the city guard.

"No, we have not seen the fugitives since this morning. My daughter reported this to another guard already. We saw them appear in front of our shop and then they ran back towards the gates. No, she is asleep. Why do you need to speak to a little girl? We just told you what we saw…"

Jon and Thea listened as the guards tried to gain access to the back of the forge. If found they would put Lene, Horst, and the children in further trouble. Jon nodded at Thea and she knelt down to Anke.

"It's no longer safe for us here. Thank you, Anke, but if we stay, they will hurt you and your family. Never speak of what you are about to see, sweet girl."

Thea kissed Anke's cheek. Jon subtly let the incubus pull just enough energy from the guards to open a portal. He gave a wink to Anke and placed his finger to his lips. Then he and Thea disappeared.

They reappeared back in the alley where they had first fought with the guard. Taking a deep breath they ran past the forge as Jon yelled taunts at the guards.

"Hey assholes, why not pick on someone your own size?"

The guards turned and ran after Thea and Jon. Jon glanced back over his shoulder.

"Well, we have their attention. Now what?"

They ran putting distance between them and the forge. They needed to pull the attention away from Anke and her family. Thea looked up at the citadel.

"Jon, I believe the time for subtlety has passed. But before we leave, I think we should impede the circle's research into magic. That they employ these ruffians to impose their will has shown them to be cruel. These people are not ready to wield such power, not yet."

Jon pointed at the Guards still chasing them.

"Maybe we should deal with these two first?"

Thea skidded to a halt and turned on the guards.

"Agreed. These city guards are nothing more than hired thugs to terrorize the populous."

Thea conjured her Hellfire and launched a ball at the guards. She hit one and he dissolved into ash, but the other roared before charging at her.

"I am going to enjoy interrogating you."

Thea launched another ball of Hellfire, but the guard raised his shield and the Hellfire died on contact.

"Jon, their shields are enchanted."

The guard brought up his sword to strike Thea, but Jon blocked with his sword.

"It's not polite to hit a lady, especially my mate, you overgrown gorilla."

The guard turned on Jon, and Thea took the opportunity while his back was turned to run him through from behind with her sword. Several more guards appeared from another alley and Jon nudged Thea.

"As much as I would love to teach these punks a lesson, if we stay on the streets we'll be overrun."

Thea nodded her agreement. She began taking her Dragon form and Jon unbound his wings.

"Ok, let's cause a little mayhem."

* * *

Chapter 37 - The Circle of the Silver Blood

As soon as Thea had fired her first shot of Hellfire, the residents on the street had scurried into their homes, and the roads were now deserted but for the city patrols. The guards stopped when they saw Thea in her Dragon form.

Even as small as she was for a Dragon, she was still imposing with her Hellfire glowing between her scales. She gave a roar so loud the ground shook beneath them. To further warn them off she presented a short burst of Hellfire.

The guards stood their ground with their shields raised. Jon took the opportunity while they were focused on Thea, to call up the incubus and prayed he could put the genie back in the bottle afterwards. He drew in their life energy. Some fell dead where they stood. Then Jon fired ice bolts at those left standing.

"Come on, Thea, I can hear more coming, and pretty soon they *will* find a way to take us down."

Thea bobbed her head and she began to climb up the walls of the building so she could take off. Bits of white stone crumbled and fell as her claws dug into it as if it was nothing more than chalk. Jon took a running start and beat his wings so he could take off over the heads of the guards just entering the road.

As they made their way towards the citadel, they heard the city troops organizing below them.

"Where are those crossbowmen? We need to stop them before they reach the citadel."

Jon dodged a bolt and turned to fire back. His ice bolts falling like deadly rain to neutralize the shooters. He turned back to follow Thea towards the citadel. They landed inside the walls of the black structure, and Thea took her human form as Jon dispelled his wings. Jon called up his sword.

"Now we end this once and for all."

Thea understood that the Circle had proven themselves incapable of shouldering the responsibility of magic use but was torn over killing novices. The guards were brutes, but surely students and scholars could be contained by simply burning the volumes of their knowledge.

"They do not have the Dragon ability to remember vast amounts of knowledge. We can just destroy their texts–"

Jon disagreed and cut her off.

"No, remember what Caris told us about these races. If anyone is left, they will rebuild. We have to remove all traces and that means everything: books texts, scrolls, and everyone from archmages to novices. If they were supposed to learn magic they would, on their own. Not by taking short cuts and stealing it from the Faye. Maybe if they learn it in their own time, they might also understand how to use it responsibly."

On cue a group of mage scholars ran around the corner wielding magically bound weapons.

"The rogue magic users must be destroyed. But make sure the body of the female is saved. Reports say she is a Dragon. Her blood can be collected and studied."

Thea and Jon stood back to back as the mages attacked and deflected their weapons as best they could, but even so Thea took several nasty cuts, and Jon could see they would fall if they didn't get out of this corridor. The need to protect Thea made the incubus rear up inside him, and the mages began to fall over one by one. Thea could see Jon was battling to bring the monster back under control.

"Jon!"

He turned and his eyes had gone from their usual pale grey-blue to a dark murky almost black colour. Thea was frightened but tried to reason with him.

"Jon, you need to slow down and disperse the excess magic the incubus is taking in."

An idea took form.

"You are correct we cannot leave any trace of magic, but perhaps the monster can be of use."

Thea was hopeful that draining the scholars would prove as humane an execution as her Hellfire and she called out to him again.

"Jon, this citadel is made of black stone. Do you understand?"

Jon blinked a few times before his eyes reverted back to their normal appearance.

"Sorry, what? What about it?"

Thea prompted Jon as she knelt, just as more mages came around the corner.

"Can you direct your incubus to send me the energy?"

Jon nodded.

"Ok, but I hope you know what you are doing."

Thea gave him a confident smile.

"Mount Pyrosis."

Jon still didn't understand but did as she asked. He allowed the incubus to feed and again the mages fell but instead of pulling their energy into himself he directed it to Thea and he felt the incubus lament the loss. He was finally beginning to understand her plan.

"Not this time, we need to sustain, Thea."

Thea closed her eyes as she received the energy. The floor beneath them began to shudder and shake. Dragon magic was elemental. Thea was relying on the fact that stone did not come from the earth neatly formed. She was using her command of it to revert the rock of the citadel, back to its natural state. She would literally erase all evidence of the Circle and their hateful fortress.

By now Jon was pulling energy from all over the citadel. The flow was immense. Even more than what Thea needed and Jon's eyes were pitch black as the incubus gorged on the surplus life-force of the acolytes. The part of his brain that could still register what was happening switched on, and Jon knew he needed to slow down or he would lose himself completely to the monster.

"Thea, I can't... do you have what you need?"

Thea looked up and shouted at Jon.

"Stop!"

He fell and Thea went to him. Her plan had worked. The citadel was caving in on itself now, and she no longer needed to maintain her control. Much like her old home, she was pulling the structure down around the remaining inhabitants. She knelt next to him cradling his head.

"Jon, we need to portal out. This structure is collapsing. We must escape now or be buried alive. Jon, wake up."

She slapped him a few times to revive him before his hand came up as she was about to strike him again.

"It's me. You can stop hitting me now."

He blinked a few more times before he opened a portal under them and they fell through.

***

Chapter 38 - Safe Magic Dispersal

Thea and Jon landed with a hard thump back in front of the forge. Jon groaned.

"I don't know how many more of these I can take today."

Thea gave him a kiss.

"I am sorry for landing on you."

He gave her an amused smile.

"Usually I don't mind you being on top."

Thea gave him a playful swipe before helping him up. Even though the streets were now full of people, most were staring up at the chaos ensuing at the citadel and didn't notice Jon and Thea's unusual arrival. Horst and Lene came over to them.

"Why have you returned? The guards will still be looking for you."

Jon pushed them towards the back of the forge.

"This place is about to go to hell, pardon the expression. Grab only what you can carry and you can't live without. I'm taking you and your family somewhere safe."

He and Thea helped Lene and Horst gather as many of their possessions as they could and Jon opened a portal inside the shop. He gestured for them to walk through.

"I can't chance anyone else seeing you leave this way. There will already be too many questions, but trust me, this place is no longer safe for you."

Thea grabbed hold of Anke's hand.

"We shall take you where the city guards and the Circle can no longer harm you."

The family hesitantly stepped through and found themselves back at the cave where Thea and Jon had first appeared. Thea consoled the startled family.

"This cave will have to serve as your home for the time being. It will keep you dry but more importantly safe. It is not so far from the city should you wish to return once the chaos has died down."

Jon was feeling lightheaded from all the energy his incubus had guzzled. It was more than he could handle and he needed to diffuse it. So, he set about making the inside of the cave more liveable. He made beds for the family and a fire pit for them to cook over and keep the space warm. He moved outside and made a forge for Horst before finishing with a secure door for their new home to keep thieves and other unsavoury types out. He pointed toward the hill behind the cave.

"There is a field of darra roots growing just beyond that hill that should keep you fed for a year and a clean natural well just to the east. By then hopefully, you'll be able to have your little farm up and running."

Horst and Lene looked around.

"This ground will never support planting."

Thea and Jon lowered down to the ground and using the last of Jon's surplus energy healed an area big enough for a small vegetable patch.

By the time they were done they were both exhausted. They felt safe enough this far from the city to pass out.

Anke ran into the cave and brought out a blanket from her bed and placed it over them as they slept.

***

Thea and Jon slept for the rest of the day and part-way into the next. When Thea opened her eyes Anke let out an ear-splitting shriek towards her parents.

"They are awake now!"

Jon groaned.

"Oh my god, please stop yelling. I feel like something the cat yacked up. And I think I swallowed part of the field."

Thea giggled at Jon's comment.

"I do not know what *yacking* is, but it does not sound pleasant. I too feel less than optimal."

She reached down and while most of her cuts were now dry and crusted with blood and dirt, one continued to ooze.

"While I am rested, these injuries must be cleansed and dressed."

Lene was marching towards them with a steaming bowl, and Anke was now trailing behind her holding a tray.

"Good, you are awake. Now you can eat and I can clean those wounds. I'm sorry, Thea, but this will hurt."

She indicated the steaming bowl.

"The best way to fight infection is to burn it."

Thea smiled.

"Do not worry. Heat and fire do not bother me."

Jon gave a snort and she elbowed him. She reached into the bowl that Lene has set down beside her and with her finger caused the water to come to a rolling boil, then taking the cloth from her, she dipped it in and bathed her cuts. Dropping the cloth back into the water she again used her finger to conjure a small flame of Hellfire and proceeded to cauterize the wounds she could reach as a shocked Lene and Anke watched. Lene pulled herself together enough to see to the wounds on Thea's back, stitching and bandaging the worst of them. Thea winced, but once it was done, she was able to relax.

"I do not think we will have time to allow my sores to fully heal, so this will have to do for now. We will stay for a few days to rest, but we cannot stay for much longer."

Anke's face dropped. Thea gathered the little girl to her.

"Our own daughter waits for us, little one, and as much as I have enjoyed meeting you and your family, I miss ours terribly."

Jon stood, dusted himself off and helped Thea to stand before handing the blanket to Horst who had walked out from the cave.

"We appreciate your help and hope everything works out for you. This realm is not ready for magic use. Who knows? Maybe one day it will be."

Horst nodded.

"Though I never feared magic like some, I never felt it was right in this world. I do not mourn its loss. Rest as long as you need, and I hope your journey home is a swift one."

***

Chapter 39 - Sleeping Rough

Another realm, another night sleeping under the stars. They were stretched out in a grassy meadow. It was now three weeks since they had left Horst, Lene, and their children. Thea sighed at the memory.

"Another night sleeping outdoors. At least this realm looks to be in its summer."

Jon rolled his eyes.

"Some of those winter realms were brutal. Beautiful, but fuck if my balls didn't crawl up into my tonsils with the shock."

Thea giggled at the comment.

"And at least we are keeping out of trouble. With the exception of Artiscaena, we have been lucky to have found relatively peaceful realms…"

Jon slapped his hand over Thea's mouth.

"Damn it, if you didn't just jinx us."

Thea's eyes narrowed as Jon removed his hand.

"What is to jinx?"

Jon sighed.

"I suppose it's a human thing, but when things are going good and everything is smooth sailing, you *never* say that they are. It just seems to bring on all that bad shit like you were asking for it."

Thea shook her head.

"I did not realise the Faye were such a superstitious race. I am surprised you subscribe to such nonsense."

Thea looked up at the sky. Though not familiar, it was peaceful. As tired as she was, she still could not sleep.

"Jon, what if we never get home?"

She heard Jon turn on the ground and knew he was as wakeful as her.

"I don't think about it."

Thea turned on her side to face Jon's back and continued.

"I do not say it to be disparaging but surely it is something we must discuss."

Jon sighed and turned to face Thea.

"So, I guess neither of us will be sleeping. Yes, I have thought about it, and yes, we probably need to talk about it. I guess I just didn't want to upset you."

Thea reached to out and trailed a finger along Jon's jaw.

"I know my tears increase your guilt and I am sorry. It is the hope that eats away at me. If I did not hope so much to be back and to hold Darcuna and see Gath and Gerard… The hope makes their absence all the more painful."

Jon shifted so Thea could lie against him. He wrapped his arm around her. Once she was settled, he kissed the side of her head.

"So, we keep hoping, no matter what. I know what it's like to just survive, and you don't want that. Caris said something to me that seems appropriate. She said hope is the one gift the celestials gave us to see us through hard times. If we give up hope then we are completely lost. I'm already geographically lost; I don't want to be emotionally lost as well. I don't know how long it will take, or what we'll have to deal with along the way, but I do know I made a promise and I intend to keep it."

He knew Thea was a sucker for poetry and having no talent to compose it himself he often appropriated it as needed. He wasn't much of a singer either, but he knew it made Thea smile so as they lay there, trying to go to sleep, Jon thought about a song written by another John. He wasn't really a Beatles fan but Mr Lennon's love song to his *woman* sprang to mind. He started singing softly and it wasn't long before he got the desired effect and Thea was quietly snoring against his shoulder, a content smile on her lips. The song apparently had a narcotic effect on him as well and he yawned.

"Thanks John."

***

Jon was appreciating the sight of Thea whizzing around overhead in her true form. He never got bored of the sight of her in flight. Her inner fire glowing between her dark black scales made her resemble a comet streaking across the sky. The effect was amazing and only made more striking when he'd stroked her head. He would feel her purr and the glow would intensify.

This realm looked to have been abandoned either by choice, or the more worrying thought, by force. They could usually tell by the look of the rubble if the cause was neglect or destruction. The land this time wasn't lush but neither was it totally barren. There were no buildings that either of them could see. And the lay of the land was flat enough that they could see for miles.

Thea flew passed. Knowing she could be airborne for hours, he closed his eyes. He tried to doze off, but his thoughts kept churning like a witch's brew. So far, they had been extremely lucky. They had not travelled through many hostile realms. Luckier still, those realms in the midst of conflict were non-magical. Throw magic into the mix and the shitstorm would be unreal.

He rubbed his face, trying to will his brain to shut down. He needed sleep if he wanted to refrain from relying on the incubus. Jon tried to rest when he could. Lately he'd been pushing his portaling abilities as far as he dared without waking the incubus again. He would still pull small amounts of energy to keep his skills sharp, but he was consciously limiting and thus controlling the incubus. He was getting better. Thorikill would be proud to see how far he'd progressed.

He sighed, trying again to relax, but it was not enough to fall asleep. Thea's comments a few weeks back were haunting him. It was taking forever to get home and for the millionth time he was wondering how Thea's brother had managed to build a machine capable of harnessing the magic to portal them so far away. It nagged him and led to him wondering what happened after he and Thea went through. The machine was ripping itself apart and would have probably killed him and Thea had he not made the decision to push them through. If luck was with them, he hoped the machine left enough carnage behind to not just to disrupt the camp but destroy it.

He didn't think anyone close to them would be hurt or in danger but the destruction of the portal would leave Black Heart and his flunkies trapped in the Dead Grounds. Once it was established that he and Thea were missing, Ash would go to investigate. Gerard would be able to get him there safely. Once they saw the state of the camp they would report to the rest. Everyone would assume he and Thea were dead, but they would be ok without them. Crusher and Gath were more than capable leaders. It was inevitable, but it made him sad. He wished there was some way to let the ones left back home know they were alive and slowly but surely trying to make their way back.

"And if wishes were pennies, I'd be a rich man... damn."

His eyes were still closed but Jon felt the ground shake as Thea landed close by. She took her human form and went to sit next to him. He could feel her staring at him, and he cracked an eye open.

"Can I help you with something?"

Thea's expression was inquiring.

"I looked to see you were sleeping but your face was troubled. I thought you might be having a nightmare."

Jon pressed his palms into his eyes.

"Argh! I am trying to sleep, but my stupid brain won't shut off. Too much garbage that I can't do a damn thing about. It's like a mosquito buzzing next to my ear that I can hear but can't see, so instead I'm stuck listening to it buzz, buzz, buzz... No hon, you have to be asleep to have nightmares and I am completely, and very much awake."

Thea pulled his head onto her lap and tried to sooth him with some positive news.

"My Dragon memories are becoming further organized with each day. Some are clearer than others, some are still only impressions. I am not yet at a point where I can make sense of it all, but I do have a better understanding of the stories Grandfather shared with me."

Jon smiled.

"Well that's good. Anything we can use? Like a map of the realms?"

Thea gave a regretful laugh.

"No, nothing so practical. But rest assured if something as valuable as that becomes known to me, I will share with you. The things I remember are like half-forgotten dreams. It's still mostly a jumble, but I would not be at all surprised if by the time we travelled home I was able to organize them."

Jon could not help the melancholy laugh that escaped.

"Figures, doesn't it? We have to get home to figure out how to get home... but to get home I need to sleep and to sleep I need to relax."

Trying to help him unwind, Thea stroked Jon's hair and began humming a tune from her newly discovered Dragon memories. The melody seemed to have the desired sedative effect and soon Jon's breathing was slow and even. She leaned over and kissed him as he slept.

"I believe you will get us home."

***

Chapter 40 - Acallaris War Zone (or Murphy's Law)

Thea stepped through the portal but before she could get her bearings, Jon shoved her down as an explosion went off next to them. Grabbing her hand, Jon pulled Thea up and ran across what looked to be right in the cross-fire of a full-scale war. He was yelling to be heard over all the noise.

"I knew it. I fucking knew it. Everything was going too smoothly. Watch out!"

Thea ducked as a projectile raced passed her.

"What in all the realms is happening?"

Jon zig-zagged them through the onslaught trying to avoid what looked to be magical missiles.

"It wasn't enough to land in a hostile realm; no, we had to walk into the middle of a fucking magical war... Holy shit!"

He dove again, shoving Thea down under him. Thea spat out the dirt in her mouth.

"Jon, can you not put us closer to the outlying edges? If we stay here, we will be killed."

Her head swivelled around before her eyes lighted on a possible spot.

"Look, there, I can see a small copse on the edge of this field. While not particularly strong it might provide us some cover."

Jon nodded.

"Anything has got to be better that this."

Jon opened a portal next to him and rolled, pulling Thea with him. They landed behind the trees. They could hear stray missiles whizzing passed them, but at least now they were not in the middle of the fighting. Thea's runes were glowing so brightly she had to hold her hand over her wrist to keep them from giving away their position.

"Jon, the magic, it must be Faye or at the very least its roots are Faye. My runes are reacting very strongly to it."

Jon closed his eyes and lay back to think. He began to rub his temples.

"What the fuck have we wandered into?"

He opened his eyes to see Thea moving away from him.

"Thea, what the hell are you doing? Where are you going?"

Thea crawled over to get a better look at the fighting. On her stomach hidden in the bushes she studied the battle.

"We assumed we were caught in crossfire, but look, the artilleries are moving in only one direction. See, the other side has their shields raised. They must have Faye magic, because I recognise the aura. It appears similar to Evan's shields. They are not returning fire. Those shields must be formidable. See, they show no signs of wear."

Thea chewed her lip as she thought out loud.

"They are possibly waiting for the other side's weaponries to diminish before they begin their own assault..."

Her expression was grim as she recalled her classes in military strategy.

"It was a tactic my Father often employed. He would have his shield caster hold the line and wait until his adversaries had depleted their resources and were unable to maintain their position, then he would bombard them into submission. It is a cruel but effective tactic. The other side has no way to defend and must either yield or face destruction."

Jon crawled over and watched the two sides and sure enough Thea had called it, but he saw something else.

"There is a whole line of spell enchanters not engaging behind the shield casters. These guys are just toying with them. If they have the numbers and the strength to hold back, then the other side won't be just defeated, they'll be vaporised out of existence."

Thea remembered her Father's display during the Remantis revolt.

"We cannot allow the stronger side to destroy them. Not like this."

Jon was looking at Thea sideways already knowing what she wanted to do and also aware he would be unable to stop her, not that he wouldn't try.

"Fine, assuming I agree with you, which I don't, but let's just say I do. What are you thinking?"

Thea pulled them back into the relative safety of the copse.

"I know you worry for our wellbeing especially since I have previously shown I can be rash, but I have seen this play out before. My Father destroyed an entire settlement as a display to others. While I doubt there are any children here on the battle field, they will be back home beyond the fighting. But if I am correct there will be a massacre to follow. Not simply soldiers but their families. Those mages hiding behind their shields are biding their time until...until they annihilate the other side."

Jon held up his hands.

"Now hold on, we don't know that. That other side is doing all the agro. Those mages you say are *hiding* behind their shields have the ability to end this right now, but they are holding back and showing some restraint. I'd say that allows them some consideration."

Thea beamed at him, and Jon had the sinking feeling he'd just been played.

"Exactly, we cannot deduce what is happening without a closer look. I think since you are the one most adept at circumventing wards and shields that you would be best suited to speak to the mages' side. I will try to speak to the 'agro' side as you call them. Maybe between us we can help them find a solution."

Jon stared into the sky.

"And why do we have to do anything at all? Why not just quietly slink away from all the fighting and leave them to sort it out themselves? Why do you always need to butt into every conflict? You are not a saviour, Thea. Stop trying to be one."

Thea pointed out towards the field.

"Regardless of our being outsiders, *this* is not fair, Jon. I have seen what will happen because it was my childhood. Always the strong believing themselves better than the weak. Crushing any upheaval to the perceived status quo. I was unable to stop it then, and I will be damned if I allow it to happen again when I *can* do something."

Jon and Thea glared at each other for several seconds before he closed his eyes and sighed.

"You know it's hard to argue with you when you are being so fucking, god-damned noble. *Fine*, but the absolute minute this goes to shit, I will not only portal your arse out of this realm; when we arrive in the next—providing there isn't another fucking war going on— I will spank that arse until it's glowing like your fucking runes!"

***

Thea had Jon portal her a safe distance from the fighting but still within the area. She stood up on her toes and gave him a kiss even though he turned his face away in protest.

"I know you hate doing this, and you are only indulging me, but I *am* grateful."

Jon was fuming at his own stupidity for going along with this. Every time she did this to him, he told himself next time he'd react differently. And every time he found himself caving in because if he thought about his motives, he came across as a selfish arsehole.

"Ya, but the arsehole lives."

Thea heard his grumbling and pulled his chin, forcing him to look at her.

"Yes, but the arsehole sleeps alone. I will be careful. In several hours' time, if their day is similar to ours, when the sun has set and the twilight shadows can hide us, we will meet up again to exchange information. Agreed?"

Jon rolled his eyes.

"Yeah, yeah, agreed. You know one day you are going to get us killed and fuck if I don't follow you anyway. I'm a stupid love-sick moron who lets his dick do far too much decision making".

Thea kissed his cheek.

"And I love you regardless."

***

Chapter 41 - Meeting the Agros

Thea thought it best to approach from the rear, if she appeared from the battlefield, they might mistake her for an enemy. Jon told her to keep her hands visible and to not make any sudden movements when she made first contact.

"Their firing patterns are haphazard at best. It sort of reminds me of the first time I learned to cast, like they are still learning how to use magic. *That* is not good. If they think you are a threat, they could kill you without intending to. Do not, I repeat, do not give them any reason to fire on you. And for the love of all that is holy, don't tell them you are a Dragon. Please Thea, I'm begging you."

Thea agreed to be cautious. As she moved warily through the camp, Thea noticed the casters looked exhausted and frightened. More alarmingly, they were all children. All around this side of the fighting the smell of fear was almost permeable. What horrors awaited them if they allowed even a moment's respite? One caster faltered and without thinking Thea went to him. She felt a blade in her side.

"Step aside and I won't hurt you."

Thea froze but kept her voice even.

"I do not mean him any harm. I do not even know if I can help, but I wanted to try and offer some comfort.

He looks drained. How long has this been going on? Why has he not rested? Even I can see he is fading."

The young mage slowly pulled himself up.

"It's ok, papa, I can continue…"

The older man sighed.

"The outsider is right; you are completely spent. You need to rest."

The young mage stood, and Thea noticed how his clothing hung off of him. He looked hungry as well as tired. His cheeks were sallow, and his red-rimmed eyes had dark circles. Everything about this child made her heart break. She held her hand out as she'd seen Jon do.

"My name is Aurrynthea. I am not from this area but when I saw the fighting, I thought I could help. Who are those mages, and why are you fighting to the point of collapse?"

The boy spoke.

"I am fine now. I just needed a short break. Thank you Aurrynthea, but I must take my place back in the line."

Thea and the boy's father watched his son run back. He gave a sad sigh.

"He's a good boy, my Ceale. So much like my sister at the same age, until the Sentinels came for her. They took my sister and crushed her, and I swore that if any of my children ever showed signs of having the gift, I would never let those monsters take them."

Thea's expression gave no indication she understood. The man continued.

"The Sentinels are the governing body over all magic use. They train any child who shows signs of having the gift, for a price."

He glanced down at the tattoo on Thea's wrist, noticing it for the first time and his face darkened. Thea felt her stomach drop at his expression and quickly covered it with her hand. She did not know how, but he knew what it was and more importantly, he wasn't happy with what he saw.

***

Jon stood at the spot where he'd left Thea. It was well passed the time they'd agreed to meet, and he was starting to worry. She'd been so confident that she would be fine and for the hundred millionth time he was kicking himself for letting her talk him into a situation he knew was bad.

"If you are dead or chained up somewhere I will…"

"You will what?"

Jon turned so fast he almost lost his footing.

"Where the fuck have you been? I've been standing here for the last hour thinking about every possible worst-case scenario."

Thea looked contrite, but for the first time ever Jon wasn't having any of it.

"Look we agreed this was a tricky situation and I, against my better judgement I might add, left you here with a promise to meet just before the sun went down. That was over an hour ago, I have a good mind to give you that spanking I threatened before."

Thea blinked a few tears. She could see just under all the anger was a very real fear for her safety and she apologized.

"I am sorry, Jon. I found it difficult to leave after they saw my protection tattoo. I cannot explain how, but I think they know what it is and, I think I was being observed. It made sneaking off quite difficult."

This bit of information gave Jon a cold shiver down his spine.

"Ok then, we can leave right now..."

Thea placed her hand on Jon's arm to stop him casting.

"What I did find out was disturbing. Enough to make me feel I need to stay. They do not trust me – yet. I think my walking amongst them made some nervous, but I fear what might happen if I just disappear. The casters are just children, Jon, and they are so frightened. I cannot in good conscience just leave them to their fate."

Pulling Jon down to sit with her she shared what she'd learned.

"This side that you call the *agro* side, they are fighting to keep their children. It seems not all the inhabitants of this realm wield magic. The ones who show signs of having the gift, as they call it, are rounded up and taken away, never to be seen by their families. They only want to stop the kidnappings."

Jon's face was grim and he shook his head.

"I knew this was a bad idea. Well, I might as well tell you what I found out. You've got it all wrong. The mages remove the kids who show signs of having magical tendencies but only to train them properly. Seems in the past, they left the kids to develop on their own and there were fatalities, nasty ones. It was decided from then on, before the kids could do any real damage, to take the kids away for training to avoid further harm to anyone.

"True, the kids never went back, but not because they were being held. They got depressed when it was time to go home. The kids were attached to their teachers after the mages had taken care of them for so long. Some of them even felt closer to the mages than their own parents. They didn't have any friends in their villages, and in some cases their real parents rejected their magic and forced them to stop using it after returning, so they ran back to the mages, then the kids just stopped coming back at all.

"Either way this whole thing is fucked up and if either side knew what you are... Thea we need to leave, now."

The two explanations were at odds, and yet the fear in the camp Thea had seen was real. Why would the mages lie to Jon? She needed more information.

"We are missing a part of this puzzle. Give me one more day and I promise if a solution does not present itself, we will simply vanish."

Jon could see that last part was hard for Thea. He tried to give her something to think on.

"We can't save everyone, it's just not possible. And besides, Darcuna's waiting."

Thea nodded and he gave her a small kiss before he called up a portal to return to the mages' side. He turned to look back at Thea. He should have felt better, seeing that his comment had made Thea think, so why did he feel like such a shit for saying it?

***

Chapter 42 - I Am Not a Spy

Thea awoke to the sounds of the camp, and for a moment her mind tricked her and she thought she was back at home. She opened her eyes expecting to find Jon and Darcuna but instead she was met by a surly old woman.

"Come with me."

Wiping the sleep from her eyes, she followed the woman in silence. She was led into a dark tent and immediately knew something was wrong. There were four men sitting behind a table. They stopped talking as soon as she entered. There were a few others off to the side watching. One of the seated men spoke.

"We've had a report that you met with a mage last night. Is this true?"

Thea felt afraid. Someone must have seen her leave the camp. She tried to keep her voice even to avoid showing her anxiety.

"I met my mate, Jon. He is a mage, but we are…"

Thea was interrupted by a shout from another of the seated men.

"Silence! She's a spy sent by the mages to find the vulnerabilities in our defences. She reported back to them, and it's only a matter of time before they attack. Oweyn was right. The symbol on her arm is magical. She must be a spy."

Two large men each grabbed one of Thea's arms to restrain her. One of them was the father she had spoken to the previous day. He looked so angry at her she was ready to cry. There was a commotion from outside, and the man's son rushed in.

"Papa, I told you about her meeting to prove she was coming back, not so you could capture her."

Oweyn reprimanded his son.

"You stay out of this, Ceale. You are supposed to be resting. You need to sleep while you can."

The boy stomped his foot.

"Why are you doing this? Why do you always do this? You say you trust me, but you never act like you do."

Thea could see a spark of magic forming in Ceale's palm, triggered by his emotions. If she did not move quickly, the boy might hurt his father accidentally. So, wrenching herself free, she threw herself at the boy and cast a shield around her and Ceale just as he hurled a spell at his father. The magic encased in the shield had nowhere else to go but back at Thea and Ceale. Oweyn cried out as Thea and his son crumpled to the ground.

***

This time when Thea awoke, she knew she was not at home. She felt a metal collar around her neck and saw it was attached to a strong chain. The iron felt heavy against her skin. Her hands were cold as the binding on her wrists was cutting off their circulation. Another man from the tent held onto the end of the chain in a large beefy hand. When he saw Thea was awake, he yanked her up to stand. His voice was disdainful.

"Get up, mage."

Thea was now starting to understand what Jon was talking about. Oweyn may love his boy but regardless, it seemed magic users were not well liked in this camp, only tolerated. Jon had expressly told her not to say what she was. But if they thought she was a spy, she had to give them some other reason to explain her ability.

"I'm not a mage, I'm a Dragon."

The minute the words left her mouth, she knew Jon had been right. And if the expression on her jailer's face was any indication, she was very much afraid she might not get the chance to tell him so.

***

Oweyn sat by the bed as Ceale slept. The boy had woken briefly, and they'd talked. Ceale's remorse over the altercation was so strong that his father knew something needed to be done. But then he remembered Emony and how she had suffered. He was so confused. Ceale needed training, but what if he never came back? Or worse, what if he came back broken like his sister, Emony?

***

Oweyn's parents had never explained what had happened. He was young at the time, but even he could see something was wrong. The training was supposed to help Emony control her gift, instead it changed her. He didn't understand why his beautiful, funny, and lively older sister had returned a shell of the girl she used to be. She was melancholy, and she snapped at him when he tried to tease her like they used to. She cried in her room when she thought no one was listening. And then one day she was gone.

"Oh, Emony, what did they do to you? I wish I could ask you. I could really use your advice right now. I want my sister back."

***

Jon sat alone at a table. He should have tried to be a bit more social, but something was nagging at him and making him less than willing to try and make conversation with the other mages. It was like his skin was too tight. The atmosphere in this camp was as far away from what Thea had described on the other side as possible. She talked about casters being pushed to breaking before an equally exhausted replacement was brought in. Everyone looked either tired or hungry or both. She'd described a place with very little laughter, and as if to demonstrate that difference, right at that moment Jon looked up as someone at the next table was howling at something his companion said.

This could have been a festival instead of a battle camp. The shield casters were rotated enough that they were always fresh and well rested. No one looked hungry or stressed. The rest of the mages were virtually spectators come to watch the show. Damn it, Thea was right again. He did not look forward to sharing that with her. She wouldn't gloat but her eyes would sparkle with that little *I told you so* glint. Who was he kidding? She wouldn't even do that, *he* would gloat. That sparkle had nothing to do with being smug and rubbing it in. It was just that she would be happy to see she'd made a difference.

He stood up to leave and that feeling that something was off struck him again. The last time he'd felt anything remotely close to this was that day he left Thea to talk with Levi. What had he called it? Soul-matched? *He said I would know when Thea needed me.* His heart stopped and it finally hit him– Thea needed him; she was in trouble. The problem was, if he showed up now, would it make things better or worse?

***

Thea stood with her jailer as the men behind the table conferred quietly. Her jailer had drugged her. He'd actually smiled when she squeaked as he injected her. The drug left her mostly aware but it made her arms and legs feel heavy and disjointed from the rest of her body. She could not even feel the rope that bound her hands anymore – she could not feel her hands at all. She'd tripped a few times on their way to her judgement and the jailer had hauled her up roughly. Whatever else, the drug seemed to diminish any pain she might have felt from her rough treatment. Hopefully dying would be as painless.

Even with the drug induced fog, she could follow what was happening. They seemed to be in disagreement as to how she could be best used. Some wanted to offer her up in exchange for the children in the Sentinels' custody. No one had specified whether she would be living or dead when the exchange was made. The far more worrying option was to kill her, take her blood, and then use it to boost the remaining children. The thought being they could use her blood to overthrow the Sentinels once and for all.

Jon had been right. These people had no place playing with magic. These were untrained children; they would most likely kill themselves before doing any damage to the mages—all except Ceale. Of all the gifted children she had observed, he seemed the most advanced. If he could contain his emotions, he would be a competent mage; with training he could be exceptionable. If he were given her blood, he might be able to make proper use of it.

Standing there listening to them argue over her fate, Thea's mind retreated into a Dragon memory. Another young Dragon forced into a similar situation, but he was not afraid or conflicted. This world was out of balance. The mages held all the power; they not only had all the magic, they knew how to use it. When faced with a similar predicament, the young Dragon had understood that as long as one side felt superior, they would never allow the other to flourish.

Thea understood better than most the temptation of power. The words were repeated to her from the day she was born. *We do not serve, we do not rule, we remember.* A simple creed learned from a millennia of memories. Dragons understood that having power did not give one the right to rule. The pull to see her family was strong, but these children had no one of strength to fight for them.

She might die, but her memories would live on in Darcuna and while her heart broke to think she might never hold her little girl or see Jon again, this conflict would continue if the balance of power was not shifted. Jon could make it home without her; he had to for Darcuna's sake. She tilted her chin up even as tears slid down her cheeks. Interrupting her judges, her voice was small but clear.

"I understand what it is to fear for your child. I am a mother. I would kill and die for her if needed. I also understand what it is to live under a brutal regime.

Until the mages understand what it is like to lose someone they love, they will continue to steal your children and though I…"

Thea had to stop, the image of Darcuna and Jon almost undoing her.

"My daughter is safe, but your children are not. I am a Dragon; I was made to bring balance. This world is out of balance. The celestials brought me here to this place. Use my blood and bring your children home."

***

Chapter 43 - A Sacrifice

The room went silent. Thea glanced at her jailer and the shock on his face at any other time would have made her laugh. Instead she spoke. Her voice shook, no longer able to hide her fear.

"I have one request. I would be grateful if you could administer more of your narcotic to me. I am afraid of the pain and would appreciate an anaesthetic."

One of the judges responded.

"For such a sacrifice, we would be barbaric not to allow this. Thank you."

Thea tried to smile through her tears. Unable to talk she simply nodded.

***

Jon's pacing had now worn the grass flat. Thea was late again for their meeting. She always did this and usually it would make him furious, but right now that feeling from earlier was causing him to itch all over to the point of sending him out of his mind with fear. Something was definitely wrong but if he showed up, would it make it worse – or was Thea counting on him to appear? *Damn that bloody woman and her fucking noble gestures.* Right now, he hated her for putting them in this situation.

"Sometimes doing the right thing gets you a boot to the head for your troubles. No good deed goes unpunished."

Right now, he wished he could go back to that point when they arrived and just leave. Of course, Thea would have been mad, probably for a good few days, but eventually she would have forgiven him and more importantly she would be with him and out of danger.

"Ha! If I could go back in time, I'd fix a lot of shit... but I can't."

Stomping his foot down like a petulant child he decided standing here and waiting would do nothing but make him insane. Drawing up his Faye glamour around him, he made himself invisible and prayed that the camp had no wards and no way to detect him. He was pretty sure if they found him, they would kill him, maybe not on purpose but either way it would hurt a lot.

***

Thea had not come even close to describing how bad the situation was in this camp. Everyone looked shattered. He guessed they had one, maybe two days at best left before having to concede defeat. And if what Thea said was true, there would be retribution on a biblical scale. They would never recover. *How did things get so fucked up here?*

Someone would notice if tent flaps started moving on their own; so he poked his nose into any tents with open flaps looking for Thea. He found the tent where the *gifted* kids rested. He could see now why Thea had been drawn into the dispute. They were a pitiful lot. Some of them were not much older than Gaia, but all of them looked underfed and overworked. Kids should never look this burned out. A twinge in his chest told him that if this affected him it would hit Thea ten times harder.

He shuddered and stepped back out. He needed to find Thea but conceded that if they could, they would try and help those kids. Maybe Thea could shield them when the worst came? She'd kept the Dragon camp safe almost by herself. Maybe he could teach them a little defensive magic, nothing too advanced but enough to help keep them safe until the worst was over. It wasn't a perfect plan, but it was the best they could do and still be able to leave and get home. Of course, Thea would want to try and restore the balance of power. Growing up a disadvantaged Faye kid, it was usually one of the things he loved about her. But this whole situation was a clusterfuck that could not be fixed overnight, and they still needed to get back to their own family.

He continued his search for Thea.

***

The room Thea lay in was now lit up with what seemed like hundreds of candles. The leaders had specifically requested as many as they could find.

"We do not have much, but your sacrifice has touched us. May you not go into the dark but simply fade into the light."

Her restraints were gone, and Oweyn and Ceale had come to see her. Ceale's eyes were red rimmed, and Thea had to smile to keep from adding her own tears.

"I wish I could say I was brave. I am frightened, but this is the right thing to do. You have so much potential Ceale, but I would be errant if I did not give you some guidance to the use of magic. I am the most powerful of my kind, but even I cannot win a battle on my own. Use my gift to inspire those around you, friend and foe alike. Do not allow it to turn you into that which you despise. The mages do need to be brought to heel, but once they have, show mercy.

"Magic is intent given form; make sure your intent is just and pure. Do not allow either your head or your heart to rule, but allow them each their voice. Trust your own judgement, but also listen to wise council given in good faith. Love is always the better course over hate. Hate is a disease that can fester; only love allows for growth. Listen to your father, though he may make mistakes, he loves you – more than you will ever understand until you are a parent yourself."

The boy hugged her so fiercely, and she held him pretending he was her own child.

Oweyn was touched by her words.

"I am not so hateful towards magic as some. I will try and council him as best as I can. Thank you for helping us."

He gave Thea a kiss on her forehead. Before they left Ceale made a pledge.

"I promise to remember what you've said. I'll try to be good and do my best."

Thea nodded.

"That is all anyone can expect from you."

After they left Thea was laid out as comfortably as they could make her. A needle with a small tube attached was inserted in her arm. The other end of the tube was laid in a glass container to collect her blood; several more were lined up, ready for when each filled up. Her jailer, she learned, was named Serill. He spoke about his daughter as he adjusted the tube.

"My Simmy was so happy when she found out she had the gift. She said, 'I'm going to take care of you,

Papa.' So, against my better judgement, I let her go and get trained in magic."

Serill said magic with such contempt, as if the word itself was foul in his mouth.

"Simmy used to write to me almost every day. I'd get these parcels of letters all bundled up and then after a month or so the parcels got smaller and then they stopped altogether."

His face held so much anguish before it turned to rage.

"Those Sentinels, they turned my Simmy against me. Bloody Sentinels don't want anyone but them to know magic. If I had my way, I'd get rid of the whole lot. Maybe now with your help we can do that."

As quickly as it had flared up, the rage left him and he was melancholy again.

"What you are doing means no more fathers will ever have to send their children off to strangers."

He stopped short of saying 'thank you'. Instead he gave her a quick nod and she understood. He still didn't really expect her to go through with it. Thea assured him.

"I did not lie. I am afraid to do this, so if you would be so kind to administer your narcotic quickly. Maybe then you might tell me more about your daughter… and I can share with you about mine."

She pulled out Jon's gift from her shirt.

"This is my Darcuna. She's beautiful, is she not? She looks so much like my mother. When she laughs, her whole face lights up. I should warn you Dragon blood does not flow as efficiently as other types of blood. It is quite sluggish in comparison; due to the memories it holds."

Thea was rambling, her distress driving her to speak continuously. She needed to make sure of one thing.

"I know you have no love of mages, but I would ask you this one favour. My mate, his name is Jon, Darcuna's father. This pendant is enchanted, nothing so useful to anyone but us. It is compass of sorts. He will need it to get home to our daughter and family. Please, I do this only because your children need someone to stand for them, but do not penalise my little girl. If you could see Jon gets it after I... when I am gone. He will need it to... to... to..."

Thea's throat was so tight with emotion she could no longer speak. Serill held the charm reverently, only now understanding Thea was fully intent on her sacrifice. Giving the charm back to Thea, he gave her a genuine smile.

"Keep hold of it for now – to give you strength. I will see he gets it afterward. Thank you."

Thea nodded still incapable of speaking but relieved to know Serill would honour her wish. The drug would allow her to remain mostly lucid but would make her arms and legs too heavy to move but more importantly she would feel nothing as her blood and her life slowly left her body.

She closed her eyes and dreamt of the last time she and Jon were home and they were together as a family.

***

Chapter 44 - Seeing Red

Jon had been wandering for what felt like hours. There was a tent at the center of the camp that had visitors going in and out most of the day. Because of the traffic he was worried about approaching it but something nagged him. He figured it was a command tent. It was lit up like Piccadilly Circus. Something big was going on inside. His gut told him if Thea was anywhere, she would be in that tent.

Oh, for fuck's sake. It has got to be that one.

This would be ten times worse than sneaking around Incendya Domus and even then, he'd not fooled anyone. Shadow Lord had known he was there as soon as he'd stepped out of the portal. Hopefully this time he could sneak in and out without setting off any alarms. The feeling that Thea was in trouble was now nearing critical level. No matter what, he would get her out of this camp even if she hated him. If the sensation he was feeling was anything to go by, she needed him, he would deal with her anger later. He just needed to get her safe.

His mouth was dry as he neared the tent and he licked his lips. No one was any wiser to his presence. At least one thing was going right, but in all the years Jon had been alive, nothing was ever easy and he felt like a stone dropped in his stomach. The thing he'd intentionally forced himself to not think was now a voice shouting in his head.

No one was guarding this tent. Bodies don't need to be guarded because dead Dragons don't run.

He felt lightheaded and thought he might actually faint on the spot until he heard her voice. He dropped to his knees in relief.

"Thank the celestials."

He clapped his hand over his mouth. He'd been so grateful to know she was alive he'd accidentally spoken out loud. No one seemed to be the wiser, but that slip up made him realise he needed to be careful. If he were found this close to saving her and they were both killed, he'd have no one to blame but himself.

Taking a slow calming breath, Jon slid passed the tent flap and found himself looking at his nightmare made real. Thea was laying there as they drained her blood. The jar looked to have collected a little less than what she'd given Nash that first time. Not enough to hurt her but enough to make the world go red for him.

There was a moment when Jon acknowledged the incubus clawing to get out and he thought *Fuck it, go nuts*."

***

Thea turned her head just as Jon shed his glamour and could see his eyes go black. If she didn't do something, he would annihilate this entire area. The drug made moving impossible, so she did the only thing should could still do and screamed.

"Serill, run!"

Jon looked over at the terrified man, and Thea saw the colour leave Serill's face. She called out to Jon.

"Leave him alone!"

She could not physically block him, so instead she raised a shield around Jon. She hoped it was enough to slow the incubus and get Jon back in control. Serill was petrified and froze on the spot. Thea called out again.

"Listen to me, Jon. Listen to my voice."

He turned towards her and Thea continued.

"Jon, I need you to control the monster. Please."

She could see that part of him was hearing her, but it wasn't enough. She needed to get him away from the camp. He was too worked up and the monster would not let go without a fight. She tried to reason with him.

"Look at me Jon. Do you see any chains or restraints?"

This got his attention, and Thea could see her Jon was wondering why she was letting them take her blood.

***

The incubus turned it around in his head. She was always looking out for everyone except herself. He was the only one who worried about her, but she always got her way and he was the one who suffered.

Selfish bitch, it hissed in his head. He could feel the monster like it was clawing at his insides. There were too many voices in his head vying for leadership. Closing his eyes so he could refocus on Thea's voice, he tried to rein in the incubus.

***

Thea willed her body to move. She pulled the needle out of her arm and tried to roll off the table. She fell painfully off and onto the floor. Her legs were too numb to hold her up. Jon rushed to her and gathered her up, before opening a portal.

Thea called out to Serill.

"I will be back. I promised I would do this, but if I do not deal with Jon, I fear his pain will lead him to act and the consequences would be dire. I promise to return soo..."

And then they were gone.

***

Jon laid Thea down and walked away. Unable to sit up she rolled over to keep him in sight.

"Jon, I'm so..."

"Don't you fucking dare say you're sorry. Do you have any idea what seeing you like that did to me? Do you have a clue how fucking exhausting it is always having to watch you run headlong into danger without caring what those of us who care about you are left to deal with?

"You selfish fucking... bitch!"

Jon had to walk away. He could feel the incubus wanting to hurt her. After Artiscaena, he knew if he allowed it, the monster could become almost unstoppable.

Thea watched him as he walked over to a tree and punched it. His hand was now bleeding and the tension in his face could not hide the pain hitting the tree had caused. He was angrier than she'd ever seen him. She had never thought about how her actions might affect him. He was right. She was thoughtless. She had been willing to help a stranger at the cost of hurting those she loved and who loved her. He would not accept her apology, not at this stage, so she tried another tactic.

"What would you have me do? I cannot see suffering and not try to relieve it. So much of my life was spent watching those who could not defend themselves be abused by those stronger than them. What point is there having all this power if not to aid those weaker than me? Everyone seems to believe that power is for lording over others."

Thea stabbed at her temple.

"These memories which I am just starting to understand teach me that my strength can do so much more than rule. I want to do what is right. What do you want me to do?"

By now most of Jon's rage had blown itself out. He was still angry but calm.

"No, but there has to be some kind of middle ground. I know you want to help when you can, but you are going to have to learn that sometimes you can't. Not just us, and definitely not just you. Look I love that you care, really, but it's too much. You have obligations. You need to start learning that sometimes the only option that gets you out alive is to walk away."

Thea's arm was still bleeding. Jon sat down next to her and pulled her up. He held her arm so he could look at the wound. His heart had skipped a beat when he'd seen her laying there, eyes closed and her blood flowing into the jar.

"I'm not asking you to stop caring, just to think before you act. Believe it or not I'm shitting a brick over the idea of being left alone. I've done it and it sucks. If you leave, that's it—I'm on my own again...

"I want to believe we'll get home, but until then, you are literally all I have; so, if you get anymore hair-brained ideas about committing suicide by some sort of misguided hero complex, please for the love of all that is holy don't do anything until we discuss it."

Thea nodded.

"Ok. I will."

***

Chapter 45 - Musical Contemplations

Both of them were emotionally drained. Thea dropped off immediately thanks to the drugs she'd been given, but Jon was too restless to sleep. No doubt her penance would be waking up and feeling how she'd abused her body. He placed a few wards to keep anyone from sneaking up on them. He hoped she had learned her lesson. He truly did love that she was such a caring person. He just needed her to remember her actions affected him as much as her.

Often as they wandered from realm to realm, Jon found himself remembering songs from his life Earthside. It was like a soundtrack to their travels, and it helped keep him tied to home. Before meeting Thea, there were nights he would listen to the AM radio just to hear a friendly voice and remembered falling asleep to the music in his falcon. It felt like a lifetime ago. He'd been alone because of what he was and his fear of being found or worse, hurting someone he cared about.

Thea was strong enough to handle the incubus, but she was still vulnerable. He lay back and pulled Thea to his side, her soft snores making him smile. She never had problems falling asleep, bless her. She could sleep anywhere but right now he missed his bed. He missed his brother, he even missed Gath. He didn't often allow himself to think too long about Darcuna; she had him wrapped right around her chubby little finger. He missed her giggles and how she looked at him like he was the sun in her universe. His chest went tight and he blinked back a few tears.

He needed to relax, so he went through his mental music collection and the familiar intro to Boston's perennial classic, *More Than A Feeling*, started up in his mind. Music was a kind of magic. It could take him out of one headspace and put him in another.

He needed to stop thinking about what he'd almost lost and think about what he still had. He tightened his hold on Thea, and she moved closer to him in response. The music in his mind began to weave its magic as the notes lulled him enough so he could close his eyes and finally drop off.

***

Thea woke to find Jon sitting a short distance away from her. *He must be still angry at me.* She needed to make things right between them.

"I am truly sorry. I forget my actions have wider consequences, which is made all the more significant because as a Dragon I should remember everything. I forget that sometimes watching someone you love in pain can be worse than feeling that pain yourself. I forget that you worry over me as much as I do you… if not more because I forget that as strong as my magic is, I am not immortal. Oh Jon, I *am* sorry. I know this realm is out of balance, but you were right we should leave and make our way back home to the ones who love us."

Jon didn't turn around to face her, and she was afraid she'd done irreparable harm to their bond.

"Jon, did you hear me? We can go whenever you are ready."

She crawled over, not quite sure of her legs yet after the drugs she'd been given. What she saw unnerved her. Jon's eyes were closed but his cheeks were wet. She'd never seen him cry before. She'd hurt Jon so badly; he'd finally broken down.

Jon opened his eyes to look at Thea.

"Sometimes I do wonder if you hear anything, I say."

He paused to formulate his thoughts.

"Thea, seeing you there on that table with your blood draining into that vial, was every nightmare I've ever had. I know you want to help when you can, and I love you for that, but I can't un-see that. That's going to be with me for a very long time. I need you to understand that first."

Thea threw herself at him crying.

"I swear I will never do anything like that ever again. Please, Jon, I need to know you forgive me, please."

Jon held her face between his hands and wiped away her tears.

"I do, I'm still mad but yeah, I forgive you. I know *why* you did what you did. Even if I don't agree with your method, I understand why. Those kids are in bad shape, and if it was Gaia, or someone else we love, then maybe we'd be forced to do something as horrible. But the fact is giving one side more magic will not fix what's wrong here only postpone the inevitable. They need to talk… and maybe we can try and help with that."

He pulled Thea's face closer and forced her to look him in the eye.

"I never want to see you offering yourself up like that ever again. You have a daughter who needs her mother and a mate who needs you more than you can imagine."

Thea nodded.

"I *will* remember that."

Jon kissed her on the forehead.

"I love you."

"I love you too."

"Now as to facilitating some sort of truce between the sides, *that* is going to be tricky."

***

This time Thea took Jon with her into the camp. For Jon's safety she kept him close enough for her runes to protect him until she could explain herself. She noticed Serill backing away from her.

"It is ok. Jon is no longer a threat. I promised you I would help, that has not changed, but Jon has reminded me that I have a family and obligations to them as well. My dying won't solve your problem or bring an end to the conflict. Jon has offered to take a small delegation to speak with the Sentinels. We will offer a guarantee of protection to anyone who agrees to speak to the other side. We cannot end this for you, but we can help you to be heard and we have the means to protect you if they refuse to speak and attack."

She cautiously stepped towards Serill.

"Perhaps you can speak to Simmy and tell her how hurt you are by her silence. Maybe if she could see you, then you could talk. She is your daughter and as one who had a complicated relationship with her own father, I know regret. I did not know my father's heart until it was too late, and I would help you to avoid the same fate. I hope you will take our offer."

Serill fidgeted with his hands. Thea could feel he was conflicted. She made one last attempt to reach him.

"You owe your daughter a chance to reconcile. She is all you have, let her know she is still your little girl and you love her."

Serill kept his eyes lowered by nodded.

Jon looked over to Oweyn and Ceale. He addressed the boy.

"Thea tells me you are gifted beyond the other kids. If she sees potential then I believe her."

He turned his attention to Oweyn.

"I know how hard it is to learn to control something inside of you that you don't understand. I was lucky I had a magically trained mother. She taught both me and my brother how to use magic safely but even then, there were accidents. You can't just hope everything works out. Ceale needs training if not from the Sentinels then from someone who understands how to control magic."

He stopped to look over at Thea before he turned back to Oweyn.

"I can try and show him a few methods my mother taught me to control my emotions so that you don't have as many accidents. I can't and won't promise anything beyond that. Magic sometimes seems like this living thing that can have a will of its own. A lot of times it can feel less about controlling it and more about working with it."

Jon looked back at Thea; she gave him a bright smile. It was clear that this was the right thing to do.

"We're here to help, in whatever way we can."

***

Chapter 46 - Negotiations

Thea stepped through the portal first. She surrounded herself with an earth shield before Oweyn, Ceale, Serill and Ade, one of the elders, joined her. The air around the group crackled with the energy of the shield, enough to display they were quite safe. Jon stepped through last but left the portal open behind him, both as a precaution if things went sideways and as a show of strength. He addressed the startled mages.

"Some of you might have seen me here. I've brought members of the other side to negotiate a ceasefire. If anyone has designs on attacking us or the other side, I've given a guarantee of protection while they are here to talk. I will enforce that along with my mate, Thea."

Thea gave a short display of her Hellfire but did not speak or otherwise give away that she was a Dragon as per Jon's instruction.

"We're here to try and start a process to end this conflict. I'm not asking for a miracle; we just want to talk."

An older mage was making his way through the crowd towards Jon and Thea. Jon stepped forward and introduced the mage to the small delegation.

"May I present the Palatine Archmage of the Sentinel Order, Didrayl."

Thea joined Jon at the head of the group.

"Though outsiders, we understand this dispute can only be resolved if both sides are willing to discuss concessions. I've spent time with these people and know them to be honest and hardworking, only trying to do what is best for their children and you've seen Jon among you. He tells me you are wise as well as astute. We only wish to help secure some sort of peace between you if we can."

Thea gestured for Ade to come forward.

"May I present the Elder Father of the Huemily, Ade. I am confident a truce between you can be reached if both sides are committed to deliberating in good faith."

The two men stood facing each other awkwardly before they tentatively shook hands.

Thea and Jon looked at each other before he whispered.

"Well it's a start I suppose."

***

A tent was cleared for the purpose of the talks, but all inside knew that the entire camp was listening from outside the canvas walls. Jon cleared his throat.

"These people have been sending their children to you for training only to never see them again. I know the reasons, but their parents don't. I think it's only fair to have a few of the kids present to speak on their behalf, since all this fighting seems to be about them."

Didrayl nodded sagely.

"We too had the same thought and have asked a number of them to join us. They are being pulled out of their classes and brought here as we speak."

Serill stood as soon as the children arrived with their guardians; his daughter was among them.

"Simmy, I need you to come home."

A girl with bright green eyes and brown curls ran back to her carer.

"Please don't let him take me. I don't want to go back. I want to stay here with you."

A woman similar in age to Serill held her. She looked sad.

"I know you do, poppet, but he is your father. You must tell him why. We have always told you, you must tell the truth. He should know why."

Simmy turned to face her father and her expression was full of wrath.

"He hates magic, and he hates me. He just wants me because I look like Mummy, but he'll make me stop doing magic because he can't do it."

Her outburst did not shock the mages as much as the parents. Serill looked like his head would explode.

"Where did you get that idea? They put it in your head. They turned you against me."

Thea laid her hand on his arm.

"Why would Simmy believe her father hates her?"

The guardian held out a sheet of paper and began to read its contents.

"I miss being able to do things with you my angel, before all this magic got between us. I can't wait until you come home and we can put it all behind us."

She looked back up at Serill.

"These children are rejected by their own parents. Of course, we cannot send them back to this environment. We've raised and loved them. To send them back to a community that sees their aptitude in magic as an affliction instead of the gifts that they are is criminal. We are not so heartless."

Serill's face fell.

"It's only that I miss you so much it hurts. And of course I miss your mother, don't you?"

Simmy burrowed her face into her guardian's skirt. Her voice was muffled by the fabric.

"He said I killed Mummy, and he wished I'd never been born."

The tent went quiet. The only sound was Simmy's crying. Serill's face was white. Thea could feel her own heart break at the little girl's words. For so much of her own childhood, she'd felt like a disappointment to her own father. It was only after receiving his memories that she knew of how much pride he'd felt in her and her accomplishments in spite of her size. That she refused to let it hinder her or cow her with her brothers was a huge source of pride for him. But only Dragons had their parents' memories. Thea was compelled to speak. She knelt by Simmy.

"I too fought with my father about my magic. He was the most powerful of all the fire demons and when I finally presented as a fire demon, at first, he was so happy. But females in my world are not thought of well, and I always felt like I disappointed him. But then before he died, he told me how proud he was of me and my accomplishments. I only wish he had told me before."

Thea turned and beckoned Serill forward.

"You must tell her now before it's too late what you told me. She cannot go on believing you hate her or her magic."

Serill wiped the tears from his face.

"I lost your mother and now I'm losing you. I'm all alone Simmy. You're all I have left, and I need you more than you can ever imagine. Please come home. I miss you. I know I can't do magic like them, but I don't care about the magic. I just want my little girl."

The guardian pointed at Serill.

"You see, he does not care about her magic but it is part of her. I love all of her including her magic. I've held her after every nightmare, and I dressed her wounds after every fall."

This seemed to anger Serill.

"I never had a chance. You lot came in and took her away and never gave me or any of us a chance. We're not fancy mages with our own magic. We have to tear our hearts out and give 'em to you for training. We have to live knowing we'll never understand our own flesh and blood."

Jon decided to step in.

"Look, can we at least agree that we *all* want what's best for these kids?"

Serill and Simmy's guardian grudgingly nodded.

"Ok, progress."

He knelt down to the little girl.

"Simmy, you have a dad who misses you so much, he's making all of us as miserable as him. I know you're scared. My dad tried to kill me, but yours loves you."

He looked up at the carer.

"Maybe we can start with visitation for the parents if the guardians are worried about how the kids are treated when sent home. And in return the guardians can try and guide the parents on how to deal with magic even if they can't wield it themselves. You know, help the parents understand what their child is dealing with."

Everyone looked at Serill before he gave a nod. His sadness was evident in his voice.

"I would do anything if I got to see my Simmy again."

Thea prodded the guardian.

"These parents need their children more than the children need them. The anger is a mask for their grief and frustration. They do not understand the burden that magic places on the user. It is up to you and the other guardians to not only teach the children magic, but also the parents who do not wield it. It is more than was expected of you, but magic demands a high price for the power it grants us. I know this lesson all too well. Above all, these children need guidance and support from both sides."

Thea addressed the Archmage and Elder Father.

"While we cannot stay overly long, I feel it would be remiss of us to start these negotiations and leave before they are properly underway. We have a child of our own waiting for us, so our time is finite, but we will offer what assistance we can."

Thea and Jon's eyes met and while his expression was not happy, he gave her a nod to say he agreed. A little while later, he was able to grab a quiet word with her.

"We can't afford to stop too often, but it's ok, I get it. Since stepping into this, we have just as much responsibility as the guardians to see these kids and their families reconciled. I'm asking though, between us, if we can set a soft deadline before we leave them to settle on their own."

Thea was upset but agreed.

"As you have repeatedly reminded me, we have obligations of our own before taking on any more. If our soft deadline approaches and they have not reached a solution, how long will we stay? I think it best at this time to not make too much of our leaving and instead concentrate on these discussions so that when we do finally go, we can without worry."

Jon wasn't going to get a firm yes or no from Thea, so he took what he could get and ran with it.

"As long as you *are* still planning to go home, I can accept that."

***

Chapter 47 - Armistice

It took roughly eight months before Thea and Jon saw a relatively stable armistice between the mages and the parents. The number of families managing to re-establish ties encouraged the leaders on both sides that the end of hostilities would benefit all.

Serill was over the moon to have Simmy back in his life. And now that her carer understood his anger sprung from missing his daughter and needing her, she was helping them to rebuild their relationship.

Just as they had suspected, Ceale, was proving to be an undeniable magical talent. He was advancing through his lessons faster than his tutors could believe. With Jon's help he was now able to control how his emotions affected his magic.

Oweyn looked on his son's achievements with so much pride, he would boast to anyone within earshot.

"That's my Ceale. Look how gifted he is. Why he may lead the Sentinels one day."

The boy took his father's boasts in stride and though he would not say aloud, his smile was all the proof needed to see how much he appreciated his father's words.

Thea was overjoyed to see so many parents reconnect with their children. There were a few who refused to let go of old hates and it broke her heart to see some children's parents unwilling or unable to reconcile.

Jon had to remind her.

"You can lead a horse to water, but you can't make it drink."

Thea swallowed down the lump in her throat.

"I understand, but it does not mean I do not mourn for those children denied their parents' love."

Jon pointed to the carers.

"No matter what, those kids will have someone who loves them. You did good. I wouldn't worry too much."

Thea took Jon's hands in hers and faced him.

"No, *we* did good. I could not have accomplished this alone. I am indeed lucky to have someone who cares for me enough to remind me that I am not infallible. My initial plan was flawed; you showed me another way."

Jon's eyebrows shot up so fast that Thea laughed out loud.

"Perhaps I should listen to *your* wise council more in the future."

Jon lost his footing and would have hit the ground had Thea not caught him.

"Can I get that in writing, signed and notarised?"

Thea punched him in the arm.

"You jest, but I am serious. I am truly in your debt."

Jon pulled Thea over so he could plant a kiss on her head.

"You don't owe me anything, but I'm glad that it's finally starting to sink in."

* * *

Chapter 48 - Three Long Years

Thea was heartbroken over how long they had been trying to get home. She checked the lines on her arm. Since Artiscaena and missing Darcuna's first birthday she began cutting a line to commemorate the year as penance for her part in sending them away. Calling up her sword she carved a third line onto her arm. Jon hated the gruesome reminder that he'd yet to get them home.

"Why do you keep doing that?"

Thea cauterised the cut leaving a mark.

"It is so I do not forget our little one."

Jon rounded on her, ready to lay into her that she could never forget anything and that he did not need to be reminded that he was a failure, but he stopped short when he saw her. She was trying to keep from crying again, but he could see her lip trembling and he blew out a dejected sigh. He knew why she did it, and his bruised ego was not making it any better. He moved to gather Thea into his arms.

"I'm sorry…"

Thea laid her finger on his lips.

"I hate that you still blame yourself. It was my pride which took us away from her, and it is my mark to bear. I do not do this to make you feel guilty. I do it to emphasize my failure and mark my time away from

Darcuna. If I did not have you to pull me through each day..."

She did not need to finish her thought. Jon knew she didn't blame him. He blamed himself for not getting them home. With no way to precisely chart their progress other than the vague fluctuations of the pendant, they might well wander forever. The races they encountered since stumbling into the war in Acallaris were sympathetic to their plight and allowed them a few days rest and some food until they again made another blind jump, hoping this time they would end up either Earthside or home.

Thea stepped away but gave him a weary smile.

"Before we attempt to portal again, I wish a chance to wash myself. I feel as if I carry a thousand years of dust. Amara told me about a series of pools where the water springs from the ground warm enough to feel exquisite. We can wash our clothing and rinse some of this travel dirt off of us. Will you join me? I can sense your tension."

Jon had to admit he felt grungy as well. And his clothing, while enchanted, probably could do with a wash. Caris had provided Thea with enchanted clothing, but it looked like it could do with a good scrubbing as well. Thea grabbed his hand and gently pulled him.

"I think we are both suffering. If I had to bear this alone... at least we have each other. Come with me, Jon."

He allowed Thea to pull him along. She steered them towards the Vandi pools. He got a few nods from some of the Aerie Naga. As the pools came into sight Jon had to admit the rising steam looked inviting. They chose a small pool away from the others.

Stripping off he slipped in and couldn't help a sigh slipping out. Closing his eyes, he lay back and swore this was the best thing he'd ever experienced until he opened his eyes and saw Thea slip in across from him.

She dipped her head back to wash the grime that had built up in her hair, and when she came back up, he coughed, the air in his throat catching at the sight. Thea had long since removed the enchantment from her hair, and he loved how when it was wet like this, it resembled liquid fire. He floated over to her. She met him in the middle of the pool and he hovered over her face.

He noticed little things that weren't there when they'd first met. Since regaining her Dragon memories her eyes had lost their innocence and it made him a little sad. They stayed that way for some time before Thea pulled him down to her.

Grabbing a handful of her hair he deepened the kiss and he felt Thea push herself against him. He pulled her legs up to wrap them around him then broke the kiss long enough to latch onto her neck.

Thea let out a soft moan and ran her hands over his skin. She felt the new scars he'd picked up on their journey.

She held onto Jon as she leaned back to give him better access to her neck before pulling his head back up to kiss him again. Jon smiled against her lips and moved to whisper in her ear before something caught his attention. Pushing her hair aside he saw it—the mark of a Dragon's pregnancy. Jon's face lit up.

"Thea, how long have you known?"

Thea smiled at him sadly.

"It has not been long, but I was afraid of your response with everything we are already dealing with."

Jon grabbed her face and kissed her. He broke the kiss to look at Thea again.

"You're not happy about this?"

Thea blinked back tears.

"A child is always a blessing, but we are not yet home. We are constantly moving. As my pregnancy progresses it will become harder to move quickly, what if we meet up with another race like the Sommner? Or the Orimyar? We barely made it out of their realm alive. What about another war-torn realm? I am not unhappy Jon; I am frightened."

Jon wrapped his arms around Thea to try and soothe her, but she went on.

"Already you feel the strain of caring for me. A child will put additional pressure on you to get us home. I did not wish to add to your burden."

He pushed the hair off of her face before he kissed her forehead.

"You're right. I'm feeling the heat because I promised you I would get us home to Darcuna, and so far, we are…hell, I have no idea how long it will take to get back to Hell, but this is good news. I love you, Thea, and maybe this will be the thing that turns our luck…"

Thea tried to interrupt him, but he clamped his hand over her mouth.

"We'll deal with this, like we've dealt with everything the celestials have thrown at us. I am ok, *we* are ok. This is good news—fuck, this is awesome news."

As if to prove the point, Jon hoisted Thea up and whooped as loud as he could.

"We're having another baby!"

Thea giggled at his display while trying to climb down.

"Jon, others are starting to look…"

He laughed at her.

"Hey, I've tried to tell you to cover up, but you seem hell-bent on the nudity thing."

He laughed even harder when Thea tried to pry his arms open to let her go. He finally dropped her into the water and laughed so hard he couldn't breathe when she came up glaring at him.

Thea tried to keep her face straight but had to concede to his laughter. She splashed him and he splashed her back, and by the end both of them were feeling better about the days ahead than when they had woken up.

As they lay bare waiting for their clothes to dry after scrubbing them clean, Thea gave Jon a kiss on his cheek.

"You will get us home; I believe that with all my heart."

***

Chapter 49 - The Ethereal Sanctum

They stood in the valley looking up. This realm was covered in mountains and it looked like at the top of each one there was a temple only reachable by a set of long and winding stairs carved into the rock. In the valley, areas of woodland had been cleared to make room for farms. Thea and Jon were hidden away in one such wooded area on the edge of a farm. Jon was staring at Thea's belly trying to decide whether they should keep pushing or plant themselves here until the baby was born. For the last few days they had seen no signs of conflict and no aggressive species.

Because Thea's curse had been lifted, they were now looking at a more typical Dragon pregnancy and if his math was right, Thea was due to drop any day now, a week at most. He was charged up so he could portal if needed, but was apprehensive over what the next realm could hold.

"Jon, I do not relish climbing all those stairs."

She rubbed her lower back, and Jon stepped in. Gently pushing her hand away, he massaged her back. Thea groaned in appreciation.

"Ah, thank you. I did not suffer so with Darcuna. This pregnancy feels much different. My body feels heavier and slower. I am sorry I am delaying us…"

Jon gave her a kiss on the cheek.

"It's fine. I'm happy. Sure our timing, as usual, is crap, but for the first time in a long time I am actually happy. But I want to take a look around these farms and see if we can hole up somewhere down here. I don't relish climbing all the way up there any more than you do."

Jon lowered Thea to the ground so she could lie down while he scouted around. He wasn't worried about Thea. He knew her power was at maximum due to her pregnancy. If anyone tried to mess with her, they'd be in for a world of pain. All the same, he subtly laid out a few protection wards. He heard Thea laugh.

"I can see your wards, Jon. Thank you. I am so tired these days that perhaps some sort of warning trigger would be wise."

Jon left her leaning against a tree dozing as he wandered towards the closest farm. He stopped when he saw the farm workers had no eyes and backed away slowly. His first though was he'd missed something and they'd wandered into another possibly hostile realm and he needed to grab Thea.

"You there, where did you come from? How did you get here?"

"Shit."

He held up his hands hoping that he could talk his way out and grab Thea.

"I'm not looking for trouble."

Turning he saw it was a younger woman wearing what appeared to be monk's robes. She was pointing a wicked looking staff at him. He paused wondering if he should mention Thea's state. He crossed his fingers that Thea would wake up if things went sideways. He raised his voice hoping to catch Thea's attention.

"I'm here with my mate. She's pregnant. We were just looking for someplace for her to rest and maybe barter for some food."

The woman lowered her staff but did not put it away.

"Why are you yelling? I've never seen you before. You're an outsider. You should not have been able to get passed our wards. What are you?"

Jon hoped the truth wouldn't get him killed.

"I'm part Faye. I kind of have the ability to get passed most wards."

The woman raised her staff again.

"Why are you sneaking around?"

Jon called out to Thea.

"Um, Thea honey, can you come out here and tell this nice lady I am not a thief or a mugger?"

The woman had her staff pointed at Jon's chest when a few seconds later Thea came out from the trees.

"Jon, what are you yelling about...? Oh, hello."

Thea saw the staff and moved to stand next to Jon.

The woman seemed to instantly recognized Thea as a Dragon.

"By Kiydarr! We did not expect one so exalted as you would ever visit us, and with child as well. This is an incredible blessing."

She turned to the nearest farm worker.

"Quickly find the mother and tell her we will need a stretcher. Oh, and perhaps we should gather more of those delicious helie berries for our guest. And maybe we should send word to the other temples..."

She seemed to only remember Jon afterwards.

"Why are you here? Are you here to cause trouble?"

Thea stepped in front of Jon.

"He is the father of my child and perfectly honourable. And if you revere Dragons, his father was one as well. But I must ask, where are we?"

The woman introduced herself.

"Oh noble one, I am Nushala and this is The Ethereal Sanctum. We are honoured by your appearance. By Kiydarr himself, a Dragon, here."

Another neophyte arrived.

"Nushala the other novices are waiting on you to start the lesson."

Nushala pointed towards Thea and Jon.

"Mordan, are you blind? We have a Dragon in our realm."

The neophyte turned startled to see Thea and Jon.

"A Dragon?"

She looked at Thea's belly.

"She is with child!"

She fumbled in her robes for a book.

"We have practiced your teachings faithfully."

Jon was starting to get fed up with the whole *exalted Dragon* routine and cleared his throat.

"Ok, we get it, she's a Dragon and she's pregnant. Why are you all so excited?"

Mordan and Nushala bobbed their heads.

"We have not seen a Dragon in this realm since Kiydarr first showed us how to use our healing magic to take care of our realm. While other realms around us faltered, we alone stayed true and now we are visited again. The high priestess must be told."

Nushala elbowed her companion.

"Well, don't just stand there. Run to the temple and tell the high priestess. I will see to our guests and bring them to her. Go Mordan."

The younger novice ran as Nushala looked around.

"Where is that stretcher?"

Thea tried to dig for further information.

"Tell me, I heard you say to Jon this realm was hidden. How have you hidden an entire realm?"

Nushala gave a proud smile.

"We fashioned the wards ourselves. Clever, eh?"

Nushala went on to explain the realm was usually hidden away by magic to keep it safe from raiders.

It was just dumb luck that Jon had been able to portal them here at all. His ability to move passed wards and enchantments that hindered most meant he could enter realms that were usually inaccessible to outsiders. This realm was home to a mix of two races: the Yeosti who practiced a sort of monastic lifestyle, and the blind Xilios who were simple labourers.

The Yeosti lived in the temples high up. Each temple housed a different order and each order spent their days in prayer and study, but all of them followed the teaching of Kiydarr. In the valleys below were farms where food was grown and animals kept, tended by the Xilios. Born blind, the Xilios were taken in by the Yeosti when their own realm was destroyed by raiders. In exchange for tending to the farms of the orders, they were protected by the Yeosti's magic. The two groups had enjoyed the cooperative relationship for several thousand years.

The most remarkable feature of this realm was its use of magic to maintain the land, much like the Dragons had done in Earthside. When the young Yeosti novices had seen Thea and her swollen belly they instantly believed it was divine providence that she and Jon had been sent here. Dragons were not just known but revered by Yeosti.

"Kiydarr was a Dragon from Earth realm who saw how our healing magic could be used like the Dragon's elemental magic to maintain our realm. So, after his family was killed and he abandoned his home, he came here to live with us. He taught us how to live in balance."

Jon could see the wheels turning in Thea's head. He waited until Nushala stepped away to see about the stretcher. He kept his voice low.

"What are you thinking? I can actually see the gears in your head turning. Something wrong?"

Thea shook her head.

"No, nothing like that. It is only that I know the story they speak of, and the Dragon was not Kiydarr. His name was Kadir and his family was not dead only hurt."

Jon stood with his mouth open.

"No... wait, are you telling me you know who they are talking about?"

Thea twisted her hands together.

"Yes, he was related to me by blood—my father's blood. That is why I know of him."

Jon clapped his hand over Thea's mouth. He lowered his voice even further so no one else would hear him.

"These religious types always make me nervous. What if they see you as the next coming of this Kiydarr and try to keep you and the baby here?"

Thea gently pushed Jon's hand away and spoke in the same hushed tones.

"While I agree, I am nervous over keeping such a secret, especially if I am forced to birth our baby here."

Thea's lip trembled and Jon knew she was trying not to cry again, but her pregnancy hormones had made keeping her emotions in check even harder. He gathered her to him and kissed the top of her head.

"I know, I know, and it's ok. This isn't your fault, last I checked I played a vital part in this. We'll have to stay, but for now let's keep mum about your ties to Kiydarr/Kadir. And don't worry, we are all leaving. No one is getting left behind."

* * *

Chapter 50 - A Gown For a Princess

As much as she loved them, Thea's hunter shirt and shorts were now tight to the point of being uncomfortable. As the first to greet her, Nushala made it her mission to be Thea's personal attendant. She realised that Thea required new clothing. Thankfully the high priestess, Daphine, was in agreement and the celestials had made their will known.

"We are honoured that you will be with us for the birth. I hope these meet your needs."

The priestess presented Thea with a robe made of pale silk. As beautiful and luxurious as the material was, the design was kept simple. Sleeveless, with a high waist to remove the pressure off Thea's womb and a cowl neckline that would allow her to comfortably feed her child once born.

Later Jon snickered quietly to himself, as Thea constantly had to keep pulling the shoulder up, but he couldn't deny she looked like a princess. He stood behind her as she studied herself in front of a looking glass examining the dress.

"It is beautiful but it feels very impractical. I am so short that the regal length keeps tripping me so I am forced to either lift the hem as I walk or slow my pace to that of a snail."

Jon slid the shoulder down to Thea's chagrin. That is until he began to trail kisses down her neck and shoulder. He spoke between each kiss.

"I know …you think …it's a pain in the arse, but …you really do look beautiful. You don't call yourself a ruler …but damn if you don't act like one, so …why not look like one for a change?

Thea spun around to look at him pulling the dress up over her shoulder again.

"Jon, I am serious."

Her hand went to the pendant with Darcuna's face before she raised her arm up to show him her line scars.

"Four years, Jon, almost five. We have been away from her and now it will be longer because of me. I am trying to be happy, but then I think of Darcuna and it is like I am being unfair to her. This child will forever be in her shadow because I cannot think of it without thinking of the one before."

Jon pushed her hand down and held her at arm's length. Thea could see him swallowing and knew he was not as unaffected as he appeared.

"We talked about this. You need to worry about the baby we have here with us and trust that Gath and Gerard are doing right by Darcuna. I hate that we aren't home yet. I hate that you are suffering, and most of all I hate that I can do fuck all to change it. But we both agreed that we had to set all that aside for the sake of this baby. I'm not talking about forgetting Darcuna, but she's at home with an entire Dragon settlement to look out for her. This baby,"

He poked Thea gently in the belly.

"Has no one but us to look out for her. As much as it hurts, we both have to learn to suck it up."

He straightened the pendant, and Thea could see Jon blinking back his own tears as she did the same. She even attempted a smile.

"You are right of course. I am being selfish."

Jon pulled her close.

"No, you're just being an emotional pregnant Dragon. It's ok. Are you better now? Want me to leave you, so you can have a good cry while I pretend I'm not doing the same somewhere else?"

This time Thea's smile was more genuine.

"No, I think I am ok now. Oh Jon, will it always be like this?"

Jon tried to be optimistic.

"Hopefully the sprog will join us, the hormonal tidal wave you're riding will subside, and you and I will be too tired to feel anything other than relief when it's asleep."

She rubbed her stomach thoughtfully.

"Soon you will join us, little one. I hope we are ready."

Jon kissed her again.

"Of course not, but we'll muddle through like we did before and pray we don't screw up any worse than we did."

This made Thea laugh and also renewed her enthusiasm to meet her new child.

***

Thea woke with a start. It was dark, and she could just hear the sound of the acolyte's night time chanting. Her back spasmed again. Jon mumbled from under the covers.

"Are you ok?"

The spasm radiated across her back and forward under her chest. Thea poked him repeatedly.

"Jon, it is coming."

He turned over and rubbed his eyes, trying to wake himself up. Yawning, he swung out of bed. Grabbing his trousers, he went to find Nushala. She was sleeping in the room next to them. Banging on her door, he called out to her.

"Nushala, it's time."

She opened her door fully dressed and immediately ran passed him to Thea. Jon wasn't even sure if she had actually been sleeping. Nushala began by pulling back the bed clothes and placing them aside. Next, she arranged Thea's pillows and pulled her up to lay back against them. She ran out into the hall and shouted as loud as she could.

"It is time!"

Within a few minutes, several other attendants arrived and Jon was pushed aside. He and Thea had discussed what form Thea would take for the birth, and as hard as it was the first time, they decided for Thea to remain in her human form. Taking her dragon form would require her to sleep outside and even with her Dragon memories she'd already experienced birth in human form. She would know almost exactly what to expect. He could see Thea's face contorted in pain as the first contractions hit. She called out to him.

"Jon, where are you? Please don't leave me."

He took that as his cue and bullied his way back to Thea's side. He then proceeded to toss her pillows aside and kneel behind her, propping her up against him. She grasped his hands and gave him a weak smile. He kissed her forehead.

"Don't worry, baby, I am not leaving you."

Though at the moment her next contraction hit he wished he hadn't given her his hands. She squeezed so tight he was sure she was going to break something. He barely registered that Thea was undressed as he watched her stomach ripple as their child fought to be born.

She contorted with each contraction. It was so similar and yet nothing like Darcuna's birth. That time he'd stood back as Aliyah had helped Thea with the birthing. Having had Gaia, her familiarity with birthing meant he and Thea trusted her to see her and the baby safely through. This time he was all Thea had, and short of someone physically removing him, he was staying put.

***

Chapter 51 - Here We Go Again

Several hours later, Thea's head lay back against him as the pain of the last contraction receded. Sunlight was filtering into the room and Jon could hear the late morning prayers beginning. He pushed Thea's hair away from her face as she moaned. She looked absolutely shattered. The labour was sapping all her strength.

Nushala's eyebrows drew together.

"You say she has previously had a child? I do not understand why this labour has gone on so long. The child should have arrived already."

Jon looked down at Thea. She was struggling to push, too tired to continue for much longer. He had an idea. He wouldn't chance it with anyone in the room directly involved in the birth. He spoke to Nushala.

"I need acolytes who won't mind if my incubus draws out their energy. Look at her. She's fading; she needs help. I can give her a boost so that when the time comes, she can push."

Up until now, Nushala had not given much thought to Jon's incubus. It frightened her, but if they did nothing, Thea wouldn't be strong enough to bring the baby into the world. She gave Jon a nod.

He reached out and felt the incubus absorbing small amounts of energy from the other followers in the temple. He fought to keep it from overtaking him and let the energy flow through him and into Thea. Her complexion went from pale to a healthier colour, and he could feel her squeeze his hands to let him know she was receiving it.

Thea blinked as if she was waking up, and as the next contraction began, Nushala yelled at her to push. The birth finally seemed to be progressing.

"Now, I can see the head, but you must continue to push."

Thea bore down, and with a scream she pushed as hard as she could. As the spasm subsided Nushala nodded for her to stop. Jon leaned over and kissed her forehead.

"That's it, baby, just a little longer..."

A few moments later, Thea's grip tightened as the next contraction started, and Jon almost blacked out as she crushed his fingers. Thea let out another scream, and the baby slid out.

"It's a female."

Nushala wrapped the baby, but Thea kept pushing. Passing the baby to an assistant, Nushala looked.

"By Kiydarr, there is a second child."

Jon's head whipped up.

"What the fuck?"

Thea heaved and pushed and within a few minutes a second child arrived. Nushala was in tears.

"It's a second female."

Jon leaned over Thea to look.

"Are there anymore?"

Nushala shook her head as she passed the second child to her assistant.

"No, but her work is not yet done. She needs to push out the afterbirth."

By now Jon could feel Thea was running on fumes so he dug into his own reserves and pushed the energy towards her.

"Just a bit more, and then I promise I will let you sleep for a week."

Once the afterbirth had slid from her body, Thea fell back against Jon, no longer having the strength to sit up. Nushala motioned for Jon to take Thea aside. Once he had her in his arms, several more novices moved into the room to clear away the soiled sheets and remake the bed. Another carried in a bucket with warm water and a sponge.

Jon took the sponge and washed the worst of the blood from Thea. Then once the bed was ready, he laid her down and pulled up the covers to her chin. He placed a kiss on her brow. They looked over at the cradle the high priestess had provided.

***

Next to the bed Thea could see her two babies laying facing each other.

"Jon can you help me up? I want to see them — please."

Jon arranged the pillows for her and brought one then the other to her.

"I never expected twins."

She nuzzled them while Jon sat next to her.

"No, I don't think we even considered it. This definitely complicates things, but you know what? Who cares? They are perfect. Just like their mum."

Thea blushed.

"I think they are beautiful and perfect as well. Now names... what shall we name our two perfectly beautiful daughters?"

Jon was struck with an idea.

"How about Solys and Luna? They're twins but I've never known a set of twins to be identical in anything but looks."

Thea's eye's twinkled at the suggestion.

"Yes, I agree. See even now, look how one dozes peacefully while the other is staring around intensely. The peaceful one shall be Luna and our animated one shall be Solys. Our sun and moon."

Thea yawned, and Jon took the babies one by one and placed them back in the crib next to the bed. Thea turned on her side so she could fall asleep watching them. Jon lay down next to her and they both fell asleep, dreaming of their new family.

***

Chapter 52 - Solys and Luna

Just like before with Darcuna, Jon could see the gears stop and the lines of worry disappear as Thea sat down to nurse. She would not admit it out loud to anyone except Jon, but the dress did make feeding much easier. Nushala for all her pushiness was turning out to be an astute attendant to Thea. She made sure anything Thea required was ready almost before it had been requested.

Jon held Luna while Thea fed Solys. They'd learned quickly that Luna was far more willing to wait than her sister. Jon was letting her gum his finger for the time being and chatting with her.

"Now just because she is louder than you, does not mean she will always get her way. I know it means our ears will be ringing, but fair is fair. Plus, she'll never be as loud as your eldest sister. I know a thing or two about siblings and your mum, well, let's just say you two will never have it as hard as her, but don't you worry, there are like, a hundred Dragons who can't wait to meet you, so you will get all the fussing you can handle."

Thea carefully passed Solys to Nushala while she reached for Luna. The attendant placed Solys in her crib where the baby promptly fell asleep, full and content.

"Ah, one is done. Jon if you could please."

Jon passed Luna to her. Once the baby latched on, Thea asked Nushala to give them a moment. After she was gone and Jon was seated close enough for them to speak quietly without being heard, she began.

"I have asked for an audience with the high priestess, Daphine. She does not seem as fervent as Nushala in the teachings of my ancestor so could be a wise ally for when we are ready to leave. She said something to me that I think hinted that she might already be aware of our secret."

This made Jon nervous enough to stand and pace the room.

"I don't like this. Not one fucking bit."

Thea reached out and pulled Jon to sit again.

"She did not say it as a threat. I believe it was a warning."

Jon raised an eyebrow.

"And why do you think she is keen to help us?"

She shook her head.

"Having had time with my Dragon memories, I have learned that there is neither rhyme nor reason to why some crave power at all costs, while others are happy with the briefest caress and then allow it to slip away like a breeze. The high priestess, Daphine strikes me as one who does not crave power or influence, even though both have been bestowed upon her."

Jon was not convinced.

"I don't have Dragon memories, but my experience has taught me, better to be prepared and happily proved wrong than caught out because you gave the benefit of the doubt to the wrong person. This is my family and I won't take chances with it."

Thea laid her hand over his.

"Then let us agree to move with guarded optimism. We should both speak to her together. Agreed?"

Jon did not answer right away. He thought of all the ways this could go pear-shaped before he finally gave a reluctant nod.

"Ok, but I will portal us away the minute I feel anything hinkey, understand?"

Thea gave him a smirk.

"I would not expect anything less, my love."

***

Jon was holding Luna while Thea held Solys. Daphine asked her attendant to close the door so they could speak privately and gave her instructions to knock should she need to interrupt them. The attendant bowed and left.

"So, how are you feeling, Thea? I understand the birth was not an easy one."

Thea shrugged but her expression was amiable.

"I look forward to attempting a birth in my true form. I am told it is much easier, though my mother was fond of reminding me that the best things always require the most effort."

Jon chuckled as he added his own opinion.

"You realise I will not be holding your hands if you are in your true form. You've got some wicked claws. I'd end up shredded once those contractions hit."

Thea gave an amused smile.

"Ah, I will have to trade one comfort at the expense of another. Such decisions require careful thought."

She turned back to Daphine.

"As amusing as such joking is, we have come to speak to you regarding something altogether more pressing."

Daphine nodded.

"Yes, what to do about your bloodline shall we say. I had my suspicions after a dream I received several days before your arrival. Well not quite a dream. Each priestess of Kiydarr is required to spend a few nights alone without food or drink beyond water to meditate in the highest temple. While there, it is not uncommon to have visions.

"The priestess is not required to share what she saw, and in most cases the visions are so disjointed and unclear to make interpretation almost impossible. Most will not admit that it is ordinarily a time to simply recharge and rest. The last vision I had, I knew something or someone was expected. I heard a single phrase. *She is of my blood and she is coming.*"

Daphine gave an involuntary shiver at the memory, and Thea placed her hand on top of hers. Daphine smiled and continued.

"I was not afraid of the voice, only awed that it should speak to me. It was both powerful and comforting. It was not a command or a warning, only an announcement. So, when poor Mordan rushed in, out of breath and panting, I knew who you were even before you were announced. I also understood that Nushala and others like her might try to make you into a living god."

This time she placed her hand over Thea's.

"You have spoken on many occasions of the daughter and family you left behind. I would never allow you or your children to be separated. I will ask that while you are here, treat this place as your home. Your girls will need a little time before it will be safe to travel with them. Let them grow up a bit, in peace so that when they arrive home, they will have only happy stories to tell."

Jon fidgeted. Daphine understood. There was only one other answer he was looking for.

"I will keep your secret."

***

Chapter 53 - The Honey Heist

"Solys!"

Nushala was screeching at the top of her lungs in frustration. The little girl had once again got into the honey comb and left a trail of sticky drops leading out of the larder. Jon's insight about his twin daughters was proving right. Taken separately the girls looked identical but behaved diametrically opposite to each other. But when it came to how they functioned together as a team, they might as well have shared a brain. Thea was reminded of her brothers, Devourer and Destroyer, and if her instinct was correct Solys might have been the thief but Luna would be the brains of the operation. If she found one, it would undoubtedly lead her to the other.

Luna and her sister liked to sit in the garden behind the hedges. Thea would listen to them whisper and giggle together when they thought they were alone. Like their big sister, they had Jon's dark hair but while Darcuna had Dark Haven's luminous blue eyes, the twins had green eyes that Jon recognised as the same as his mother's. When they were happy their eyes reminded Thea of bright emeralds, twinkling with mirth as their childish squeals rang out. When they were upset or angry, they became dark like moss in the deepest part of a forest, shadowy and foreboding.

If Solys and Luna wanted someplace to enjoy their ill-gotten bounty it would be in the garden away from Nushala and her reprimands. Jon was in agreement.

"If we go after them it means our secret is out too. They'll know we've been listening to them, and we may never find their next hiding spot. But if we let them get away with it, I'm pretty sure Nushala will have a breakdown. I suggest we employ a little parental treachery. Follow my lead."

Jon led them to the garden, but before they could reach their hiding spot he started to make as much noise as possible to alert the girls and hopefully flush them out.

"Thea, can you see them?"

He made wild gestures to let Thea know to act as if she was clueless. She gave him a thumbs up and replied.

"No, I don't know where they are. Poor Nushala is beside herself that with no honey she can no longer make honey cakes for the girls."

Jon took over.

"She was really looking forward to making them for the party. I guess they forgot about it."

Thea and Jon heard a squeak from the hedge. Jon gave Thea an ok, signalling it was working.

"The party is only a few days away, and we won't have time to collect enough before then. I hate to think the girls won't have any birthday cake to look forward to…"

Luna and Solys appeared from behind the hedge holding the bucket filled with honeycomb between them, their little faces smeared with the sticky nectar. They looked so repentant; Thea was almost tempted to forgive them. Jon was intent to be less lenient. That is until both girls stood before him, eyes teary and spoke in perfect unison.

"We're sorry daddy."

His head dropped and he gave an audible sigh.

"Women are going to be the death of me."

***

Once the girls were cleaned up, and the honey returned to Nushala with proper if not wholly sincere apologies, the family settled on the grass in a little clearing as Thea told the girls a story. She liked to frame them as stories, but Jon could see the patterns. She was remembering Darcuna and everyone back home.

Jon sat, leaning against a tree with Solys lying in his lap. He was contentedly drifting in and out of consciousness as Thea's voice lulled him to sleep. He glanced down to see Solys give a yawn before sticking her thumb back in her mouth. She'd be out soon. Luna was serenely sucking her thumb already and breathing heavily, no doubt tired from an afternoon of honey thievery and daddy manipulation.

He was ready to drop off when Solys' sleepy voice startled him with an unexpected question.

"Daddy, will we ever get to meet our sister Darcuna?"

Thea looked at him as if to ask the same. Jon didn't need to think of the answer.

"Yes, pumpkin, we will... When you and your sister are big enough to travel, we'll go and see your big sister and my brother, your uncle, and even the gargoyle that raised your mummy."

Luna didn't open her eyes but popped her thumb out long enough to blurt out,

"Gath."

Jon smiled.

"Yep, Gath the grumpy gargoyle."

This made the girls giggle and even Thea grinned at the description of her guardian.

"He is not always so ill-tempered."

Jon nodded.

"No, you're right. After he got to know me, he was less hostile. I even miss him and that miserable git, Fenris.

Jon paused and thought about all the family that were waiting for them to get home.

"No girls, don't you worry, we'll get back to see them, I promise."

His eyes met Thea's and he gave her a nod. She nodded back.

***

Luna and Solys were seated next to each other in front of their cake. It was now their favourite tradition three years running. Nushala's honey cakes were a special treat reserved for their birthday. Jon was the one to introduce the candles to mark the years as a nod to his Earthside upbringing. Thea counted five candles and had to bite her lip to keep it from trembling. They were now old enough to start planning to leave.

Thea wiped her eyes and planted a smile on her face. It was a celebration of her babies growing up, and she refused to dampen their spirits by letting them see her upset.

***

Jon glanced sideways to see Thea wipe away the tears and could not help the little twinge in his own chest. His girls were now five years old. It was only a matter of time before he was no longer the hero in their eyes. Eventually there would be boys who would steal their hearts. He'd be cast as the mean old troll who barred their true loves, that is until those true loves broke their hearts and he was once again called in to defend their honour… He turned to see Solys shove cake up Luna's nose and breathed a relieved sigh. He still had time.

***

Chapter 54 - When Is the Right Time?

"Now girls I know you're sad to leave Nushala but your sister Darcuna is waiting for us."

It was eight weeks after their birthday. They had waited so the girls could enjoy their special day, but now it was time to go. Solys and Luna were clutching onto each of the acolyte's hands.

"Why can't we stay? Why can't Nushala come with us? What if Darcuna doesn't like us?"

Thea and Jon were both on their knees trying to negotiate with their daughters. They had been prepared for tears, but it was still hard to see their little girls so afraid to leave. Nushala had of course initially objected to them leaving, but Thea had reminded her that their first daughter was still waiting for her parents to return. Nushala could not hold her ground without coming across as selfish.

She had even petitioned the high priestess for permission to leave.

"They need me. I could protect them..."

"No, I cannot in good conscience send you out into an unknown future. My first responsibility is to keep you safe. Thea and Jon cannot bring you back. You would never again see The Ethereal Sanctum.

You would be alone in their realm. Yes, the girls are small now and welcome your attentions, but they will grow and require your help less and less.

"And while I know you revere Thea, you are also of very different minds at the best of times over issues with the girls. She knows you love them, but they are not your children. You must start thinking of yourself, Nushala.

"Once the girls are grown, you will resent them for abandoning you. Let them go now and keep your memories of them pure. Kiydarr teaches us that the one who holds on too tight risks killing that they wish to keep. Let his words give you the strength to let them go."

With tears blurring her vision she kissed each girl on the head and pushed them towards their parents.

"While I will always love you and remember you, Solys, Luna, you have family to meet, adventures to share. I have done all I can for you; it's time for you to make your own stories. This realm is my home. Yours is waiting for you."

Jon readied the portal while the girls waved sadly to their nurse. Thea knew that the acolyte was unhappy about letting them go into an unknown future and hoped to leave her with something that would take the sting out of their departure.

She grasped both girls by the hand but just as she stepped through with them, she called out to Nushala.

"His name was Kadir and his several times great-granddaughters will never forget your kindness. Your name will forever be part of their Dragon memories and mine."

The expression of shock on Nushala's face, before it turned to joy at the honour, made Thea smile. Jon followed and closed the portal behind them.

***

Chapter 55 - Family Travels

Thea and Jon were planning their next jump. They turned when Solys gave a sleepy whimper. Luna reached for her sister and they both settled back to sleep. The girls were huddled together taking a nap while Thea and Jon watched the pendant swing.

The decision to try and limit their interaction with the local population in each new realm was mutual. This was both to protect the girls as well as to avoid pulling them into any conflicts that might further delay their arrival home. To that end, they avoided moving too far from their jump sites. They travelled only as far as they needed to find a secure spot to rest and find food and water.

This realm was so scarcely populated they had little trouble keeping to themselves. The pendant's movements had not changed for some time so Jon tried to divert Thea's attention.

"That was a nice thing you did for Nushala. She'll be dining out on that story for a good long time."

Thea put the pendant away and thought about the acolyte.

"For all her many faults, she did love them. I hope she gains some peace through that admission. And it is true, they will never forget her, she is now forever retained in their Dragon memories. It is a kind of immortality."

"That's a hell of a parting gift. Still I hope she doesn't abuse it."

Thea tapped her nose thoughtfully.

"I cannot say with any sort of certainty, but I do not think Nushala will. She holds me in too high a regard to sully my gift to her. I believe it might even temper her pride."

While Jon wished he could provide more for the girls, he kept promising himself he would make it up to them as soon as they got home. The going had been slow, but Jon and Thea agreed that for the girls' safety, neither of them could afford to let their energy reserves deplete.

As a precaution, Thea's shields were always up when they initially went through the portal. Then once she was sure they were safe she would let them drop. Sometimes it was a matter of hours, sometimes it was days. But once they were settled, each jump was then followed by an extended period of rest. Depending on how long Thea was forced to use her shields, they could spend a day to a week recharging.

"I have other things to discuss with you. Do you think that because the girls were born after my curse was lifted, they will have a more Dragon-like progression as they grow? I was very magically advanced at their age. My primary aspect presented much earlier than normal. Ordinarily a Dragon child ages slowly, to allow their Dragon memories to develop before their magic. Because I did not have my Dragon memories, in some ways I was very emotionally immature when my aspect presented; so, while I had tremendous power, I did not have the mental faculty to properly comprehend the responsibility of it."

Jon sat down and patted the ground next to him. He waited until Thea was seated.

"I've been thinking the same thing. They're half Faye as well. My magic didn't manifest until I was a teen. On one hand it's good; it means we have time to prepare. We can talk to them about it and even start their training so when their aspects present, we don't have chaos. On the other hand, them being able to defend themselves would be a bonus for us. We know what's out there. We know exactly what is hunting us."

Thea rested her chin on her knees.

"I also worry that bringing them up as we are, we are making them too insular. I love that they are close, but how will they cope once we arrive back home? Will they be able to integrate with the rest of the Dragon community, or will they shut themselves away? What about Darcuna? How will they react to meeting their eldest sister? I constantly question myself and how we are raising these girls. I have Dragon memories of not just good parenting but also of bad parenting done under the guise of good intentions."

Jon reached out and grabbed Thea's hand, giving it a reassuring squeeze.

"Nothing is absolute. We can't constantly be rechecking our decisions or we'll end up paralyzing ourselves. There are too many variables to deal with. We just have to do what we think is right in each moment and cross our fingers that it doesn't come back to bite us in the arse later. And think about it, me and Gerard grew up in a similar situation and we turned out mostly ok and so will the girls."

Thea gave a long sigh.

"Even with all these Dragon memories, I am still at a loss with raising our children. Being a parent is difficult. I wonder how my mother remained so calm with me?"

Jon tried to offer some advice he remembered Aliyah had given him when he was feeling out of his depth after Darcuna's birth.

"We'll do fine as long as we remember the first rule is to love them. Yes, they will try our patience and, yes, some days it might be hard, but as long as our decisions are guided by love, everything should flow from that. My mum had two boys who argued a lot. And one of them was especially ornery."

Jon pointed at himself.

"Not that Gerard didn't give as good as he got, but Solys and Luna are as thick as thieves, so our only concern should be them conspiring against us."

Thea covered her face to hide her mirth, but a giggle still escaped. Her expression then turned thoughtful.

"I am just now remembering a singular instance where Devourer and Destroyer and I operated jointly. Spawn often organized hunts with Crusher. Black Heart had no interest and Rage was too unstable to be let out unsupervised. Crusher suggested bringing the twins and I. I believe their plan was to embarrass us, but I could see how the twins acted as one and used that to form part of my hunting tactic.

"When we separated, I told the twins I would take no credit for the kill on their assurance that we work as a team. My wings gave me an aerial advantage. I could reach vantage points for tracking with ease but Destroyer and Devourer could move about on the ground, in silence, as one.

"As we were the youngest, we were not expected to be successful, so it was satisfying to return with a significant kill. The twins of course appeared dragging the large carcass, but it was not unnoticed that I trailed behind covered in considerable blood. A silent mark of my involvement.

"When Spawn asked if I was a hindrance, Destroyer would only comment that I was not without some use, but at the time it was as close to praise as I had ever received from any of my brothers."

Jon brushed a tear from Thea's cheek. She had so few good memories surrounding her brothers. He could tell this was more significant than she let on. Thea wiped her face.

"Having my brother's and my father's memories has given me valuable insight into their actions. What I once thought of as cruel was not always done with malice, sometimes it was merely pragmatism. The girls will have my memories, so while they may complain about rules we make, they will also have access to my reasons. They will vaguely understand in a way I did not at their age."

Jon gathered Thea closer to him.

"If nothing, it will certainly make parenting these two more interesting."

* * *

Chapter 56 - Remembering

Thea was splashing about in the water with the girls as Jon tried to nap, off to the side. Luna and Solys loved to have water fights and their peals of laughter would reassure Thea and Jon that the girls were having some fun as they made their way back home. So, they tried to find a lake or stream whenever they portalled to a new realm just for the girls. Even though he was partially a water aspect, Jon was not fond of the element, so he decided to take a nap while the girls played.

"Go on you three. I'm fine lying here in the dry, while you loons splash about."

He cracked his eyes when Luna gave an ear-piercing scream when Solys sprayed her from behind. Luna launched herself at her sister and they went under. Both girls came up laughing. Jon had called it when he'd commented that the twins while identical had opposite personalities. Solys was loud and outgoing while Luna was often in quiet contemplation.

Luna did speak her mind when it suited her. If anything, she was far more bull-headed than her sister. Solys was as flighty as the wind, and would change her mind without any real push while Luna stood her ground. Solys was light and airy. Luna was more serious.

That's not to say that Luna never laughed. She laughed all the time, but not in the same way as Solys.

Solys was silly, Luna was thoughtful. If Luna was laughing you could bet there was something more to it. But with all her acuity, she had a particular blindness when it came to her sister. *She* could scold Solys, but she would pounce on anyone who tried to do the same. Jon was reminded of his own childhood.

Gerard had been a vicious bastard at times, teasing and taunting Jon, but if anyone else said as much as boo to him, Gerard would be all over them. It was ok to banter between them, but he'd defend Jon to anyone, no matter what. When things got intense, he would grab Jon into a tight embrace before pulling back and looking him in the eye.

"Family is different. We can make jokes, but you're my brother and no one messes with my brother – ever."

Jon brushed away a tear. Gerard was always in the back of his mind, but he didn't often find himself getting emotional. If he opened that can of worms there was no telling if he could put the lid back on.

He loved watching the girls together. Because they were sisters, they could tease each other mercilessly, but they would defend each other no matter what, because that was family.

***

Thea made another mark on her arm while Jon looked away. He didn't turn back until he could hear when she finished cauterizing the cut. The tension in Jon's shoulders made Thea sad but he understood her macabre ritual. Another year away from Darcuna.

"Why are you hurting yourself, Mummy?

Before Thea could answer, Jon spoke up.

"Because Mummy is remembering your eldest sister."

Thea was pretty good at keeping upbeat in front of the girls, but just around the time of Darcuna's birthday, she'd let her mask slip. Of course, Luna and Solys had Thea's memories of Darcuna. They knew that Thea got sad but didn't really understand the meaning of the cutting. Solys spoke again.

"I know it's Darcuna's birthday, but why does Mummy hurt herself?"

Her sister elbowed her in the ribs.

"She still thinks it's her fault."

Solys kept on.

"Do you wish you had stayed with her, Mummy and not had us?"

This stopped Thea in her tracks. Of course, the girls would feel her guilt and see how she tortured herself. They had the memories but not the adult comprehension yet. She was in a way telling them she regretted her decision with her actions. The realization shook Thea to the core. She gathered both girls to her.

"Never. You are both the best and most unexpected blessing we were given on this journey. I only now see what my marks must look like to you."

She glanced over to Jon who was attempting to hide, without much success, a triumphant smirk. He coughed to hide he was laughing.

"Out of the mouth of babes."

Thea had to admit her defeat. The corner of her mouth kinked before she made her announcement to the family.

"This is the last time I will celebrate Darcuna's birthday with such a mark."

Luna tugged on Thea's arm.

"Mummy, why don't we light a candle for her, like Nushala used to do for our birthday?"

Again, Jon coughed.

"*Told you.*"

Thea kissed Luna on the head.

"I think that is a marvellous idea. Should we also have something sweet, like fruit or maybe cake if we can find it?"

This caused both girls to jump up and down and squeal.

"Yes! Yes! Yes!"

By now Jon was not even trying to hide his smile.

***

Travelling with small children is difficult at the best of times, and because they were girls the learning curve for Jon was steep. But travelling with twin girls presented its own kind of hell for him. Luna and Solys loved each other, but it didn't mean they didn't fight.

Jon vividly remembered some of his and Gerard's arguments; a few of them deteriorated into all-out brawls only ending when his mother dumped a bucket of cold water on them to break them up. But he'd never before observed a fight between sisters and it was proving to be eye opening.

The twins fought hard. They knew each other's secrets so well, they could deliver insults with razor precision. Luna was slow to anger, so it usually started with Solys pushing her buttons until she lost her temper. So, when she did finally blow it was brutal to watch.

There was hair-pulling and scratching and some of the foulest language used that he could only assume the girls had tapped into his memories of the worst of

Nash's tirades. Thea was looking at him and shaking her head. There would be a quiet discussion later between them about that, he was sure.

It wasn't his fault. He'd never believed that he could have sex much less kids, forget that they were three quarters Dragon with the ability to remember their parent's memories. He could never in a million years have believed this would be his life.

He pulled the girls apart.

"Ok, Frazier and Ali, I'm calling a time out. Now what started it this time?"

Both girls started yelling over each other, and Jon closed his eyes and took a deep breath before he lost his own temper.

"That's enough. You,"

He nudged Luna towards Thea.

"Sit with your mother and calm down. I'll get your version in a second."

He pulled Solys away so that they could talk without Luna glaring at him like he'd just become the most traitorous dad in the known realms. He knew exactly who started it. He just needed to find out why.

"Ok, now tell me, why did you pick on your sister?"

Solys sputtered with indignation before she saw that Jon was not having any of her drama.

"Look, that might work with Mum, but I *know* who started it because that was me when I was your age. Just tell me *why* you started it. I promise to listen if you just talk straight with me."

There was a moment where Solys' lip trembled before she huffed.

"Luna said we would never get back to Earthside."

Jon rubbed his temple. Luna may have been the thoughtful one, but Solys was showing herself to be the emotional one. Her voice brought him back.

"Daddy, are we ever going to get back home?"

Jon was at a loss. Of course, they would eventually get home. He'd be damned if his girls never saw Earthside, but he couldn't give any sort of definitive answer as to how long it would take. At least nothing that two little girls would understand. So, he kept it simple.

"I know it's taking a long time and that it's not always nice where we have to sleep, but I promise you, no matter what, we will get home. Luna is just as scared as you, so take it easy on her if she says things like that. And about some of those words you and Luna were using, for the love of all that's holy never *ever* use that sort of language when we get home or your mother will kill me."

Jon gathered her into his arms and kissed the top of her head.

"Yes, Daddy."

***

... Meanwhile at home

Chapter 57 - Raising Darcuna

(A Few Years Earlier in Hell)

Gath's pace was relaxed as he returned from another meeting with Crusher. The weekly visits helped him cope with his loss. He shuddered. He didn't often dwell on the day of Thea and Jon's disappearance. Some days it was more like a bad dream.

***

When Thea and Jon were overdue to return, Gerard and Ash were sent to find out what happened. Their surveillance report of the state of the camp to the war council was grim. The machine had torn itself apart and taken some of Black Heart's followers, along with a good portion of the camp. There were so many bodies. But primarily, it had taken down the wards. Destroyer was the first to suggest that a large assault was now possible. If Thea and Jon were being held, they would liberate them at the same time.

The original assumption had been that the capture of Thea and Jon would crush the morale of their rebellion. Amazingly when word about them spread, it lit a fire under the entire camp. Everyone was energized – except Gath. Something was not right, but he could not explain, even to himself, what felt amiss. He vaguely remembered the war council shouting around him.

Plans were finalized and then, with no recollection of his part in it, a full bombardment of the camp was carried out. No trace of Thea or Jon was found.

In the confusion, Spawn, Rage, and Black Heart had managed to escape along with a small number of their most fervent followers. It was galling, but it was still a blow to the cult, and the net was drawing ever tighter around the rogue brothers. It did not overshadow the inevitable conclusion—Black Heart's days were numbered. It was only a matter of time before he was finally brought to heel for his crimes. The camp was levelled; all trace of it disappearing back into the wastes.

In the aftermath of the battle, Gath wandered the debris looking for some trace of Thea and Jon. All his years looking after Thea had given him a sixth sense. He could tell when she was hurt or needed him. His instincts screamed that they were not dead even though the overwhelming evidence was no one in the camp when the machine exploded could survive. But still, where were they? Was he losing his mind? He would have vanished into the wastes as well if Gerard had not found him and brought him back. In a sorry state, unable to cope with the loss of his former charge, the old gargoyle began to fade.

He stopped eating. He barely spoke to anyone and his mental ability to care for Darcuna was called into question. With Gath so demoralised, Ash and Aliyah temporarily took in Darcuna while Gerard and Fenris took care of the aging gargoyle.

They worked to keep his body going but, it wasn't until a conversation with Crusher, that Gath was able to pick himself up.

Crusher was reflective.

"As one who regularly communes with the dead, I have yet to feel my little sister's presence. Black Heart might be a far more authoritative speaker to the dead, but a necromancer can also talk and listen. And I have been listening for her and Jon. None who have passed over has given any account of meeting them. True, it is possible that the portal could have destroyed her soul and yet in my heart... I do not believe she is dead."

He paused and wistfully chuckled.

"She is... resourceful."

Crusher turned to face Gath before laying a hand on his shoulder.

My friend — how strange that I should now count you as a friend? Take heart, Gath. She will return to us, because I wish to believe she escaped. I keep faith that at some point she *will* return to us. I will not accept anything less, but more importantly I do not think neither will she."

They embraced, and the old gargoyle's shoulders shook with the effort to keep himself together.

***

Those eloquent words gave him some hope--something he'd been sorely short of, since hearing of Thea's disappearance. Crusher was right, Thea was stubborn. If Thea was dead, her body would have been displayed for the sake of her pretentious brother. That no body was present could only mean she escaped. The bigger question was, where was she now?

For now, he had a more pressing priority who needed him as much as he needed her.

***

Darcuna woke up with a start. She cried out.

"Gath!"

The old gargoyle rushed into her room. She'd had nightmares since her mother left. Barely out of diapers, she was a serious child. It was his fault. He'd allowed his own sadness over Thea and Jon's disappearance to taint Darcuna. When he saw her sitting up in her bed, she didn't look frightened or sad. In fact, she looked excited.

"What woke you, child?"

Darcuna squealed in delight.

"I have a new dream protector. She is a Dragon, and she is so pretty. She chased my nightmares away, and now we have adventures together. Well, I watch while she has adventures."

Gath was relieved to hear this but chided Darcuna.

"I am glad to know you have a dream protector. Maybe now you can go back to sleep. Your grandfather's lessons are tomorrow. I am sure he would prefer you to be awake and alert."

Darcuna huffed.

"But I want to tell you about our adventures."

Gath eased her back into bed while pulling up her covers.

"I want to hear all about your dreams – in the morning. Good night, little one."

He placed a kiss on her forehead. And even though she was scowling, she closed her eyes.

"Good night."

***

Chapter 58 - Understanding Dragon Dreams

Gath smiled when he caught sight of Darcuna playing with Gaia and Brix. She would meet up with her friends after her lessons. Gaia loved Darcuna as her little sister and Brix felt it was a privilege and her way to honour her Reyma.

Gaia was well on her way to becoming an attractive young female Dragon. Athletic with golden hair and bright green eyes, she was never short of admirers. They mooned over her trying to strike up conversations with her, until she spoke. She was fearless with her opinions, and had little time for dreamy-eyed suitors.

At three cycles, Darcuna now stood just shy of a head taller than Brix. Gath smiled fondly remembering a set of similar blue eyes inviting him to be her friend.

"Ah Mistress, sometimes I see you staring out from those bright blue eyes. I wonder what she might think of you, or you of her? She tries my patience, and yet she has such a tight grasp of my heart…"

When Darcuna noticed him, she broke off from the group and ran towards him.

"Gath!"

He scooped her up and she threw her arms around his solid neck.

"I want a sword like Gaia."

Gath chuckled at her request while giving a wave to Gaia and Brix. They both waved back before heading toward their homes.

"I have told you, little one, you will have a sword when Gerard deems you ready and no sooner. You have no need to learn so young."

Darcuna pouted.

"I want one like Gaia and the pretty lady."

Gath sighed. Darcuna's imaginary dream friend 'the pretty lady' was a constant source of amusement. Darcuna would tell him about her adventures as they ate together. She continued to prattle on as they walked.

"She has two swords. She calls them her Dragon claws."

Gath's heart tightened at the familiar term Thea had once used for her twin short swords. Levi must have told her about them, and now Darcuna's imaginary friend had the same. He placed her back down and held her hand as they walked.

"You are getting too big to be carried around. If you are old enough to wield a sword, then you are old enough to walk on your own. Come, Gerard is waiting for us. You can tell us how your magic lessons are progressing. What has Fenris taught you recently?"

"He is trying to show me how to make water fairies. I don't understand why though; they seem silly. He says daddy could cast them and that it would be nice to learn."

She rolled her eyes and Gath could only sigh. An obsidian—like her mother and grandmother. Her rock-like stubbornness was only outdone by her water-like impulsiveness. So much like her mother at the same age, and yet he would not change her for all the magic in all the known realms.

"Indulge him, Darcuna. He once promised Gaia he would show her how to cast them before her aspect presented. It reminds him of your parents. He is not a Dragon like you. He has human blood and is aging. Can you promise me you will try and be mindful of his feelings?"

Darcuna huffed.

"I will try but if I do, *then* can I get a sword?"

This made Gath laugh out loud.

"We shall see, little one. We shall see."

They arrived at Gerard's dwelling. It had been decided that Darcuna would come live with him. With the exception of Brix, who tended to Thea's little daisies reverently, Thea and Jon's house had been left undisturbed at the head of the lake. Gerard sidestepped Darcuna as she ran inside.

"She may look like her namesake, but she is Thea through and through. Did she tell you about the pretty lady's weapons? Seems 'the pretty lady' carries twin short swords. On one hand, it melts my heart to hear her talk like she remembers her mother, and yet I know she was too young…"

Gath nodded with a wistful smile.

"I too wish she had some memory of her mother beyond vague impressions, but to hear her talk it is like she remembers small details… her Dragon blood could be a factor."

Darcuna ran out with a sheet of paper clutched in her tiny little hands.

"I made a drawing of one of our adventures, so you can see my friend the pretty lady. See she has two swords just like I told you."

Gerard took the drawing and pointed to a second dark haired figure.

"Is this supposed to be you with her Darkling?"

Darcuna exhaled impatiently.

"No, that is her mate. They are travelling now, but they always talk about coming here. Every night I see them. They get to visit so many places and meet so many people. She fought a great beast called a magbear. That is it there."

Darcuna pointed at the large figure in the picture.

"It had giant teeth and claws, but the pretty lady took her Dragon form and roared and pushed the beast back saving her mate and her friends."

Gerard's eyebrows drew together in thought. Something bothered him. His voice was measured as he asked Darcuna about her picture again.

"This mate, does he have a name? What does your pretty lady call him?"

Darcuna smiled.

"His name is Jon, like daddy. Isn't that amazing?"

Gerard felt like the wind had been knocked out of him. He sat down while tears formed in his eyes and Darcuna rushed to him.

"I'm sorry, Uncle; I didn't mean to make you sad. I know you miss Daddy and Momma."

Gerard pulled Darcuna to him and hugged her.

"No, my little Darkling, it's ok. It is a lovely thought, now go wash before we eat."

He gave her a kiss on her head and sent her off before turning to Gath. The gargoyle's face was usually hard to read but his eyes were wide.

"By the stars, is it possible? Could Darcuna's pretty lady and Thea be one in the same?"

Gerard was pacing.

"I don't know. Could the curse placed on Dark Haven finally be weakening?"

Gath shrugged.

"Perhaps Darcuna is not affected."

Gerard nodded.

"We need to speak to Levi and the other Dragons to find out if such a thing is possible. But if it is, her dreams are not simply dreams, but living Dragon memories and Thea and Jon are alive. They are travelling back to us, but I don't understand why it is taking them so long. We assumed the explosion that destroyed the mechanical portal killed them, but maybe... maybe they were thrown through it; they were sent somewhere where they can't travel back... I don't know what to think."

Gath's stony facade could not hide his smile.

"Regardless, they are alive, and Darcuna is now tapping into her mother's memories. I agree we should discuss this with the others, but the news that she and Jon are alive is tremendous. I... I..."

He could no longer keep his emotions under control and the two of them embraced while laughing.

"They are alive. By the stars, they are alive."

***

Before You Go

If you have enjoyed this book can I ask you to take a moment and leave a review on the site of your choice.

As an independent author I rely on reviews from readers.

Your time is always appreciated.

Thanks.

Nadine Thirkell
www.demonality.org
www.twitter.com/DemonalityBooks
www.instagram.com/demonality_books/

CPSIA information can be obtained
at www.ICGtesting.com
Printed in the USA
LVHW022332290721
694057LV00003B/318